the WOLF HOUR

Sarah Myles began to write fiction after graduating in literature from Monash University, and studying at the University of Western Australia. She has trained and worked as a nurse, travelled through Europe, the Americas and Africa. She is the author of *Transplanted.* Currently she divides her time between writing and family, living in inner Melbourne and on the west coast of Victoria.

the WOLF HOUR

SARAH MYLES

ALLEN&UNWIN
SYDNEY • MELBOURNE • AUCKLAND • LONDON

First published in 2018

Allen & Unwin
83 Alexander Street
Crows Nest NSW 2065
Australia
Phone: (61 2) 8425 0100
Email: info@allenandunwin.com
Web: www.allenandunwin.com

NATIONAL LIBRARY OF AUSTRALIA

A catalogue record for this book is available from the National Library of Australia

ISBN 978 1 76063 251 9

Set in 13/17.5 pt Adobe Garamond Pro by Post Pre-press Group, Australia
Printed and bound in Australia by Griffin Press

10 9 8 7 6 5 4 3 2 1

MIX
Paper from responsible sources
FSC® C009448
FSC www.fsc.org

The paper in this book is FSC® certified. FSC® promotes environmentally responsible, socially beneficial and economically viable management of the world's forests.

For my family, everything

Once you lose someone it is never exactly
the same person who comes back.

—Sharon Olds, 'Feared Drowned'

1

Northern Uganda

8 March 2008—Morning

Tessa stood with the men, women and children who had gathered in the centre of the compound—some forty villagers, jostling, talking. There was dust in her throat and her heat-swollen feet were tight in her hiking boots. The braids she had plaited that morning hung like weights. She watched the boy's family approach him; among them was a lean man in a yellow shirt followed by a woman whose lips had been cut—punishment by the rebels for accused treachery and in accordance with their reading of Psalm 12:3, *May the Lord cut off their flattering lips and silence their boastful tongues*. The man was the boy's father, and he carried a basin of water in one hand and a broad-bladed panga in the other, his face solemn, his eyes fixed. This was ritual, a tribal affair. There was none of the glossy exoticism of tourist guides, no drums or dancing, or women in bark skirts with jingling *gara* on their legs. This was village business.

Dominic Oculi stood nearby. He wore an open-necked shirt, which revealed the gold chain and crucifix that hung around his neck. He touched the tiny gold body of Christ then lifted his head. Tessa caught his eye, and he nodded, but without his usual calmness. His eyes darted from one person to the next in a way that suggested he was unsure how this ceremony would go.

They had brought Oraako, a twelve-year-old boy from the rehabilitation centre, here. Driving for more than an hour through grasslands dotted with kigelia trees, their odd sausage-shaped fruits hanging like Christmas decorations, the jeep had bumped over the powdery red road while Oraako nursed his festering foot and pressed his face to the window with the same vacant look he'd had since returning from the bush.

Tessa watched him now. He was small for his age, with brambly hair and a stalk-like neck, but above his top lip there was a fine nimbus of hair. He looked into the distance as though he would rather be somewhere else and, balancing his weight on his good foot, Tessa could see tension in the way he held his shoulders, the way he listened. People here wanted to know: had he turned into a *bedo lee lee*, a wild thing, after so many years in the bush, or was he still a *dano adana*, a human person?

As his father shuffled forward, the crowd pressed closer. Behind him was the boy's mother, whose scarred lips formed an ugly inward pucker. They had healed, but they were lumpy, a keloid reminder of what should or should not have been said. All the while she kept up a soft mournful moaning which seemed to come without any movement from her distorted mouth. In her left hand she carried a chicken whose feet were bound, although its wings were free and it flapped wildly, making a frantic *bawk*ing sound as it struggled. The crowd talked loudly, but as soon as Oraako's parents came to a halt they fell silent.

The boy's father nodded and Oraako sat down on the branch-swept earth. Placing the bowl at his son's feet, the man dipped his gnarled hand into it and sprinkled water on Oraako's wounded foot, then took the chicken from his wife and with one deft spin broke its neck. Tessa watched. She would record the details later, noting the way the boy's father laid the bird on the ground, how he used the panga to cleave it in two, then wiped its blood and faeces onto Oraako's hands and infected foot.

The boy flinched and straightened. Tessa felt the sting too. Would such a ritual make his infection worse? She thought of the antiseptics her mother, a doctor, had insisted on using for the smallest cut. Tessa tightened her arms against her chest and looked on in silence. Faith is one thing, she told herself, science another—or perhaps they are the same; you just need one to rule the other out.

The crowd formed a close semicircle around the boy and began a rapid chant in Acholi as the suppurating wound was caked in chicken shit. The panga, which the boy's father placed on the ground, shone in the sun. The blade was sticky with blood and had already begun to attract a swarm of tiny black flies that congregated in a dark line along the sharp edge. Again, Tessa recalled the way her mother tended wounds, whether a deep knife-cut or a jagged laceration; how her brow would gently furrow with concentration, and how she had once removed a fishhook from Stephen's forefinger. Stephen had howled that day, his blood dripping into the bait bucket. The sound of her older brother's gulping cries had made Tessa bold. You're such a wimp, she had said daringly, although she winced now as Oraako held his foot. The boy's nose oozed with snot; he stared at the blood that soaked into the earth in a dark irregular shape then looked back at his father's hands. A flicker of alarm crossed his father's face, but at last he nodded and Oraako bowed his head before limping back into the crowd, where he seemed to dissolve into the shadows of those who surrounded him.

All around, women's voices lifted in high-pitched ululations—discordant at first, like instruments tuning in an orchestra pit, until together they found their fast pulsing rhythm and the crowd moved together and began to clap.

When Dominic closed his eyes, Tessa was unsure if he actually swayed or it just seemed that way. Of course, this kind of thing helped to heal. The Acholi people were deeply superstitious. How else could the Lord's Resistance Army have gained such a stronghold in this country if not for a willingness to believe? 'People want to be led, and for many Joseph Kony is a god,' Dominic had told her. 'His followers say he is invested with the power of the Holy Spirit, that bullets do not harm his soldiers.'

Tessa had heard the stories, and pursued them. She wanted to understand the mess that nightly news reports claimed *brought children back without a childhood*. There were so many questions, they nagged, they burnt. She stepped closer to Oraako's mother, who wore a loose-fitting *gomesi* in a swirling pattern of blue and green. It was faded and frayed, except for the patch of plaid on the sleeve that had been carefully sewn on with red thread. As the clapping quickened, Oraako's mother lifted her arms as if to pull the strength of the sky towards her son. She was not old, although she looked it. Her mouth like melted wax, her body stooped. She moved towards Oraako, who stepped back into the crowd, and her eyes filled with tears, then suddenly—in a gesture that seemed part lunge, part dance—she held out her arms to her son. Oraako's grave expression did not change; instead it suggested that he had no idea who she was. But then without warning he dropped to the ground and another woman took him by the arm and urged him to stand again, her loud wailing like metal scraping over metal.

A warm breeze had picked up and Tessa could feel the sweat evaporate from her skin. Her own tangy scent filled the air. She had tried several times to interview Oraako—once on her own, and twice through an interpreter. He answered in Acholi with a smattering of English, but for the most part he did not want to speak to her about what had happened to him. All she knew were the accounts others, particularly Beatrice, the social worker, had given—that when the rebels abducted him they cut his mother's lips and forced him to watch, that he had been gone for more than three years, raiding and killing across the border, but had escaped several weeks ago, his feet shredded and ulcerated from the long distance he had walked.

Two months earlier, when Tessa arrived in this part of northern Uganda to overwhelming hospitality and constant questions, huts of mud and thatch, red earth under cloudy skies and low hills, it smelt like nowhere else she'd ever been—sour cassava, dusty cow manure, frank sewage, burning rubbish. There were things that unnerved her: the raw stump of an amputee, the blind eyes of a child—smoky white orbs, like the eyes of a baked fish. For all her travel and education, a privileged world had filtered the details of the lives she was only beginning to witness now. She half listened to the advice her parents gave her and nodded at the cautionary tales from her colleagues and friends, but mostly she wanted to understand more. She was trying to find a way into her work and wanted to make her research count. In the early 2000s, when images of thousands of children taking refuge in the town of Gulu first hit mainstream television, she had watched from a distance. Now her research in post-traumatic stress in children had brought her to these former child soldiers. It was estimated that upwards of twenty thousand children had been abducted in the last two decades of civil conflict. These children had been indoctrinated and damaged, yet some were less likely to develop post-traumatic stress than others.

Why? Because they had family support or were naturally resilient or, as some argued, they were predisposed to violence? She was collating data and wrote her observations in the academic language she'd learnt, drafted and redrafted to shape the material she felt was required of her. It was slow work, invisible work, and she had to check her impatience. Sometimes, when it was going badly, she wondered if she was pushing too hard, looking for conclusions that didn't exist. What she wanted was to be authentic. There was pressure to be original, to do more fieldwork, and she had been advised that in order to get a postdoc position, she would need to publish at least one substantial paper. Something groundbreaking. She was unsure and anxious, but she had been lucky enough to get a small university grant and had self-funded the rest. Her networking had brought her here, and then there had been a generous offer by Dominic to stay as long as she needed.

As the chanting continued, Oraako's father smeared blood on his son's chest, his long finger moving in an arc just above the heart. For some time he let his fingertip rest there—a light, almost tender touch—then slowly he took his finger away and washed his hands in the basin of water. Afterwards, he spilt what water was left onto the ground and immediately the earth changed colour, the dry soil becoming a deep fertile crimson.

The sky was overcast. Long grey clouds marbled the west. The day's heat was building. Soon the wet season would come and the weeks of billowing red dust would turn to a dark sticky mud. People had been making offerings for good rains too. In the middle of the night food was left in certain trees where it was believed their ancestors' spirits were most active. Ceremony, ritual, seasonal shifts—Tessa was increasingly drawn to such markers. The passing of time was becoming a drumbeat: *What are you going to do with your life?* Perhaps it had always affected her in this onrushing way, but it was stronger now, brewing—a heart-in-the-throat feeling that came with a wave of panic in the knowledge that today was her birthday and already she was thirty.

Then, as if a stage direction had been given, the clapping slowed and the women's tongue-trilling cries crescendoed before softening again. Oraako's mother carefully scooped up the slaughtered chicken's liver and its stringy intestines and placed them in an empty bowl while the other villagers watched and continued to stamp their feet. When Oraako's mother walked away with the bowl of entrails balanced on her head, a large man in a shirt with an elaborately embroidered collar lifted his hand and the crowd began to break up into smaller groups. They dispersed, and Dominic moved through the crowd to join her. He looked in the boy's direction. 'You saw that this boy, Oraako, was not getting better?'

Tessa nodded and Dominic continued. 'We have to be open to the beliefs of the child and those of his family when they trust that this will cure him.' He spoke in the soft manner of his people, his English strangely formal. He reminded her of an old-fashioned teacher, someone who believed in politeness. She liked him—he had acted as her guide and taken time with her. He was kind, but possibly a bit damaged too. He said his dreams plagued him.

'They are worried he has *cen*,' Dominic added. 'That evil spirits are in his head. The intention is to cleanse him of any demons that will cripple him in the future.'

Tessa looked at Oraako, who remained with his father and the man in the embroidered shirt. 'Will he go back to the hospital and get them to care for his foot there?' she asked tentatively.

Dominic shook his head. 'That is not possible; the hospital is overrun. Besides, he has already had a course of antibiotics.'

Tessa tried not to sound argumentative although it probably came out that way. 'True, but those drugs were more than four years out-of-date—and what's to say it's not a fungal infection or that it hasn't got into the bone?'

'I thought you were a doctor of psychology?'

She allowed herself to smile. 'Yes,' she said sheepishly, 'I am.'

'Well then, you know that this is not just about tribal medicine, it's about the boy being accepted back by his family. His father and his uncle here believe that because his wound will not heal, it is a sign of his wrongdoing. They are ashamed by the killing he has done. Most important now is reconciliation. That is true healing.'

The men's voices rose then sank again to a murmur. Oraako looked on. His arms were thin, although his hands were large and callused. He had picked up a stick and was using it to spread the blood that had spilt on the ground.

'You know we are desperate for peace,' Dominic continued. 'After more than twenty years we would try anything to close this chapter of hatred—I would try anything.' As he spoke, he made a gesture of insistence, tapping his own chest so that the thin fabric of his shirt stretched and the crucifix was knocked aside.

He was an Acholi man, he had grown up in the township of Gulu, and although only ten years older than her, it seemed as though he had been dealt a terrible blow and absorbed it. She'd heard a rumour that he was a returned soldier himself. For a while she wasn't sure whether he'd been with the government forces or the rebels until one of the staff members at the centre mentioned that he had been with both. Apparently it was not that uncommon.

'I like to read,' he told her when she first arrived. 'Reading is my passion. In Kampala, I bought myself the *Encyclopaedia Britannica*, and now I'm reading it little by little. I cannot eat without reading. When I eat, I like to have a book lying open in front of me.'

She had seen him do this and admired his self-taught education, his patience. There were books in his office to rival those in her father's study: *The Rape of the Nile*, the Bible, Dante's *The Divine Comedy*. In pride of place he kept a tattered blue board edition of the *Acoli Macon* which, he told her, was a record of his people's tribal history. It contained myths and stories compiled by some missionary or other. He invited her to borrow his books, which she did, drawn to the *Acoli Macon* but also to *The Divine Comedy*, so gruesomely realised by Gustave Doré's detailed illustrations. She had leafed through each page, followed each canto, a witness to so many terrifying punishments that she had yearned for the end and the place where the two tiny pilgrims could once more walk beneath the stars. The Christian idea of *legge del contrappasso*—the law of retribution or equal suffering in retaliation for a crime committed—seemed at odds with any notion of reconciliation or forgiveness.

When Oraako's uncle walked off, the boy's father picked up the bloodstained panga, wiped it carefully across a stone then slung it into his belt. He put his hand on his son's shoulder and Oraako raised his head and moved forward, hopping on one leg with a skill that adjusted itself to his injury.

'*Timokeca*,' Dominic said, bowing as they walked past. 'Now you begin again.'

Oraako's father nodded, but the boy showed no sign that he had heard Dominic.

Tessa watched them walk across the compound. '*Timokeca*?' she asked.

Dominic turned to her. 'You have heard this word before? It means to pardon.'

Tessa studied Dominic's face, for here was his belief in rehabilitation—as an arbitrator he had given advice at the peace negotiations a month earlier: if not forgiveness, then reconciliation, restorative justice.

'As in *mato oput*,' he said now. 'The ceremony where both sides drink the bitter solution from the root of the *oput* tree. They taste it upon their tongues and take it into their stomach. By so doing it allows those offenders to get back their senses. Then they can accept responsibility for their wrongdoings, and those who were once enemies can live in peace.'

Tessa pressed him. 'Yet some people in the ICC say that *mato oput* is not enough to absolve the rebels. That proper justice is not done. They are not punished.'

'I have heard that,' replied Dominic. 'But who can say what is best? Can you? Can I? The International Criminal Court should not be a stumbling block. We do not need cosmetic justice—what we need is real peace.'

'You want to bury the hatchet?'

'That is another way of putting it.' Dominic shrugged. 'The war between the government and the rebels has been one of attrition. For twenty years each side trying to wear the other down; a voodoo war, a brutal civil war, and for the past eighteen months, the peace talks have been stalling, marred by many walkouts. But we cannot stop, we must keep trying.'

The breeze had dropped. Tessa could feel the sun's heat on her back and as Dominic moved away, she followed him. She felt whiter, more a *muzungu* today—a tourist at the ceremony she had just witnessed, not the academic she strove to be. It worried her that she was just one more spectator gawping at these people, at their rituals and their mud huts with floors of pressed cow dung. What could she really know of these children who had been abducted by the rebels? Of the terrible things they had been made to do? This was only the second village she had visited outside the rehabilitation centre. In the first, there had been a massacre by the rebels twelve months earlier. Eighteen children abducted. She had seen the charms hung in doorways to appease the spirits—brown and green snail shells as large as her hand that had rattled against the bleached bones or swirled in the breeze like spinning tops.

'Does anyone know where Kony is now?' she ventured. It was a question asked constantly by everyone, from the myth-making media to the army.

Dominic laughed flatly. 'Ah, you know, that is the problem! Joseph Kony is always moving. The word is that he has crossed from Sudan into the Congo. There are hopes he will meet with us, but we are afraid that everything might go quiet again.'

'You have met him before?'

'Yes, I have met him. A long time ago. Some say he is a shapeshifter, others say he is a spiritual leader, a true Christian, that he is one of the chosen ones. But there are still others who believe he is a devil who devours his own people. You have read of Ugolino in Dante's *Inferno*, the one who gnawed on the bones of his own children?'

She nodded.

'That is what some people say about Kony, except the door has never been nailed shut on him. He has never been imprisoned; he has never been left to starve. Nor has he been granted amnesty. No *timokeca*.'

A UN truck with its blue logo arrived, raising in its wake a cloud of dust. The villagers now reappeared and rushed to meet it. Tessa watched as the vehicle idled in front of a windowless schoolhouse its half-finished roof covered in a tarp of black polythene.

'So you will go with the delegation?' she asked.

'I have been invited,' he said proudly, 'and it is my hope that this time we may get somewhere.'

She wanted to ask him how a veteran combatant, now the director of the rehabilitation centre, became a respected mediator. Did he sympathise with the rebels? Did that bring him closer? She watched him run his hand over his scalp. His hair was cropped close and tiny droplets of sweat beaded his forehead.

He smiled. 'I am not on anyone's side, if that is what you are thinking. I am on the side of resolution. My father was a *rwodi*, a traditional chief. I am part of that lineage.'

They walked back through the village to the jeep. Somewhere nearby a hammer fell with a steady repetitive bang. A purple heron flew across their path, and to either side of the red earth road, sunlight shone through the grass. High and green, it looked like a vast swaying seabed. About twenty cattle moved ahead of a herdsman, some of them lowing or turning their heavy heads, dark brown, speckled, all with impossibly long horns. A calf trotted on spindly legs. Tessa watched it skitter and breathed in the scent of the earth it stirred up. She had encouraged Africa's seduction—even before she came to Uganda she had allowed it to begin its work on her. There were the nature documentaries her father produced—Gondwanaland, Pangaea, the vast supercontinent that once united Africa and Australia. She thought of their family holidays—camping safaris and mountain treks on which she observed her mother's resourcefulness and was challenged by her father, who teased her mercilessly for being afraid of the dark, for failing to light a campfire with damp wood. The year she finished high school they travelled to the South African savannah to witness the huge elephant herds trudging in blind family faith. Afterwards, she went to university and filled up on study—abstract theories, statistics—but her thoughts were already shaped by the dream of coming back. She had said to her parents, 'I just want to go to the furthest place I can. I want to go beyond what I know. I want to do something with my life.' That was what drove her now, yet at the same time she feared she would fail in some way and that what she hoped to do might disappear out from under her.

When they reached the jeep, her mobile phone pinged with a message from her mother. She was grateful to her parents; they would do anything for her—too much, she realised. She loved them, but for now she craved distance and independence. She hesitated then flicked her phone onto silent before quickly returning it to her pocket. They would want to speak to her on her birthday. Home and family would flood back. Not yet, she thought, as she climbed into the passenger seat. She would call later, she promised herself. Maybe tomorrow.

2

Melbourne, Australia

Leigh put her phone down and looked at the family photograph on her desk. It was several years old. They had all changed since it was taken, or perhaps they had just aged. Her children looked like adults now, though she worried about them just as much. She picked up the frame and brushed her fingertip across the glass, recalling the conversation with Tessa the week before she left. 'Oh, darling, why do you always have to leave everything to the last minute?' she remembered herself saying as she punctured the honey-coloured skin of Tessa's left arm. 'I shouldn't even be the one giving you this.'

'Mum, you're a doctor.' Tessa smiled, pressing the cotton-wool swab onto the thin trail of blood. 'It's just a yellow fever injection. I thought I'd already had one.'

'When?'

'When we went on one of those family trips.'

Leigh had dropped the needle into the plastic sharps container, where it clattered against the others. 'Yellow fever isn't a problem in South Africa; Uganda's another story. Haven't you even looked into this?'

Tessa grinned then stroked her eyebrow with her middle finger and lowered her eyes—a reflex whenever she was embarrassed. 'No, I thought you'd save me the trouble and tell me,' she said and looked up again.

Leigh had given an exasperated groan. The sensation in the pit of her stomach was like she'd drunk coffee all day without eating. 'Rabies, typhoid, malaria, tsetse flies, bilharzia, AIDS—do you want me to go on? And now they're talking about Ebola.'

'Mum, please, don't worry,' Tessa chided.

But of course, she did. Only this morning a girl who was thin and pixie-faced like Tess had entered her consulting room, and as Leigh went through the examination procedure it was as if she were watching her daughter from across the desk. She wanted to tell the girl that it was her daughter's birthday, that she had just turned thirty and was in East Africa, maybe even produce the recent photograph of her eating banana kebabs in a crowded marketplace. The girl across from her twisted the large silver ring on her thumb, and again the resemblance was uncanny. It might even have been Tessa—the same dark brown hair in a scruffy braid, the same heavy arched eyebrows and intense dark blue eyes.

Instead, Leigh deferred to her professional-self; she listened to the girl's anxieties and printed out a prescription for Ativan and, in her lunch break, left a brief message for Tessa on her voicemail, saving her concerns until she arrived home. By then Neil, following his usual homecoming routine, had already opened a bottle of wine and begun to sample the cheese he'd set out on a platter.

The heater was on and Leigh took off her coat. 'A girl came into the surgery today,' she began, 'except I didn't really help her. I was distracted; I kept thinking of Tess. I don't think I did my job very well.'

'Try to unwind,' Neil said. 'Eat something. Relax. You can call Tessa later. Stephen too.' Then he drew her to him and his arms surrounded her like a great seawall.

Against his chest Leigh felt her face flush. She put her hand up and gently pushed him away then stepped back. 'I tried to call Tess this afternoon but she didn't answer.'

'You can try again later.'

'I don't think you understand . . .' Leigh had felt this way a lot lately, that Neil's optimistic outlook made things easier for him. He had been the one to encourage Tessa to go to Africa. *Go*, he'd said, *you'll regret it if you don't. Young researchers travelling the world are the people of the future. Make something of your life.* It was the kind of speech he'd given at their children's twenty-firsts, his words loaded with pride and expectation.

Leigh looked around the kitchen. 'Do you remember how thin she got as a teenager? Anxiety, anorexia, except we agreed not to call it that? I just need to talk to her. Check that she's okay. I'm worried.'

'I worry too,' Neil replied.

'I know that, it's just—'

'You worry more.'

'Yes.'

She looked over his shoulder and there on the table was the

bowl of roses she'd bought at the market earlier in the week. Full-blown now, they drooped with exhaustion. The days were getting shorter and the nights were suddenly cold. Autumn had come, yellowing the European trees and putting new growth on the gums. There was the scent of the season's change too, the damp reek of decomposing leaves raked into piles, the earth grateful for rain. It was her favourite time of the year, nostalgic and softly lit.

Neil raised his wineglass. 'To our gypsy children.'

They clinked glasses. Leigh sipped the peppery wine then put her glass down and heaped cheese onto a biscuit. 'I know it doesn't make sense,' she admitted, 'but I worry less about Stephen. I assume Stephen can look after himself, yet with Tessa it's another story. For someone so keen on learning, she can be pretty naïve.'

'She's young,' Neil said. 'If you think of a person's lifetime as a twenty-four-hour clock, then Tessa is at the lunchtime of her life—maybe morning tea. She's barely started. Think what you did at her age. What you wanted to do with your life.'

'I'd had two children by the time I was Tessa's age.'

'I know, quite a feat.'

She smiled and took a deep breath. 'All right,' she conceded. 'But I was never as consumed by wanderlust as Tessa. That, darling, was always your approach.'

'You mean I was reckless?' Neil put a generous amount of cheese on another biscuit and handed it to her. 'Anyway,' he said, 'they have their lives to live and our role is to let them live them.'

Raised Catholic by a family of Irish descent, he'd been brought up on stories of The Troubles—really a euphemism for three decades of ruthless civil war between the unionists in the north, who favoured allegiance with the UK, and the Irish nationalists. He'd rejected all that, choosing instead the natural world, initially photographing for *National Geographic* and later making documentaries for them. Leigh, a medical student, had contacted him when she fell in love with a black-and-white photograph he'd taken of an elephant and its calf. The wrinkled hide and broken tusk. Giant tenderness, she said, familial instinct. To this day, the photograph still hung in their hallway with other images they both treasured.

'Our role?' she asked. 'You mean like a bit part in a play?' She finished eating and picked up her glass of wine. 'What about our responsibility? You say you worry, but you don't sound that concerned about our children.'

'That's not true. I worry about them all the time. I worry about you. I worry about you when you go out for groceries. That's life.' He shrugged.

She shook her head and smiled at him; how could she not? They had been married for so long now that even their sense of humour was part of each other.

After they'd eaten, Leigh stacked the dishwasher then went across to the table to blow out the candles. The roses had begun to drop their petals, reminding her of the way Tessa used to discard clothes on her bedroom floor, scattered in the excitement before heading off to a party or packing for a festival—although the image she had of her daughter these days was one Tess had contrived for herself: the photograph taken in the market, and another in which she wore a brightly patterned bandana and was surrounded by a group of African schoolchildren. In both, she looked fit, her olive skin deeply tanned. An indigo-eyed, dark-haired beauty—a romantic ideal that, if anything, was enhanced by Tessa's determination and stamina. Her strong-willed daughter, who thought nothing of entering a triathlon or taking on another degree. Resolute, persistent, she was stubborn and difficult, yet familiar. A lot like herself, Leigh had to admit, only more intense.

She dialled Tessa's number again and heard the phone ring out in that hollow way that signals no one is going to answer before it switched to a brief recording. It would be the middle of the day in Uganda—lunchtime, *the lunchtime of her life*. Perhaps she was celebrating her birthday. In an earlier phone conversation Tessa had described the festive food, honey and *simsim* butter, and the Kidandali gospel music the staff members at the centre loved to play. Over the past few weeks, whenever Leigh read Tessa's emails there was her cheerful voice, *Hey Mum*, but also her evasiveness: *I'm doing fine.* Days passed before her phone messages were returned, and emails (when they did come) were brief. Occasionally she included short descriptions of her research—children, twelve years old and younger who'd used machetes and garden hoes to murder, yet touched her hair in wonder because it was a lighter colour than their own.

Tessa's desire to be an activist had been there from the start. She was so different from Stephen who, four years older, had always been more focused on his personal freedom. Stephen was unconventional, wild, and you never knew whether he really meant what he said, but Tess was adamant about 'making a difference' in some way. When she was at school she wanted to know more about international conflicts and how they might be addressed; she obsessed over the ethnic cleansing in Bosnia and the East Timorese crisis, and wept with disbelief when she saw the horrific swiftness of the Rwandan genocide. As a university student, she protested against the war in Iraq and was arrested for carrying placards that were deemed offensive. She wanted a better world, rallied for it with the passion of youth, but something else motivated her too. It was personal and unapologetic, as though she had brought an expectation of responsibility into herself and made it a part of her life, an expectation that was now like a force constantly moving under its own weight.

Leigh left a message on Tessa's phone, the kind of stilted monologue that inevitably peters out, then finished her wine and phoned Stephen.

'Are you busy?' she asked him. After his cool greeting, her voice lost its exuberant tone, and in the long-distance echo she heard her words sound like both an inquisition and a criticism. It was not what she intended, but the effect was already there.

'Yeah, I'm busy,' he said casually. He sounded distracted.

'All right then, I won't keep you. But can I talk to you for a minute?'

Someone coughed, and she realised he was not alone. A touchy subject, since the last time Leigh spoke to Stephen he'd told her he'd broken up with his girlfriend of the last two years. There were photographs of Cherie, a blonde and stylish girl from Durban whom Leigh and Neil had not met, although

Leigh had spoken to her a couple of times on the phone; she remembered Cherie had a laugh that checked itself. Apparently, she was a model for a cosmetics company.

'I've been trying to phone Tess,' Leigh went on hurriedly, 'but there's no answer.'

'No shit.' Stephen laughed. 'Tessa's out of range? Mum, she's in Uganda, what did you expect?'

And suddenly any goodwill Leigh was aiming for evaporated. Did he have to be so glib? There was a silence in which she pictured Stephen and Tessa as teenagers. How Stephen goaded with an older brother's knowingness. *You're so stuck up*, he would say, *like you think you know what's going on when really you don't.*

'She'll be all right,' he said in an offhand way.

'I'm not so sure,' Leigh replied. 'Have you tried calling her?'

'Why?'

'Because it's her birthday.'

'Yeah, but birthdays are overrated. You know that, right?'

Leigh closed her eyes. She heard Stephen exhale and could picture his face, how it looked when he used that particular tone.

'Tess has gone there for herself,' he continued. 'You should ask her what she thinks she's getting out of it.'

He sounded even more dismissive than Leigh remembered. Why was he behaving like this? Was it because he had broken up with Cherie? He hadn't told her what had happened between them, and—as was so often the case with Stephen—Leigh felt she couldn't ask.

'Anyway, I don't know what good Tess thinks she can do; the place is a tinderbox.'

'What do you mean?'

'I mean it's a mess, especially in the north. It's dog-eat-dog. Haven't you heard? Joseph Kony had Vincent Otti, his second-in-command, killed because he decided he'd been making a deal on the side.'

All Leigh knew was that the last peace talks had been put on hold—and there it was again, a kind of floating feeling as if she were in a trance. She felt isolated, distant.

'Would you like to speak to your father?' she asked in a bid to extend the conversation.

'No, tell him I'm working. He'll appreciate that.'

A metallic taste filled Leigh's mouth. She thought of the girl who'd come into her rooms earlier that day and for some reason she couldn't shift the image of the girl's distressed face from her mind—that compulsiveness she had seen in so many young people lately. Were they more anxious now? Was OCD on the rise, as some medical journals suggested? 'It's just that Tessa has stayed on much longer than she said she would.'

'So?'

'So, I'm concerned. I thought that maybe you could go up there and visit her.'

There was a prolonged pause.

'Well, why not?' Leigh demanded.

'Because I'm working. I'm trying to run a business here.'

'With Matt Reba?'

'Yes, with Matt Reba.'

'Matt Reba's father's business in Cape Town? Firearms?'

'Sporting equipment,' Stephen corrected her.

Leigh heard Neil finishing up in the kitchen, the noisy

clink of crockery and the kettle whistling before he took their tea upstairs.

'Could you at least think about going to see Tess? It would only need to be for a day or two.'

'Mum, don't you think you're overreacting? Tessa went there for a month and now she's decided to stay on—what's wrong with that? It's her choice, isn't it? Besides, I'm four thousand kilometres away. I'm in Cape Town, remember.'

'I know, it's just—'

'Look, I get it. I understand what you want, but I'm not about to do it. Tessa goes to the arse-end of the earth, maybe she wants to see for herself how crappy life can be. It's her choice.'

Leigh flinched. 'You could take an interest . . .'

Stephen laughed. 'Come on,' he said. 'It's who she is—a bleeding-heart liberal who sometimes acts like a medieval saint.'

'You're being unfair.'

'Am I? She wants to save the world. Great. What should I do, drop to one knee?'

Leigh's face tightened. 'Really, Stephen, listen to yourself. Besides, if you want to bring honesty into it, why not tell us what it is you're doing exactly? You say you're in the import-export business; that you've gone into partnership with Matt. What about the money we loaned you? You haven't been clear about what you've done with that—'

He cut her off. 'I have to go.'

'No, wait, I haven't finished.'

'Well, I have. If you have problems, lay them on Tessa, not on me.'

After he hung up Leigh slammed the phone down. She tried to be reasonable—calm down, accept it. He led a sybaritic life. He was different from what she had hoped he would be; was that so unusual? Children did not always do as their parents wished.

When she went upstairs Neil was already in bed. His glasses were set on the end of his nose, the book she had given him for Christmas held at a distance. There was a cup of tea for her on the bedside table. She felt she should join him, but she hesitated. It was such a deliberate thing to go to bed, it felt as if she were giving up. She cleaned her teeth and came back into the bedroom, where she undressed and put on a soft T-shirt.

'It's Stephen,' she said, picking up the tea and taking a sip. The toothpaste had ruined it. She pulled a face.

Neil looked at her over his reading glasses. 'Let it go for now, you've had a long day. There's no point trying to work everything out tonight.'

That was his method: wait, have patience, let these things play themselves out. She wanted to take that approach too. It made sense—*first do no harm*. But she couldn't.

'You always play things down,' she said.

'You always play them up.' He smirked and she smiled back at him.

'Okay, okay,' she said. She groaned as she got into bed, and when she lay down, she felt his arms around her, the touch that knew her body, all the sore points, the tired muscles and old pleasures. There was the sensation of his warm chest against her back. She closed her eyes and the image of the girl in her consulting room came to her again. She could see the big silver ring on the girl's thumb and the way she rotated it as if to hurt herself. Her deep blue eyes just like Tessa's.

In the dark Neil drew her towards him. Leigh reached back and ran her hand across his thigh, then she felt for his hand and held it in her own. They lay close, but she could not bear it for long; her body was like a furnace.

3

Cape Town, South Africa

Stephen hung up.

'My mother,' he said, and looked across at Matt Reba with a bemused smile. Then he moved to the drinks cabinet on the far side of the room. Ceremonies, especially those he arranged himself, gave him pleasure, and the day's first whisky was a favourite. A heavy-based Waterford glass, two blocks of ice, the turn and twist of the cap. He went about the process with a bartender's flourish, then offered Reba a glass and raised his own.

'I've just been reminded it's my sister's birthday. Here's cheers.'

Matt lifted his glass. 'To Tessa, younger but wiser!'

Stephen laughed. 'Perhaps, but then you're not always a good judge of character.'

Matt flipped him off and Stephen grinned, then sat down. When he spoke again it was of market values and supply and demand, the difficulties with transport costs.

'So, it's agreed? We make a move on this?'

Matt shrugged. 'What if I still have reservations?'

Stephen rolled his eyes. 'Then the opportunity will pass us by and you'll regret it.'

'So you say.'

'Only because it's true. The way I see it, your father's business was in pretty good shape while he was alive, but then things changed. Life moved on, and since you took over what have you done?'

'Plenty, we're doing fine.'

'Come on, the whole setup would've folded without me.'

The whisky smelt oaky, seventeen years, top-shelf notes of cocoa and sherried peels—Stephen felt it warm the back of his throat. He leant back and slowly spun the chair round to face the window. The harbour beyond looked like a perfect functioning model. Tiny trucks drove along the dock to load up beneath gantry cranes that were painted red and white and moved robotically against a cobalt blue sky. Stephen watched as the boom swung, shifting a container. He'd been waiting for this shipment for the last six months, tracking the ships that plied their way between the Ukraine and Yemen; twenty-eight days after that to reach Cape Town. It was a new venture and it put him on guard, but it thrilled him too; some of the contacts he'd sought had finally come through and he saw this as their big chance.

'All right, so you've brought in a lot of new business,' Reba conceded. 'Got me out of a financial mess. But why keep building it up? What you're proposing has risks. Huge risks that might get us fucked over if they don't ruin the business's reputation in the process.'

Stephen waved a dismissive hand. 'Reputation's not that important,' he said. 'Except when you can make money from it.'

'The reality is—'

'Come on,' Stephen interrupted. 'Reality is an illusion.'

Reba put his drink down. 'Shit, man, you always want to go that one step further.'

'Well, maybe that's the important difference between you and me—besides, the best thing about this country is that there's no such thing as going too far. What we need to do is expand, and stop using trucks to transport. The roads are crap anyway. We fly it.'

'Fly it?'

'Yeah, fix a lease. Keep our hours up.'

They had gained their pilot licences within six months of each other and although Reba was first, they both knew it was Stephen who was the natural. He learnt quickly, had a keen sense of judgement and could easily adapt to changing circumstances. It was an adrenaline rush for him, like fast cars or making a quick bet—all those things in life he was told he shouldn't enjoy but were what he called oysters and champagne.

Reba straightened and Stephen saw that he had his attention. He lowered his voice. 'You know, that's the thing I learnt the first time I went out on safari—you have to stay in control. Right? Be assertive, but it was a group of six rogue lions who'd migrated up from the south, who really summed it up for me.'

Matt took a sip from his glass, then wiped his hand across his mouth and raised an eyebrow.

'The local guide called them the *Mapogos*.'

'*Mapogos*. Sure, it means gangsters—like the thug security company in Joburg.'

'Yeah, well, they were smarter than that. They were looking for new territory and since there wasn't much choice, they had to take over the pride that was already there.'

Reba shook the ice in the bottom of his glass and studied it.

'You get how it works?' Stephen asked. 'Those lions, those *Mapogos*, had been stalking the pride for nearly ten days and had already killed one of the male leaders, but they were intent on wearing the second one down. We tracked them for more than a week, hunting into the wind, and on my last morning we caught up with them. We watched them from the jeep. It was just before dawn and all six were closing in on the remaining male. They drew around him like a pack of wolves, the circle getting smaller, and then—you should've seen it. It was incredible the way they grabbed the old alpha by the throat and pulled him down, and even before they killed him you could hear their roars of victory. You know that sound? It stops you in your tracks.'

Matt Reba scoffed. 'Anyone who has been on safari has a story like that.'

'So, it makes sense, doesn't it?'

'What makes sense?'

'That we take our lesson from that. Look, it's simple: I'm here to do business, so first we have to decide what we want, then we do what we have to do to get it.' Stephen lifted his glass. 'Plus,' he added, 'it will double our profit margin.'

4

Gulu, Uganda

From across the courtyard Tessa could hear a wooden pestle pounding cassava into flour. Laughter came in a burst, and there was a fragment of a song—a snatch she didn't recognise from a local radio station—that rose above the banging.

She lay beneath the gauzy mosquito net in the small hut that had been provided for her at the rehab centre and listened to the voices of those who were already up and moving about. She thought she heard Beatrice, the social worker, with her warm laughter and easy affection. Light came in where the thatch had weakened; someone called and clapped then stopped.

A part of her knew she should contact her family—she ought to Skype or send an email, but something held her back. Her parents would want to know why she hadn't contacted them—four days now since her birthday—but she would not be able to give them the answers they wanted. Tomorrow, Tessa thought, or the next day, and she tried to push aside the anxiety she felt, something to do with the need to make her own way and the feeling that she could not explain herself, at least not fully. Avoidance behaviour, she was good at that.

She got up, dressed, and cleaned her teeth with bottled water. It had become her habit to take a shower and wash her hair once a week. The showers were housed across the compound in a communal bathroom, which she loved for the way the girls joked, swapping stories and tending to each other's braids. It reminded her of her own school days, in the change rooms after swimming, though here she felt shy and self-conscious, welcomed, but not really part of the group. On the other mornings, she began the day by raking her hair back with her hands and tying it in a thick hair-elastic then using a small amount of soap to wash before rinsing. It was her morning custom, this birdbath from a plastic bowl. Afterwards she would brew a pot of coffee on a small primus and swill down her antimalarials, disguising the taste with a banana or, if she was lucky, a slice of ripe mango.

She heard the muezzin's call to prayer. The sound went through her and found a place just beneath her ribcage. This country with its layered religions, its tribal rituals and violent history—what had really brought her here? Was it the chance to do the kind of research she believed worthwhile or, as Stephen implied, was it just another brand of tourism, a voyeurism that morphed into something less worthy than she hoped? She recalled Stephen's smug smile when she'd had her bag stolen on arriving in Cape Town. 'The real African experience,' he said with a sardonic edge, then grinned, which had only heightened her determination to be different from him. She would make her mark, she would do something that mattered. 'You don't get it,' she'd said when she visited him before flying on to Uganda. 'What don't I get?' he replied. 'That you are a perfect human being and I'm a perfect arsehole?' He pulled a face and they caught each other's eye, then both burst out laughing. It was automatic, reciprocal. He knew her. As kids, they had always been competitive; she pitted herself against him and, even if she'd lost every fight for the first fifteen years, she knew there were times now when she didn't.

She glanced at the notebooks on the floor beside her bed; testimonials and case studies. She had let them slide there last night when sleep overtook her. *The story is our escort; without it we are blind.* The words of Chinua Achebe, a writer remembered for his famous novel, *Things Fall Apart*. Individual stories, Tessa argued, the stories of returnees like Oraako, were needed to establish techniques that would help others to cope in the future.

The centre currently housed about sixty returnees. More than seven thousand children had passed through in the last decade, sheltered and rehabilitated for a time with limited resources. Most children stayed for a few weeks, some stayed on for more than a year, but what then?

Two days after the cleansing ceremony, Oraako had come back. 'There has been trouble,' Dominic told her. 'As I feared, his uncle is against anyone who has been in the bush with the rebels. The boy is not wanted by his family. He will have to try his luck someplace else.'

'So what happens now? Where does he go?' Tessa had asked tentatively.

'He will stay here for as long as we can keep him, but eventually he will have to go to another village.'

'Which means he will probably end up in one of the displacement camps?'

Dominic had looked past her. 'Sometimes, when they come back, the anger in them rises even more. Maybe it is because they are no longer held by the rebels' laws. I have heard of those who turn on their parents—they are filled with hate.'

'And so the family breaks down.'

'Yes.'

It seemed that Dominic was trying to tell her something about himself but was unable—or perhaps she was just unable to read him. 'Which means there are times when forgiveness only goes so far?'

Dominic gave a deep sigh. 'Maybe it is as you say. Forgiveness is not without limits, but as we like to say here, hope is a vulture; it can pick away the bitterness.'

When Tessa had re-entered Oraako's name in her data collection she wondered whether his story as Chinua Achebe said, would be able to *escort* or guide anyone else or, despite Dominic's insistence on hope, become lost like so many others.

'Too many; it is like a plague,' Beatrice had told her. 'Too many; how can we cope? In the end, they all become one. There are days when I cannot rest, I feel the weight of all those children upon me.' Generous Beatrice, with her natural affection and soft eyes, but for Tessa, it was the kind of acceptance that felt like despair. 'I pray to my Lord. My Lord helps me,' Beatrice had said. 'He tells me this is the way life goes.'

Beatrice was Dominic's cousin; their mothers were sisters and they shared a common purpose. Both were practical, although Dominic was more optimistic—or perhaps he was just more determined. Hope was what mattered, he insisted. Tessa admired his dedication and his beliefs although, like her colleagues at the university, she felt that scientific research would support better ways of coping in the aftermath of trauma. She wanted to understand what such children had experienced as soldiers and how they dealt with those experiences. It was driving her, a hot hurricane in her head.

Walking towards Dominic's office, she rehearsed what she would say. This would be a chance to gain the kind of observational data that might help. There was other work being done in the area of trauma and memory. In her thesis, she had written that PTSD 'was a memory disorder'. It didn't affect everyone, but for those it did affect, a never-ending past could deprive the present of meaning. What were the trigger warnings, what were the path-breakers, the safe spaces? One thing for certain was that there wasn't a one-size-fits-all solution, only the absence of trauma would allow for that. She would make it clear to Dominic that she wasn't asking to be involved in the peace talks at any level, that for her it would be an opportunity to observe a rebel camp—a chance to see where and how the child soldiers had been living.

As she crossed the compound, a boy ran past her, rolling a bicycle tyre with a stick. It was a game played in the local streets that reminded her of a snapshot from some old-world childhood. 'Hello, Aunty!' the boy called in a shrill voice as he ran on ahead, his bare feet powdering the dust. *Aunty*, *Miss Tessa*, *Sister*—she was amazed by the affable familiarity, the openness of the people here. They wanted to feed her, make her comfortable, and in turn she wanted more than ever to return something to them.

It was still early morning but already people were moving about. About half-a-dozen girls in blue pinafores headed across to the classroom where the week's sewing lessons were held. They waved to her and giggled. Among them was a girl with a sway back and a walleye. Tessa had seen her pull at her hair repeatedly until it came out in tufts. She now linked her arm through that of another girl so that she might whisper something to her and laugh. Last week, in a counselling session with Beatrice, the same girl had plucked her eyelashes out and smacked her own face until it swelled—persistent self-cruelty that begged the question: if our earliest experiences shape who we are, what if those experiences are violent? If we are forced to do something wrong, can we ever move on?

Dominic's office was in a low concrete building. The roof lacked gutters so natural rainwater channels had formed in the soil beneath the barred windows. Rising damp had crumbled the walls to produce a lattice effect beneath a large mural along one side—blue-armed children played soccer amid giant butterflies, and beneath the window there was a longhorn cow with a striped face. The effect was celebratory, almost cartoonish. When Tessa first arrived it reminded her of a kindergarten. She liked its shabby, almost whimsical optimism, but after two months it was easy to see what often began with great enthusiasm could easily flake away.

Things Fall Apart. 'Everything turns to shit,' was how Stephen put it when she was in Cape Town. 'The Africans can't maintain anything, they let everything go.' It was the final thing he'd said to her before she left; a sour culmination of their last argument, and in seething frustration she hadn't spoken to him, or about him to her parents, since.

Dominic's door was open. Tessa stood for a moment, and when he failed to look up she knocked on the doorjamb. She had made an appointment to see him and felt certain that he knew she was standing there.

'Hello,' she said, and knocked again, a light, slightly urgent sound.

Finally, Dominic glanced up and nodded for her to enter. As she stepped forward he held up the book he had been reading. It was his copy of *Acoli Macon*. He cocked his head to one side. 'In here,' he said, 'there is an Acholi saying, *Ibino ma atakka pyeri opong*—you have come dressed for a big part in a dance, you have come full of ambitions.' He smiled and cast a critical eye over her. 'But, be warned, the dance might not be as easy as you think.'

She gave him a lopsided smile in reply.

He put the book down, pushing others aside. On the desk in front of him there was a clunky old desktop computer. It made an audible hum that seemed to keep time with the generator—and, like the generator, frequently lost connection, often for the better part of the day. For now, though, it worked, and as Tessa sat down on one of the plastic chairs, Dominic lifted his chin in the direction of the screen. 'There is an email addressed to me from someone you know,' he said and moved closer to the computer as though his eyesight was poor.

Tessa squared her shoulders and waited.

'You have been busy,' he added.

'You mean I have a colleague who is one of the delegates.'

'This one here, John Alphington?'

She nodded. 'He's from the ICG.'

'Ah yes, I see that, the International Crisis Group. Like so many others—Pax Christi, World Vision, Invisible Children—these NGOs they help, they hinder. Gulu has become an NGO city. Everywhere you see their white Toyotas.'

Tessa shifted uneasily. 'Maybe, but I don't belong to any organisation—political or religious. I don't have an agenda.'

Dominic tapped his index finger against his lip. 'Really? *Everyone* I know has an agenda.' He pointed to the computer screen and nodded. 'I know your colleague, John Alphington, and he does have an agenda, although it is one in favour of the ceasefire and retraction of the indictments, so I happen to agree with him.'

'I'm sorry, Dominic. I wanted to speak to you before he contacted you.'

Tessa noticed the pulse beating in Dominic's throat. The gold crucifix shone. For a time neither spoke; there was just the humming of the computer and voices outside calling to each other.

'There are claims that the talks will go ahead this week,' Tessa said, breaking the silence.

'Yes, there is to be a face-to-face meeting.'

Tessa glanced around the office. It was stuffy and cluttered. A dusty old-fashioned fan stood in one corner, its electrical cord cut, most likely appropriated for some other appliance. Beside it there was a filing cabinet, and on the wall above a whiteboard on which a list of returnees' names was written in smudged blue and red. Papers stacked in cardboard boxes were stored along one wall, and along the other two walls were crammed bookshelves.

The gold lettering on the spine of *The Divine Comedy* stood out like a challenge, although beside it there was a large photograph of Dominic shaking hands with the government minister, Betty Bigombe. Dominic had spoken of his admiration for Bigombe's efforts to initiate contact with Kony in the nineties. The photo, mounted in a plastic picture frame with scrolled corners, was covered in red dust, although there were fingerprints on the glass as if someone had recently wiped it with their hand.

Unlike the system of divine punishment in the *Inferno*, Dominic wanted reconciliation, he wanted peace, as did Betty Bigombe; they held on to the idea that things could change. An amnesty, a permanent ceasefire. Dominic sat at his desk in his baggy gabardine pants, his beige socks and slip-on sandals with his white shirt open at the neck, and Tessa felt a sudden tenderness for him; he looked weary and the thought came to her that he was always tired.

She said very carefully, 'Why do you think Dante says: *Abandon all hope ye who enter here*?'

'Ah, so you think that is where I am going?'

'You *are* going?'

Dominic nodded. 'But I do not think it will be Hell. I am not a medieval Catholic.' He lifted the gold crucifix. 'This was my father's,' he said. 'He spoke both Acholi and English. He went to church, but he was also a traditional healer. I am a reader of the Bible, but I believe in the ancestors' spirits too. I also use Western medicine. Ibuprofen is very good.' He smiled.

'We have this saying in Gulu: *God help me, but I'm going to run as well.* We think both ways at once.'

'And now you believe that peace is possible.'

'Anything is possible. I see that in America a black man is running for president. That the war in Iraq may end.'

Tessa sat forward. Feeling a nervous catch in her throat, she swallowed. 'Dominic,' she said, 'I want to come with you.' There was a small warning voice in her head that reminded her this was a breach of etiquette—she was asking too much of this man who had been her advocate and host. 'I'm physically fit. I can take care of myself,' she said, then waited, hoping there might be other tacit understandings between them that would carry their own weight. There were the benefits: she could think of many—international exposure, maybe extra funding for the centre, help with the new school.

Dominic picked up a pen and twirled it in his hand. His nails were yellow and split. He stared at her and raised his eyebrows then put the pen down.

'I don't think so,' he said. 'This is to be a sizable delegation, but it will be an arduous and possibly dangerous trek into the Congo. Besides, Kony and the LRA are very strict about who they allow.'

'If I came, it would be as a neutral bystander. I would have nothing to do with the talks. You can trust me to stay out of the way.'

Dominic waved her words aside as if he were swatting a fly. 'Ah, you are like a smouldering coal ready to catch fire! You have a dangerous will. But you are determined, Dr Tessa, I can see that, I can see you are adamant. You might have the support of another delegate, but not *my* approval.' His tone had become stern and the crease between his brows deepened. He stared at her. 'Let me ask you this: what is it that you hope to achieve?'

Tessa took a deep breath, afraid of affectation, afraid of inadequacy. 'I want to do something with my education rather than spend the rest of my life in a university without really contributing anything very much.' Immediately she felt embarrassed, sure that she had overreached. 'Dominic, please. I would go only as an onlooker. Someone to report on the conditions in the camps. You know that there is not enough information about how the rebels function or the actual extent of child participation. I could document something of that.'

Outside a horn beeped.

Through the open door of the office, Tessa saw the gates to the compound entrance swing open. An army jeep entered and, when it came to a stop, two government soldiers got out. Both wore the shoulder-sleeve insignia of the Ugandan flag on their fatigues. The taller of the two had a general's stripe; the other, who was loose-limbed and lean, adjusted his peaked cap with his thumb, then reached into the cabin for his rifle, which he pulled out and casually slung over his shoulder in a way that seemed perfectly natural.

Dominic leant his elbows on the desk and studied the soldiers through the open door of his office, then glanced back at Tessa. 'And now we have more delegates,' he said. 'But you need to remember that it is not just the LRA who have carried out crimes against humanity. Kony is right when he accuses the government army of atrocities. These men—' he nodded in the direction of the soldiers '—belong to the Uganda People's Defence Force. They are meant to protect the people against the rebels, but that has long been compromised. Why hasn't the ICC investigated the killing done by the Ugandan army?' Dominic bristled, as he did whenever the topic of the army arose. 'How it is that army commanders can inflate their troop numbers only to keep the salaries and rations of dead soldiers for themselves?' he said in a reproving voice. 'You understand how it is? They promise peaceful outcomes, but this is still a business from which they can profit—Operation Pay Yourself.' He flashed another quick look at Tessa then stood up. 'And now I must go and greet my guests.'

From inside the office, Tessa could barely discern what language they spoke let alone make out what they were saying. Dominic towered over the soldiers and it was the first time Tessa had seen him use such animated gestures. Normally it was his slow purposefulness that struck her; now, as he held his head high, she saw he was as much a soldier as those in uniform.

She moved to the front porch for a better view and craned her neck. They were arguing. Dominic raised his voice and shook his head as he shifted from one foot to the other, then he placed his hands on his hips. The soldier standing closest to him moved aside.

Across the driveway, a game of soccer was taking place. Excited cheering, then a gleeful yell as one of the boys scored a goal between the two haphazard posts. The galvanised sheeting on a nearby lean-to banged whenever anyone kicked the soccer ball into it. It sounded like a marker of time, followed repeatedly by the boys' whooping.

Finally, the soldier in the peaked cap swung his rifle around from his back and, lifting it, aimed it at the boys playing soccer. It appeared to be a joke; he laughed, lowering his rifle, then shrugged to make light of the pantomime he had just staged.

Dominic waved his hand disdainfully. It was clear he would not be intimidated, and that he had also agreed on something on his own terms, and then, almost as if he had waved them away too, the soccer players abandoned their game as the soldiers walked back to the jeep.

As Dominic returned to his office, Tessa stepped aside. He glanced at her. 'Kony has moved the meeting forward,' he said.

She nodded. 'So you will be leaving soon?'

'Yes, within the hour.'

The air was warm and Tessa's hands felt sticky. She could smell smoke and the scent of burning rubbish from the incinerator in the corner of the compound. Adrenaline rushed through her. It was that foot-off-the-ground sensation she felt whenever she gave in to a slightly reckless impulse. 'So, you will agree to let me come?' She heard the anticipation in her voice.

Dominic's brow furrowed. 'We have already been through this. It would be too difficult, too dangerous. Besides, you would not be welcome.' He straightened. 'I will see you sometime next week.'

'Dominic?'

'Again, I must say no. You are a woman. You would be at risk. And—'

'And I am white.'

'Yes, you are white. You are a white Westerner. You are a woman.'

She heard the note of derision in his voice and wished she hadn't, but as if to confirm his position he went on, 'Besides, I would feel responsible for you.' He jabbed his chest above his heart. 'If anything were to happen to you, *I* would have to take the blame.'

'Dominic, please, I will gladly sign a waiver. You are not responsible for me, but this is important—my going might eventually assist the children here.'

Dominic began to move things around on his desk. 'How can it help? What good are your reports when, as you tell me yourself, all they do is gather dust or end up in the computer system of some foreign university?'

'Don't you see? That's exactly where they will end up if I don't try to make them count. These children's stories have little meaning unless the rest of the world knows about them.'

'So you want to go to the source of the conflict and report back?'

'Yes.'

He smiled, but not happily. 'You sound like a journalist.'

'Perhaps that is not such a bad thing,' Tessa said carefully. 'If I can help these children by raising awareness, it might influence what you do here by supporting the call for more counselling. The caseworkers you need. Another psychiatrist. One that comes here more than once every three months.'

She knew she was pushing hard. She saw Dominic's acquiescence in the way he refused to look at her.

'Please yourself,' he said finally. 'But you are right: I will not guarantee your safety.'

5

Anything Tessa could leave behind she did. She packed only the lightest camping equipment—dried food, a small tent, a sleeping bag, her phone—then quickly changed into sturdy clothes and her hiking boots before joining Dominic and the Ugandan soldiers who stood in a cluster around the jeep.

Dominic introduced her as Dr Lowell, but before anything further was said a noisy *boda-boda* pulled up with two men on the back. The men got off with their packs and paid the driver, who revved the battered motorbike and drove away, raising a small trail of dust. Both men were delegates from the International Crisis Group. The first, a field analyst, introduced himself as Hans Berg—a Norwegian with sandy-coloured hair and hooded eyes. The second was the American delegate Tessa had contacted.

'John Alphington,' he said and offered his hand. 'So finally we meet in person.' He had grey, collar-length hair and sharp features, a large nose and stubbled beard. Tessa had seen photographs of him online but he looked older in real life. The crêpey waffle of skin on his neck and the crow's feet that came into relief when he smiled gave him a world-weary look. *Actually, they all look worn*, she thought. Even the younger soldier in the peaked cap—whom she had heard Dominic address as Gideon—appeared older than he should.

When the soldiers helped Dominic and the Norwegian to pack the jeep, Tessa thanked Alphington for vouching for her.

'You seem pretty fit,' Alphington commented. 'And I suspect you've played your own part by talking Dominic into letting you come along.'

Tessa shifted uneasily. 'I was hoping to observe the camp, that's all.'

Alphington lifted an eyebrow. 'Because you know this is Uganda—and in Africa there aren't so many protocols?'

He raised his head slightly and, following his gaze, Tessa saw an enormous marabou stork on top of the compound's water tower. It arched its neck and groomed its feathers with its blade-like beak.

'They've become dependent on human garbage,' he noted. 'I've seen them eat plastic bottle tops, pieces of metal, human faeces. Scavengers. Some people call them the undertaker bird.' He looked back at her.

'I promise you, I won't be in anyone's way,' Tessa said.

'That's a lot to promise,' Alphington replied, and a smile that broke across his face seemed to suggest she knew very little. 'Look,' he conceded, 'there might be some value in you coming. Like us, you're an international presence and you may well get to see some of the child combatants who are with the rebels. But these people here—' he nodded in the direction of the Ugandan soldiers '—they don't actually care what you've done. Doctorates don't mean anything. Besides, there's a ten-hour drive before we even get close to the proposed meeting site, and then who knows how long it will take to trek in—at least a day, maybe more. No one will help you on this journey and there will be no one to get you out should anything go wrong.'

He looked across at Dominic then rolled his shoulders, and there was something in his brooding watchfulness that warned Tessa to be careful and not press him any further. It's okay, she thought, she had no right to expect his allegiance let alone camaraderie. Stay neutral. Although, a moment later, Alphington turned and said almost confidentially, 'You know, this may not turn out as we hope. The odds are stacked against us. There's even the possibility that these talks might end up making things worse.'

'Worse how?' Tessa asked.

'They can always get worse.' Alphington shrugged. 'Tensions escalate. Things get out of whack. Look, I've read your work, and I assume you've read mine. I'm not an idealist; I'm a pragmatist. Anyway, people don't always help you out. Personally, I don't know any truly good Samaritans, do you?' He stepped back and put his hands in his pockets. 'I'm not even sure they exist,' he added. 'As far as I'm concerned, these talks are about getting people to agree to terms they don't want to agree to.' He smiled and Tessa reminded herself that she had met men like him before; they might dismiss you completely, or they might press you up against a bar and talk on endlessly about what they had achieved.

Alphington dumped his pack into the back of the jeep and got in after it. Gideon had already started the engine and was talking to the general who sat in the front passenger seat, his arm resting on the sill. It was a battered army vehicle—a closed-in six-seater with a second fuel tank. A long crack ran across the front windshield and a spare tyre was attached to the bonnet. There was a rifle holster and a large plastic container of water in the back. Dominic hoisted himself into the central passenger seat and Berg got in on the other side. Tessa watched them and, in that moment, she felt she was making a mistake. She had a last-minute urge to tell them she had changed her mind, but before she could give in to it she stepped onto the rusty running board and climbed in.

They drove from the centre through the township of Gulu, which she had visited a few times with Beatrice. Some of the newer buildings were brightly painted in lime green and yellow and had low verandahs, others were completely run-down. Most of the inhabitants lived in mud-and-tin shanties or under tattered tarps along the tracks of a disused railway line. Northern Uganda had seen decades of civil war, yet somehow the town had not only survived but adapted. Outlets for Western Union money transfers and mobile telephone sellers, housed in small concrete shops, had sprung up, and beside them were stallholders who sold plastic buckets and shopping bags with pictures of the Eiffel Tower and *I Love Paris* printed on them. A 1950s-style white mannequin with blonde hair modelled a colourful *busuti* with puffed sleeves. It stood rather jauntily beside the mats of drying millet while women swept the earth with acacia branches or washed their clothes at stirrup pumps before spreading them out on the grass to dry. Others had babies slung low on their backs, and helped one another to lift the loads they balanced on their heads. They stood in their brightly coloured skirts or bent from the hips like strange tropical flowers. Bending, straightening, bearing bundles of grass-tied cassava, loads of firewood and charcoal, basins of dried fish.

Along the sides of the road there were great middens of rubbish mostly made of plastic bags, and in the shade under sheltered awnings merchants sat with sweet potatoes and green oranges neatly stacked in pyramids. Butchers in bloody shirts used pangas to hew strips of meat from carcasses that still had dark hairy tails, and children in ragged T-shirts rounded up small herds of cattle. Laughing, they threw stones or called to each other as the straggling beasts walked on, heads bowed under their enormous horn spreads. Girls sat in the shade selling petrol in Coke bottles.

It was the children who most fascinated Tessa. They were everywhere, labouring from an early age with their accomplished adult gestures. Children carrying children smaller than themselves or lugging sacks of grain, while others balanced plastic water containers on their heads. Often they stopped to wave at the passing vehicle—'Hello! Hello!'—or they watched shyly from shadowed doorways. Tessa smiled and waved back, and the thing that struck her most was how young they all were. The older ones—from the age of about ten onwards—were missing. Their absence, Tessa thought, was like the last scene in the tale of *The Pied Piper* when the town's children disappeared through a door in the mountainside.

They passed a school surrounded by a low brick wall topped with shards of glass and coils of barbed wire. Within the grounds there were no students; the doors and windows were bricked up—another 'ghost school'. Perhaps this was because there was limited funding, but mostly schools like this one closed because the administrators were afraid they could not protect the children from possible attacks or abductions. Tessa had heard the stories and seen the results. Beyond the outskirts of Gulu and further north, huts had been burnt to the ground, while great stretches of land lay fallow and untended crops were choked with weeds.

They continued along the mostly deserted roads of broken bitumen, with ribbed red dirt tracks that disappeared into the distance. Every so often they encountered groups of people travelling along the road who lifted a hand in acknowledgement before moving onto the verge in single file to let them pass. They passed a battered bike saddled with a crate of rope-tied cargo or one of the overcrowded *matatus* with their cheerful philosophies on the back window: JESUS HAS THE SOLUTIONS, Tessa read, or PSALM 121: I LIFT UP MY EYES TO THE MOUNTAINS—WHERE DOES MY HELP COME FROM? MY HELP COMES FROM THE LORD. And famously, THE RICH CRY TOO. The last was a frequent slogan in northern Uganda and one that Dominic favoured; he smiled now and repeated it: 'Ah, yes! The rich cry too.'

Gideon drove, drumming his fingers on the steering wheel. He wore wraparound sunglasses with lenses that mirrored the landscape. Sitting higher, in the far back seat, Tessa watched him in the side-view mirror. Further on, the road became increasingly potholed, and the bitumen suddenly gave way to dirt, but he sped anyway, swerving in the dust. Dotted across the landscape were clusters of small mudbrick huts, many with cassava tubers drying on roofs of thatch or corrugated iron, but before long, the land levelled and stretched out. Miles and miles of thorny flatlands under a cloud-massed sky.

The jeep became hot and stuffy, and the general put on the air conditioner then began to fiddle with the radio, crackling through the local FM channels. Tessa had been trying to teach herself Acholi, with Beatrice encouraging her by repeating a smattering of common phrases, but on the radio the announcers spoke too quickly. 'Anyway, you've got a tin ear,' Stephen had told her years earlier. And what irritated Tessa most was that he was probably right: when she read, she understood, but when she listened or tried to pronounce the words herself, she failed—they were like dry stones in her mouth.

In the seat next to her, Berg roused himself and wound down the window an inch or so, enough not to let the dust in. In the front, the general switched the dial to a music channel and singing voices rose in harmony, the rhythm building—an exhilarating solo then the chorus rippling in call-and-response as they drove along the boundary of one of the vast displacement camps.

For several kilometres they passed a sea of makeshift tents, from which the mumbled sound lifted above the singing on the radio and buzzed with an intense undertone—an amplified humming as if from a beehive and as impossible to ignore as the overwhelming stench.

Berg wound the window up again, but it made little difference. Plumes of blue smoke rose from cookfires where people massed in their tens of thousands. They were like a spray of colourful dots, constantly moving so that the whole campsite seemed to tremble. Mounds of picked-over rubbish, the waft of open sewage, everywhere spot fires burning what could not be recycled.

The music on the radio broke up and the general turned it off, swatting the dial as though it were a mosquito.

'Now we are faced with people in transit,' he said.

'Yet they live out their days here,' Alphington replied as he looked out the window. 'They are born, they grow old, a few leave, but most of them are just floating.'

'Floating,' Tessa repeated. The word sounded disembodied.

'Yes, floating, like ghosts. There are some two million. More people die in these camps than they do in the war.'

Here, then, was a rival to Dante's Hell, with children too, Tessa thought, and as they passed, she glimpsed their small shapes moving among the garbage heaps.

'Perhaps it is in the government's interest,' Dominic said. It was unlike Dominic to make such a comment; normally it was his insistence on diplomacy that Tessa noticed, but it seemed as if the sight of the camp had stirred something in him and made him less reserved.

The general glanced at him in the rear-view mirror. 'You talk like a fool,' he said. 'It is a military strategy and necessary for their safety.'

Dominic rubbed his chin. His hand made a sandpapery sound. 'That is not true,' he replied. 'When ninety per cent of these people are Acholi, you have to ask: why are they refugees in their own country? Most have been uprooted without a choice. It is the Ugandan army who sends them to these camps.'

'The camps are a temporary measure,' the general replied, waving his hand in the air. 'President Museveni has promised to dismantle them.'

'So he says,' Dominic replied. 'But it is no secret that he wants the camps to remain.'

The general turned to face Dominic, and Tessa saw that he might be easily provoked. He squared his shoulders and the muscles in his neck tensed. 'I can assure you that what the president does is for the best.'

'And how you can assure me of that,' Dominic said in an even tone, 'unless it is by regarding all Acholi people as potential rebel supporters who must be monitored and controlled?'

'Have you forgotten your own past, Lieutenant? Or was that Major? Surely you have seen there is no other way around it. *Kwo odokotek*,' the general added—life has become difficult.

'Perhaps,' Dominic replied in the same low voice. 'Or perhaps the government has made it so. But what I have seen is that these camps have become permanent. The government wants the Acholi people to stay here, it wants them to be silenced.'

The general pointed his finger at Dominic. 'I would be cautious if I were you,' he warned. 'With such strong sympathies it's reasonable to ask why you are even coming to these talks.'

Dominic held his gaze. 'I do not support the LRA, if that's what you mean—nor do I support the government.' Then he turned and looked out the window, shaking his head as if trying to free himself from some terrible sound. 'The rebels say we need a fairer system, but even if I wanted to defend them in this, how can I when they are killing my people?'

'They are killing everyone,' the general replied. 'They are brutal extremists.'

'Kony—'

'Kony has not a single religious bone in his body.'

For a long time they travelled in silence. There was a CD player built in to the console but there was no suggestion of playing anything else now that the radio was out of range. Tessa thought about using her phone, of quietly pressing the earbuds into her ears, then decided against it. She kept it switched off to conserve the battery. A typical *muzungu*, she thought, with her expensive gadgets, her bottled water and pale skin.

'Unlike us, you can leave any time you like,' Dominic had reminded her. 'You are in the fortunate position of always having a return ticket in your back pocket.'

6

At the park border they had their paperwork stamped before taking a dirt road through the top end, north of Murchison Falls. Great-tusked elephants stood in a sea of grass and fanned their ears, and on the yellow plains giraffes walked in groups like towering flowers. Termite mounds dotted the landscape, lookouts for small antelope that commonly stood on them to survey the surrounding scene.

From the back of the four-wheel drive Tessa scanned the trees in the hope of seeing a leopard as she had once done with her father's documentary team. Agile, spotted, amber-eyed, they favoured the flat-topped acacias, often dragging their prey into the upper branches, a larder for small hoofstock: gazelle, impala, kob, and on occasion, monkeys. She mistook a vespiary for one; concertinaed and golden-coloured, it hung like an enormous bag of sugar. Then, on the next rise, she let out a small cry of surprise and swivelled in her seat when she did in fact glimpse a magnificent leopard with her cub. Dappled in the shade, they were draped together in the fork of a tree, and for a moment she felt cheerful, almost cavalier. Then amazed. She smiled at the warthogs that knelt to graze and, when startled by the jeep, ran off with their tails in the air, awkwardly stiff-legged as if tottering on high heels.

A few kilometres further on, Berg pointed to something lying on the grassy slope. It was the size of a large waterbuck, or perhaps it was a zebra. It looked as though it was running on its side. Unable to get up, it kicked frantically. Overhead three vultures soared on the updraft—lifting high, then slowly swirling down again. Her father, with his photographer's eye and fascination for the natural world, often spoke of survival. He would remind her, *It is always the one best suited to its environment that comes out on top; that's a fair enough law*. It made sense that he was on the leopard's side, on the vulture's side. She feigned objection. Luck, circumstance, it didn't seem fair at all.

Nature, he had replied. *The instinct that seeks life. You know that, don't you? Survival comes at a cost.*

An hour later they came to the Nile, north of Lake Albert, where they crossed over on a truss bridge. The current was swift and great green clumps of fringed vegetation sailed downstream. Buffalo grazing on a huge floating island passed beneath them and continued downriver like a living barge. In the distance fishermen stood in narrow canoes and cast their nets. The jeep rattled across the bridge and when they reached the other side they stopped and got out to stretch.

They could hear the rush of the Nile and the birdlife that was drawn to it. Dominic handed around a few oily chapattis filled with beans and egg, and afterwards they had tea from a metal thermos while Tessa offered mixed nuts and sultanas from a traveller's pack she had in her rucksack. Like picnickers on a warm afternoon, they relaxed. Gideon, in his peaked cap and sunglasses, had taken to pointing things out: a solitary shoebill with a reptilian face that stood on the shore like a sentinel, and a sea eagle hunting for fish, although the closest sea was hundreds of kilometres away. He looked back at Tessa and laughed when she began slapping at the tsetse flies that appeared. Scratching a red welt on his own neck, he asked: 'Why do tsetse flies like us? Because they must blood-suck,' and smiled wryly before telling them they had better get back into the jeep before they were swarmed. 'Especially me,' he said. 'They like celebrities—and in Africa we have very few!'

They drove west out of the park through even more fertile country where tea plantations looked like clipped English gardens. But within the next kilometre the roads deteriorated and they swerved to avoid the biggest potholes. 'They call this the African massage,' Alphington said as the jeep juddered over the uneven surface, then pulled a face at his tired joke. Tessa held the bar above her to stop her head banging on the roof as her body jolted from side to side. At the next intersection, a truck lay overturned. The passenger door was missing and the windscreen was peppered with what looked like bullet holes. The chassis was rusted, but that was not unusual.

'Keep going,' the general said curtly, and Gideon accelerated past the wreck, driving up onto the verge before he brought them back to the road.

From the back seat Tessa was unsure what she had glimpsed. Was she seeing things? Was she imagining dangers that were not even there? Neither Alphington nor Berg said anything, and when she glanced at Dominic he faced the other way. It was only Gideon who, on catching her eye in the rear-view mirror, seemed to confirm her suspicions. '*Wi-lobo*—that is the way of the world,' he said, lifting his chin.

Gravel clattered against the underside of the jeep and dust billowed behind them. They drove on and by late afternoon the vegetation changed again, becoming dense and lush, the terrain suddenly more mountainous. Local people referred to this country as the bush, although it was not the bush as Tessa knew it, more a knight's move from the dry spiky brittleness of Australia. Everything here was greener, wetter—so rich in rotting undergrowth that it seemed to breathe. When she had flown over, it was like seeing a colour movie for the first time. The wide sky and the red soil might've been somewhere in Australia, but not the light. In Australia the light was higher, brighter. Here it was green, gold, purple; it infused the landscape and held her, a place not filled with light but made of light itself. And yet something about it seemed aqueous, almost submarine.

Late in the afternoon they came to a checkpoint on the Congolese border. The general pulled out two yellow sheets of paper and passed them to the guard, who peered through the windows with watery eyes before stalking off to a glassed-in booth.

'He's drunk,' the general said.

When the guard returned fifteen minutes later, the general confronted him. 'What is it—don't you remember me? Why are we waiting here for you? Huh, what do you think I am going to do? Do you think I am about to offer you money?'

The guard coughed, a loose, phlegmy chest cough. 'I know who you are,' he said. 'You are General David Suruma. But we must check everyone. When the sun goes down, we start to worry more. Daylight is dangerous, but it is worse at night—no road is safe, and often the people who pass through here are not who they say they are.'

'The military presence is strong in this area,' the general said. 'Why do you curl your tail? Are you a coward?'

'I am not a coward,' the guard replied. 'I worry because the army does not protect us.' He leant in through the window and there was a strong whiff of alcohol. 'I have seen what can happen.' His bloodshot eyes revealed a look of terror. 'A village was raided two days ago. A whole family massacred.'

Tessa heard the thickness in his voice—true fear, that came from a place she had not known until now. Her one thought was to get past him and silence the escalating feeling that she was in over her head. Keep moving forward, she thought.

The general disregarded him. 'We do our job,' he said. 'It is you who must work with us.'

The guard started to reply, but the general put his hand up to silence him. 'Enough! We are not here to answer to you. Let us through.'

7

Dusk had come by the time they reached a small village where they met six other delegates, including a high-ranking government official from Sudan and two village elders—one Acholi and one Ma'di man.

The delegates made a polite display of handshaking along with official greetings and formal introductions. Superfluous to them except as a curiosity, Tessa kept a low profile but, looking from one delegate to the other and studying their body language and cautious smiles as they sized each other up, she wondered how they would navigate their way through the talks to come. No one seemed at ease; they spoke with arms folded, hands in pockets. Only Gideon laughed.

Darkness descended and stars massed in the clear night sky. Two women from the local village set down kerosene lamps and brought out platters of sweet potatoes, beans and millet bread. From across the nearby gorge, baboons whooped and barked, their frantic screeches intensifying to fever pitch before becoming weird echoes that stopped and started up again.

'It could be something's after them,' Alphington said. 'Usually they settle at night, but they can probably smell us.'

'There is also the smell of food in the village,' Gideon added. 'But it could be that is just how they are—they like to fight.'

The fire glowed. They sat in a circle on plastic chairs and continued to eat; next was a stew of groundnuts with banana whose mottled skins were nearly black and the soft flesh inside almost syrupy. Afterwards they drank local beer served to them by one of the women, who knelt on the ground and filled each gourd almost to the brim from a large clay pot. Sour-tasting, it mingled with the night's heightened scent and the smoke from the campfire. Tessa swallowed two or three mouthfuls then nursed the gourd in her lap and looked around uneasily. Dominic sat across from her. He no longer wore the gold crucifix around his neck—perhaps he feared its theft. They were in more hostile territory now—bandits, *boo kec*, rebels. Tessa wondered now if she really had seen bullet holes in the windscreen of the abandoned truck or if she had just imagined it. The LRA were not only notorious for the abduction and forced enlistment of children, they were also accused of large-scale massacres, murder, rape, dismemberment—all the clichés of African violence. But she needed to stop. Stay in control, she ordered herself. The worst thing would be to act as if she was scared. She hated the idea that she might be viewed as weak—the stereotypical woman among men.

Her heart thumped. She slowed her breathing and listened, taking notes in her head as she tried to gain a clearer sense of what it might be like to live in this isolated, often dangerous place. How did the children who were taken from their villages survive? The delegates were talking in a mix of languages and she strained to gather some idea of what they were saying. She heard Dominic mention Kony's name and figured they were talking about the trek to the meeting place the next morning. She knew she was fit and could handle the tough terrain, but there was something menacing in the way Gideon said, *The Congo*—the way he did not differentiate between the DRC and the Republic, but repeated, *The Kongo, the Kongo* in a way that made it sound like a terrifying place.

The conversation rose and fell. Insects were drawn to the firelight and bumped against her face; she tasted one that flew into her mouth and spat it out. Alphington smiled. Music came from another part of the village—the soft mournful sound of a *sansa*, the small thumb piano that was common but resonated differently from one village to the next. A pig snuffled—or what she thought was a pig, until she realised it was a baboon that had come in close and sat near the edge of the campfire clearing: a male with its long ruff of hair and elongated muzzle. For a moment she glimpsed its dog-like face before it turned and scurried back into the shadows.

As the evening wore on some of the group began to talk over each other while others broke off into side discussions, their voices escalating almost to the point of drowning out the night sounds that surrounded them. Fractured languages, including the English Tessa listened for.

'The rebels don't even know why they are fighting,' Gideon said. 'They call themselves insurgents and freedom fighters, when they are simply religious fanatics. Why should the indictments be dropped, why should they be granted amnesty and get off scot-free?'

'You come with the wrong mindset,' Dominic replied. He spoke like a teacher giving a lesson. He lifted his chin slightly and set his shoulders back, his eyes on the general. 'We must speak constructively with them, we must make a deal with them,' he said. 'The LRA say they have a manifesto, they have their causes. They want to end the government's dictatorship.'

'Rubbish!' the general scoffed, a look of outraged astonishment on his face. 'What was originally a rebellion has turned into terrorism. If they had a political problem, we would have solved it a long time ago. The gap has widened.'

'These talks should bridge that divide.' It was the Norwegian, Berg, who spoke, his European accent a reminder of the outside world.

Tessa watched the general rub his knees with his hands as though they were sticky. He sighed and raised his eyebrows with the disbelieving stare of a man whose patience is being tested. 'Our government has been trying to bridge it,' he replied. 'They encourage everybody to take part in the dialogue—look at all of you who are here.' He waved his hand from one delegate to the other. 'And all those who have volunteered to help mediate—even the Pope!' He laughed at his own joke and waited for them to join in. Gideon smiled his crooked smile and moved restlessly while the others looked on. There was an awkward silence. 'But Kony is insolent,' the general continued. 'He has snubbed all efforts.'

The government official from Sudan pushed a log further into the coals and the flames leapt. He was a large man with glasses and a gap between his front teeth. 'Kony is not a madman, as some people say,' he insisted. 'He knows what he is doing. For him this war has become a way of life—he has gained from it.'

He might've gone on to say more except the general was quick to interrupt: 'Then you should put more pressure on Sudan to stop supplying weapons.'

Tessa watched them. How could it work, all of this? Negotiation behaviour was a growing speciality—John Alphington had published papers on it. What was required was a careful strategy, but *when the disconnect is cavernous*, she had read in his paper or someone else's, *then each declares the other a fool.*

They began to talk over each other again.

'The rebels are hyenas,' Gideon announced. He had taken his cap off and put his sunglasses in his top pocket. His eyes glistened in the firelight. 'They should be punished,' he added, 'as a biting dog is punished.'

The village elder frowned and shook his head. 'I am tired of hearing the Acholi are a savage people, and that my brothers here—' he gestured to the Ma'di man '—are wild animals. We have been cut off, our homes and our cattle have been looted. We have no choice but to make a stand.'

'If your people are not animals, then they are *ankole*—cowdung,' Gideon said and grinned.

Alphington looked at the young soldier with interest. He put his beer down and sat forward. 'Do you think that tribalism helps?' he asked in a careful voice. 'Do you think it does any good to set one group against another?' His eyes were fierce and the lines on either side of his mouth made his face seem both grave and harsh.

The general shot him a pained look. 'We cannot deny the divisions,' he replied in defence of his aide. 'They exist everywhere; they exist the world over.' He waved his hand in an expansive arc. 'In Uganda they exist between the north and the south and it does not pay to have a short memory. Our responsibility is to protect the civilians and protect ourselves. We need peace terms that will work, we need a good military.'

The village elder regarded the general with a troubled face. 'Your military destroys us. They say they do not practise black magic, but they are *lajok*—wizards. You have been to Kampala, you have seen what a booming city it is, but in the north, we have nothing. This is what happens: old tribal hatreds split us in two.'

Around the fire their expressions were angry, conflicted. How could they possibly go into these talks and not shout one another down? John Alphington leant towards Tessa and said quietly, if sharply, 'They all have their own version of what the LRA is. These are supposedly some of the best negotiators, brought together to break the stalemate, and you see the divisions. Some want to soften the ICC's war crimes indictments on the LRA rebels in a bid for peace, others want harsher terms. In the end, it is the Ugandan people who will suffer if we cannot agree.'

Tessa said nothing. Something hard and tight had settled itself in her stomach; a kind of sick dread was filling her up. Perhaps they were rehearsing, merely thrashing out what they would moderate when the talks actually took place, but there was little sign that they would agree, let alone act as a united front.

'Will Kony even show up?' Gideon asked.

'Let us wait and see,' replied the government official from Sudan. 'First, let him meet with us. These talks must be worth the effort or they will stall again.'

From behind them came a low grunt followed by a more distant call—a fevered *wahoo, wahoo!* Tessa looked for the baboon with its grey ruff in the nearby foliage and for a moment she thought she heard something move. Someone outside the circle, one of the villagers perhaps, threw a stone.

Around her the delegates continued to argue, their voices competing—one rising, another lifting to meet it. There was the scent of steaming bananas and somewhere she thought she could smell cigarette smoke. Most Ugandans frown upon smoking, Dominic had told her. *We see it as a weakness, local beer is our vice.* She shook at her near-empty gourd, surprised she had drunk so much. Her mouth felt slightly numb, her lips swollen. She stared into the glow of the fire. It was the general who was speaking now; he said the time would be wasted—hadn't they counted how many times Kony had already delayed signing the agreement? The rebels were not sorry for what they had done.

No, Dominic insisted, that was not true; there were some who were looking for a way out and they should be granted amnesty. A ceasefire was possible if Kony would agree to the terms and sign this time.

The general glared at him. 'They are thugs, criminals!' He sighed dramatically. 'And what you call peace talks are really peace jokes. Kony will do the same thing he always does. He will make demands that cannot be met. He will not comply with the ICC.'

Tessa waited for Dominic to reply, but it was the elder who

spoke, his brow crinkled like bark. He talked of the spirit world, of using ash and placing charms in courtyards, of casting sleep by touch. 'We must listen to our ancestors.'

'Peace, uncle!' insisted the Sudanese mediator, lifting his hands and patting the air in a gesture of conciliation. 'We need to focus on unity, on moving forward. That is our only hope of ending this war. Let us build trust. This is not a local problem. It crosses borders, it affects the whole region.'

'An erratic leader keeps everyone on edge,' the general said without irony. 'He divides everyone. What choice do we have other than to go back to military action?'

'Don't you see that is the problem?' Dominic replied. 'Kony doesn't trust the army when they speak of military control.'

At which the general pointed his finger at Dominic. 'If you want to talk about trust, then tell me, why should Kony trust you, when you are a deserter?'

Dominic stood, knocking his chair over. He was much taller than the general, and for a moment it looked as though he might reach down and grab him by the throat. Tessa noticed his fist clench at his side, then slowly release again. It shocked her to see this other side of Dominic—a spike of violence before he brought himself under control. 'We have a chance to end this war,' he said. 'That is our hope. *Hope*,' he repeated. 'Hope should be our future.'

Mosquitoes whined, and some of the more daring baboons scuttled in closer for food. Two males, one large and the other a smaller, scruffier one, began to fight at the edge of the camp, screeching with bared teeth until Gideon suddenly swung his rifle around and shot the larger one.

The sound rang out through the night and, as the bullet hit, the baboon lurched with a piteous scream, causing the rest of the troop to scurry away on all fours.

The shot echoed in Tessa's brain and, following the screeching aftermath of the baboon, she heard some of the delegates laugh.

Gideon gave the Ma'di man a friendly clap on the back then, slinging his rifle over his shoulder, sat down again and looked at Tessa. 'Is that what you're hoping for?' he asked her. 'For action?' He gave a half-shrug and Tessa felt her hands tremble. She stared at the forest into which the other baboons had fled. The gunshot was like a great door slamming. Her feet felt leaden, her boots heavy and hot. You don't have to put your finger in a fire to know it will burn; simple common sense, and yet here she was in this volatile place.

Later that night, lying in her sleeping bag, she thought, I'm an idiot. Dominic was right, John Alphington was right. But it was Stephen, with his knack for seeing through her, who had given her the most stinging warning. *Africa isn't kind—it will swallow you whole*, he had said when he handed back her passport. She took it from him and stepped away. She had been careful not to let him see the bruises on her wrist from when her bag had been snatched outside the airport, careful not to let him have the last word—except he had, and maybe he was right. If she had any sense she would quit now before she got herself into something she couldn't handle.

The knot in her stomach tightened. Several years ago, Stephen had said, *You should know how to look after yourself,* when he and a couple of his friends surprised her with a visit to a shooting range for a three-hour lesson in how to use a handgun. Ridiculous, she had argued, but she'd gone along anyway. Earplugs and eye protection, clay targets, large red dots on paper sheets, the ease of the trigger and the jolting shock of the recoil. But now Gideon's precision was real—the shot was real—the baboon's corpse dragged away and she was shaking. Perhaps she should ask Dominic if she could get an escort back to Gulu? No, don't, she told herself. Be calm. You need to do this. Don't back out now.

In the dark, she could hear some of the delegates still arguing; someone coughed, then groaned. She lay awake for most of the night until eventually she dozed, fitfully at first, before falling into a deep sleep that broke at dawn when the baboons began to hoot again.

8

As the sun came up, they drank black tea and ate millet porridge before reloading their packs. Now they were on foot—a party of a dozen, with the general at the front and Gideon at the rear, armed with rifles. The pace was quick and, despite her fitness, Tessa strained to keep up. The others were more accustomed to this type of trekking and moved fast; even the older delegates walked as if their limbs were sprung with wire.

They picked their way through the first miles of thick undergrowth then began to climb a steep rise. When they reached the top, Tessa looked out across the forest. It was an endless deep green swathe, crimpled and spongy like a sea of broccoli into which, it was said, you might enter and never find your way out.

The day's heat intensified. Insects swarmed and, regardless of the long sleeves and the repellent Tessa had put on, her skin rose in ugly welts, itchy red blotches that added to the scabby half-healed bites she already had on her arms and legs. She willed herself not to scratch and focused on Hans Berg's rucksack.

A small red flag with a blue Scandinavian cross was stitched on the corner. The neatness of the stiches reminded her of the patch sewn on Oraako's mother's dress. She imagined boys younger than Oraako who had trekked through these places without food, without water, without knowing what would become of them.

Keep going, she told herself. Keep up. Her pace fell into a rhythm and her mood lifted. Bee-eaters darted through the understorey—a kaleidoscopic flare of red, blue and orange, they lit the green foliage like tiny jewels. She moved now as if through a greenish dream, at times interrupted by small-faced monkeys that scampered in the branches or lightly dropped to the ground. On one occasion an alpha male ran past her, displaying his vivid blue balls, then glanced back over his shoulder with a look less territorial than comical. It made her smile, as if the joke had been meant just for her. She stepped over the tangled undergrowth, thankful for her solid bush-walking boots, and found herself becoming swifter and more agile the further they went.

Around midday the clouds built up and it began to rain. Great heavy drops pattered through the foliage and continued to fall, drenching them for more than two hours. The general insisted they keep going while overhead thunder rumbled. Occasionally, through a break in the canopy, Tessa glimpsed lightning claw a charcoal sky. According to Hans, they had crossed the park border into Garamba and were following the route the rebels had taken after their failed peace talks eighteen months earlier. The area comprised vast savannahs, and dense gallery forests that ran along a maze of rivers, hiding remote swampy depressions and isolated grasslands where, it was rumoured, the last white rhinos existed in the wild.

When the rain eased they began to dry off, although Tessa's pack felt heavier now and the clasp of her bra dug into her back. She released it, conscious of the schoolgirl prudery that made her worry it might sexualise her appearance. Adjusting her scarf across her breasts, she forced herself to quicken her pace. She could feel her heart racing and there was a tired heaviness in her legs. A few of the delegates had begun to talk again—the syrupy sounds of their dialects coming in half-tones with occasional laughter. She listened to the murmured mix of languages, occasionally shot through with English. At one point, she gathered enough meaning from the general's murmured, 'I try to please her, but who can understand?' to work out that he was having problems with his wife and was asking for advice. Until then, Dominic had not spoken of his own wife or children, but now, surprisingly, both men laughed, at one point uproariously. Dominic shook his head and clapped his hands. His laughter was easy and infectious and strangely new. Tessa had not heard him laugh so readily before and it struck her that had these men found themselves in different circumstances they might even have been friends.

They stopped briefly to eat the millet bread and dry samosas they had brought with them then continued skirting a marsh-land that fed one of the tributaries of a bigger river. Papyrus reeds grew in the shallows and further downstream they could hear the pig-snort of hippos. 'There are crocodiles too,' Gideon announced, adjusting his cap and pointing in the direction they were going.

An hour later the cloud rolled in and a mist swirled around them. It was like breathing through a musty flannel. Alphington walked behind Tessa. She was aware of his presence and it unsettled her. She would prefer it if he walked ahead. She had an apprehensive feeling, as if she were being tested, and it weighed on her. When Alphington questioned her, it felt as if he were on the brink of discovering something inadequate about her. He'd told her he considered her work important, at which she took heart. His comment flattered her and confirmed, if not her presence in the group, then the collegial alliance she sought with him. 'But you know,' he warned her in the next breath, 'an educated person, even a smart person, can still act like an idiot. You need to know what your motivations are.'

They reached a stream that was in shadow except for a small gap where a tree had fallen; the filtered light created a luminous glow. There was a discussion about which route to take, although it was the general who, after a stuttering conversation on a satellite phone, had the final say. He pointed upstream and they continued on to a ford. They crossed, then gradually began to climb again.

The forest became thicker and deeper, so that the soldiers had to hack a way through with pangas, their blades making a *chit chit* sound as they used them to swift and devastating effect. At one point Gideon used a hooked scythe to lift the tangle of vines that blocked their way. As Tessa watched him, it reminded her of those family hikes and how Stephen would rush ahead to make it seem as if he'd been caught in the knotted branches of a fig tree—the crazy expression on his face, his eyes rolled back in his head, his tongue hanging out—and of the photos that captured the look just before they all burst out laughing. He would stop at nothing to make them laugh, especially their mother, who would shake her head and chortle with pleasure, an expression that lit up her entire face.

For the next four hours they kept trudging, their human scent mixing with the forest to become a distinct oniony odour that wafted with the reek of musk and rotting undergrowth. A red soldier ant dropped onto Tessa's forearm and she flicked it off. There was always some insect either falling into her hair or crawling over her skin. Leeches attached themselves to her boots. Wherever she looked she saw life—huge worms like long thick *pici* pasta, spiders in intricate webs. The air was still now, broken only by the bird calls that shrilled repeatedly overhead. It was like a place where someone had died, as if haunted by the *jogi* the Acholi people spoke of or—worse, Tessa thought—a place where the ghostly vengeance of *cen* drifted.

At one point a small woodland antelope slipped across their path, startling them, and when they continued Tessa noticed how the soldiers silently signalled to one another or, if they spoke, how their voices held a strange intimacy. Occasionally they brushed a tick from the shoulder of the person in front of them, Dominic pinching, between his thumb and fore-finger, a small scorpion that had crawled from her collar onto her neck, this simple grooming a mutual wordless task.

The dense vegetation pressed down on them and Tessa felt a growing sense of claustrophobia. There was a sense of urgency too; night was approaching and there was pressure to pick up their pace before darkness overtook them.

Just before dusk, they came out of the forest into a natural clearing, then made their way in single file through clumped shrubs and stiff grass thickets that were thigh-high and as sharp as blades. At the top of a small rise the general stopped to take in their bearings, and again used the satellite phone.

Ahead of them the horizon was lost in another wall of ancient trees—emergent oaks, cedars, mahoganies. Forty, fifty metres high. Tessa stared, transfixed by the unremitting broad-leaved canopy. If you stayed put it would grow over you, she thought. You had to fight to live in this place. You had to fight all the time.

Night came quickly. The sky flushed pink then deepened to crimson and purple. The last of the day's light hovered briefly over the forest's crest and then it was dark. They made a rough camp and ate beans heated in tins over a small fire. The soldiers took turns to keep watch. Lying in her sleeping bag, Tessa could hear them talking. Occasionally they laughed then mumbled again. Long after midnight, after the others had fallen silent and there were only the night sounds, it was as if she could hear the mesh of tree roots and ground insects that moved beneath her. Somewhere close by was the LRA camp and Kony. The thought of it kept her awake, charged with a strange raw energy. She thought of what John Alphington had said: Did she know what her motivations were? If she was honest she would have to answer no.

At daybreak she was the first up. They continued in the pale early morning light, and by midday the blisters on her feet had burst and begun to chafe against her boots. She stopped to tape them, then hurried to catch up again. Her legs were strong. *Keep up*, she remembered her father saying on some outback hike. *Don't let yourself fall behind*. It was not the walking that worried her now, nor the fact that she was tired and felt the weight of her rucksack, nor even that she was uninvited and mostly unwelcome—it was the strange expectant silence that had descended on them.

Their talk had all but ceased and the anticipatory mood grew. Tessa concentrated on moving forward until Gideon, who had been walking at the back of the group, suddenly rushed ahead and overtook her. Pushing past, he scaled the next rise then, placing his rifle in an offhand position, the butt against his shoulder, he took aim. The others surged behind him. Tessa stopped, the muscles in the back of her thighs pulling tight as she heard a distant shout and caught a quick glimpse of movement in the foliage ahead.

9

Melbourne

Leigh dropped her keys into the glass bowl on the table by the front door then came into the kitchen.

'Hi,' Neil said, and leant over to kiss her.

'Hi,' she replied, but her lips were uninterested and he could tell by the drawn look on her face that she'd probably had a difficult day. She pulled a magazine from her bag. 'One of the girls on reception gave me this,' she said, and handed the magazine to him with a hard smile. 'For some reason, she seemed to think I would be grateful for it.'

Neil frowned. It was a copy of *African Hunter Magazine*, a glossy production with a black-maned lion on the front cover.

'The page is dog-eared,' Leigh told him.

Neil took the magazine and opened it to a feature article on hunting in South Africa. *Plains Game and the Big Five—Luxurious Accommodation and a Thrilling Experience.* A column of text ran on, but his eye was drawn to the photograph of Stephen crouched beside the carcass of a bull rhino. He could sense Leigh's agitation, she was waiting for him to say something, but he could not look at her. He stared at his son, the smug smile, as if he'd just presented them with a straight-A report card and expected praise.

'Matt Reba is in it as well,' Leigh added. 'He's on the next page.'

And so he was, boyish and jubilant with a dead buffalo.

Leigh released her hair from the clip that held it in place and shook her head. She poured herself a glass of wine.

'How does it get to this?' she asked. She walked around the bench and stood next to Neil. Her voice was sharp. 'I don't understand it—those magnificent creatures slaughtered. And this is his idea of fun?'

When Neil flipped the page back to the photograph of Stephen, Leigh felt a hot flush begin, the tart taste in her mouth then the full menopausal heat flooding through her. She took her jacket off, and again scrutinised the photograph of Stephen, although it had already imprinted itself on her mind: his left hand resting on the slope of the rhino's head, his right clutching the barrel of a hunting rifle. He had a look not only of ownership, but impunity, and it roused in her other times when she'd felt incomprehension at something he'd done or said. She took the magazine back from Neil. The light in the picture was golden, a stunning South African light, under which the trail of blood on the rhino's tough hide appeared to have been painted on, and yet it had probably been photoshopped, just as the rhino and the buffalo had been staged to appear not as they might have fallen when they died, but as though they were resting in a dignified, even contemplative way.

Leigh put the magazine down and topped up her wine. 'What are we going to do?' she said.

'Do?' Neil replied.

'Yes—what should we do?' she repeated. 'I'm trying to fill in the blank space here. I want to find the thing that's missing. There's a nightmare factor to all this. It's sickening; the guns, the thrill of killing, and then the tacky celebration. And need I remind you, this is Stephen—*our* son.'

The wine had triggered her mood and another wave of heat flushed through her. She rubbed the back of her neck. Their son—her son. Stephen looked more like her than anyone else in the family. He was fair and handsome, but with sharper features. He had a predatory stare and resembled, disturbingly, an uncle Leigh had not liked. The first time this similarity occurred to her, Stephen was about fifteen, but she'd put the association out of her mind. Now it returned to her with renewed significance. The uncle, her father's brother, could be charming. He owned a restaurant and was considered extravagant, a real mover and shaker, but she never felt at ease in his company; there had always been something unsettling about him. He was the type of person who knew no boundaries. It worried her that Stephen might be the same. He was reckless, excessive; he always had been. Prodigal, without the repenting part, so carelessly lavish. As a teenager, there was a constant desire for something new—a mountain bike, another computer, the latest phone. Her firstborn. She favoured him and criticised him simultaneously, and if she wished they were closer, she also yearned to be relieved of the responsibility. He frightened her and it was the worst kind of fear because she could not talk about it with Neil. Not really. There'd been a couple of posts on Facebook recently, images of Stephen at a bar somewhere, one in the cockpit of a plane, but Neil would not know that, it was not something he followed, and if Leigh tried to tell him, he would say she jumped to conclusions or worried too much.

She looked at the magazine and felt her eyes well with tears. She dug in her bag for a tissue. 'What does he do this for?'

Neil shook his head. 'Who knows? The sport, the thrill of it. Come on, sit down, have something to eat.' He lit the gas burner and began to heat the oil in the pan. He would cook for her at midnight if she were hungry. Peas with butter, paella with the finest saffron he could find. He placed a wedge of soft cheese and a handful of dry biscuits on a platter then pushed it before her. She looked at his grey head as he bent forward. His insistence on caring was what drew her to him, the generous openness of his heart, but she believed it was this too—his leniency—which made it easy for his children to do whatever they wanted.

'You said you'd speak to him about what he's doing over there—his business plans.'

Neil shrugged. 'And I've tried. But he doesn't always answer my calls.'

Leigh watched as Neil diced an onion, the blade of the knife making a rapid tattoo on the board. The album he'd been listening to, a favourite jazz recording, had just finished and the chopping sounded very loud. He would withdraw from her now, hoard his thoughts, and she was annoyed at him for it. 'Don't you think we should be a united front on this?'

Neil didn't answer. He crushed a garlic clove with the flat of the knife, the heel of his hand coming down in one deft thud. The skin broke open. He peeled the mashed clove and chopped it.

'Neil?'

'What?'

'We need to be strong.'

He looked up. 'What do you mean?' he said in an uncertain tone.

She was staring at him with an implacable look, an expression he had not seen before. 'I mean we're responsible,' she said.

'Darling . . .' He sighed. He wanted to offer her reassurance or a solution, but he could offer neither.

Her face tightened; it made her look older than she was. She might have said, *You're responsible*. He looked down. 'I know you feel that,' he said, 'but Stephen—Stephen is an adult.'

'He's an adult in years maybe. He looks like a man, but he still acts like a child.' And there it was again, the anger and ugly complaint in her voice, the voice of censure—critical, without relief. She tried to soften it. 'When it comes to families and forgiveness we laugh, we say look at Richard with his restaurant and his red Ferrari at sixty-five, or poor old Uncle Gary over there getting drunk and making racist comments about refugees. We make excuses for them, we joke at their expense. He's a loser, we say, but when it's closer to home—when it's *our* children—we see how truly ineffectual we are.' She stood up and immediately sat down again, rubbing the back of her neck with her hand. 'Shit, why can't Stephen put his energy into something else?'

Neil lit the gas cooktop and placed the pan on it. 'I think he does just that,' he replied, and only then did it occur to him that he was probably right, that what they saw was not the whole picture.

The oil in the pan began to smoke. Neil turned down the flame and added the onion and garlic from the chopping board with a sweep of the knife. The pan sizzled and the aroma intensified as the onion softened. Neil tried to picture Stephen, but his son mystified him. He could recall him as an adolescent, his keen physicality—the grass-and-dirt memory of football games and the early summer mornings spent rowing. He understood his son's ambition, his restlessness and the testosterone rush that gave him such a fierce competitive edge, but not his greed. That shocked him. He was proud of his good-looking, healthy children, proud enough to sometimes overlook their selfishness. One book-clever child, one street smart—you can't expect them to be everything. But was Leigh right? Had he let them get away with too much? Had he indulged them? He remembered unhappily his own father's method of taking a firm hand, *the odd beating never hurt*, and how he'd rejected that; it was a different era. Besides, Stephen would not be reined in, he was not that type of kid. He had never tried, as Tessa had, to please them.

There were memories, so many now, particularly of one summer when Stephen, maybe fourteen or fifteen, went fishing with him, and Neil discovered afterwards that his new fishing knife, a Gerber Gator with a thin flexible blade, had gone missing. Later, the knife turned up at some party where there'd been a fight and a lot of under-age drinking, although the story of how it got there never came out. He suspected that Stephen had taken it and lied to him, but Neil said nothing without really understanding why, except that later he knew he had betrayed himself, and there was the sting of that, coupled with his fear of, and for, his son. Stephen's gung-ho approach whenever he took on something new—learning to shoot, becoming a pilot, the civilian military-style training for 'extreme fitness and strength', even the move to South Africa—were adrenaline-charged, and sometimes dicey, but if he was afraid of the things Stephen might do, then he also loved him with a father's hopeful pride and irrational loyalty, the same impulse that made him jump to Stephen's defence whenever someone else found fault with him.

They had intended to visit him in Cape Town, but between Stephen's unavailability and his own work, he and Leigh had postponed the trip more than once. He looked at Leigh now, her concerned and familiar face. 'If it's frustration you feel, I feel it too,' he said. 'But what good does it do to hold yourself accountable?'

Leigh tapped the side of her glass with her ring. 'But we are accountable.'

'Not when it comes to this,' Neil replied. 'What Stephen does,' he said, nodding in the direction of magazine, 'is a result of *his* choices.'

'Yes, that's just it—it's his choices that worry me.'

Leigh hooked her hair behind her ear and sat back. She took a deep breath and waited for the next hot flush to sweep over her, then closed the magazine and hurled it into the rubbish bin. Good. It would have caught fire if she had held it any longer.

Neil raised his eyebrows. She felt his disapproval, the implication that she might be overreacting.

'Maybe it's human nature to intensify our obsessions,' she said defensively. 'Maybe that's what makes us who we are. But this is too much. Can't you see our children have both caught the same virus, but in different ways? Stephen must have everything his way and Tessa . . . Tessa sets the bar too high. I still haven't heard from her.' Leigh bit her lip. 'The thing is, I'm afraid something's wrong with both of them.'

Their eyes met for a second.

'And what about us?' Neil said. 'What's our problem?' It was a joke of sorts, although Leigh couldn't laugh.

10

Cape Town

Stephen sat on the balcony of the Twelve Apostles Hotel drinking flavoured vodkas with Matt Reba. It was warm. A light breeze carried the scent of deep ocean currents, and gulls circled overhead, their cries high above the surf. He watched as planes crisscrossed the sky, leaving behind pale jet streams. To the west, the horizon flushed red and then became streaked with green before the sun slowly disappeared into the deep blue of the South Atlantic.

'So what happened to Cherie?' Matt Reba asked.

'She found someone else. Someone with more money, if less charm.'

'I thought you two were going to get married.'

'So did I. Turns out we aren't. She said I need a kick up the arse—well, she said *arsenal*, but then she always was a princess.'

'You're staying in South Africa, right? In Cape Town?'

'Where else would I go? Everything I want is here. We're set, the business is growing. Good for you too, right?'

Matt nodded. Both his parents were dead and there was no

other family Stephen knew of except an uncle with a debt-ridden farm near Bloemfontein. Sheep and game hunting in the semi-arid country that bordered on the Karoo.

'And we can keep it growing,' Stephen added. 'There's a chance to make a good connection here tonight. That guy I told you about, the one in the transport business.'

'You want us to meet him?'

'Just me for now. If I get this off the ground, there'll be plenty of time for you to come and join the party.'

Later, in the Leopard Bar, an opulent lamp-lit room with a bronze sculpture of a leopard and jungle wallpaper, Stephen made a quick assessment of who else was there. It didn't matter if it was a grungy dive in Melbourne or somewhere like this, where there was more money on the table, he had a knack for knowing how the night might play out. Tonight, the cards were stacked in his favour—it was only a matter of playing them in the right order, and at the right time.

In the restaurant, they ate duck carpaccio and *braaied* springbok with an expensive Hamilton Russell pinot noir. Reba ate more, drank less. He was a fitness junkie, who occasionally smoked, almost as a kind of contradiction, and then went to the gym before six. Good company if Stephen wanted someone to do push-ups and bench hops with or show him how to fire a Beanfield Sniper, but not enough bandwidth for much else. Certainly, he was no businessman.

At eleven, Reba got up and tossed a wad of rand on the table, colourful notes not unlike Australian dollars, but instead of the Queen and other forgotten historical figures, a blue buffalo, a red lion's head.

After he left, Stephen went back to the bar, where the barman put an Aberlour single malt in front of him.

Stephen nodded to the barman. He felt wired, maybe a little drunk. He scanned the decor that really had less to do with Africa now than a residual colonial idea of it—teak shutters, rattan tables, biological illustrations. Clichés, Stephen thought, then focused his full attention on the other side of the room, and the man he wanted to speak to. He knew him as Frost, although people referred to him as Han Solo. It amused Stephen, because he liked to call his father Indiana Jones, a nod to the far-flung locations his father's work took him to and because his father looked a lot like Harrison Ford. Frost, by contrast, was a heavyset man with reddish hair, well-known around Cape Town airfield as a smart operator. There'd been a good deal of talk about him lately; rumour had it he was looking to sublease some of his mid-size jets. Frost was sitting with a man known for running private charters with sideline interests in the fresh-produce market—tilapia fish, even the tulips that were grown in Kenya and exported to Europe.

When the waiter served them the round of drinks Stephen had bought, Frost nodded in Stephen's direction and indicated that he should join them.

'Ah, Stephen Lowell,' Frost said when Stephen reached them. 'This is Alex Vadim.'

Stephen shook hands with Vadim and sat down.

'So, how's the flying going?' Frost asked.

'Good,' Stephen replied, giving a small half-shrug. 'I'm looking to do more.'

Frost raised one reddish eyebrow. 'You want to upgrade?'

There was a drumming in Stephen's chest. Here was his chance, he thought, and he felt the alarming rush that woke him in the early hours of the morning.

Vadim picked up his glass and turned it in his hand. 'In Africa everything is needed,' he said expansively. He had the kind of international accent that was hard to place—one that made him sound gracious and reasonable, although Stephen had heard otherwise. 'Africa is the happy hunting ground,' Vadim went on. 'And business here is like a flowing river. You need many streams running into it, many people make it happen. But I should warn you, Mr Lowell, you must have protection, and then protection from protection, because you cannot survive as an amateur in this game. You must be careful who you trust.' Vadim put his glass down and there was a glint in his eye that suggested he was issuing a challenge. 'You listen with your mouth and you talk with your ears, hey?'

Stephen smiled then turned his gaze to Frost and tapped his hand against his thigh. He doubted whether he could trust either of them; they might just as easily fleece him as work with him, but that was the gamble. He looked back at Vadim. 'I don't intend to remain an amateur,' he said.

'Good,' Vadim replied. 'An ambitious man. That helps. That helps a great deal.'

Sitting in the back seat of the taxi as the driver took the coast road back to the city, Stephen considered stopping in Long Street and going to a nightclub—maybe he could pick up a girl or do some drugs—but he wasn't in the mood. He glanced up at the night sky. The moon shone, and a ribbon of silver light rippled along the calm surface of the glass-black ocean.

There were the streets around here where he would not go unarmed. At the Victoria Road intersection he saw a boy dressed in a garbage bag kneeling in the middle of the road with a begging bowl. Load-shedding meant the traffic lights weren't working. The usual sirens could be heard in the distance, and in the spray of headlights the youth with the bowl lifted his face up to the light like an altar boy.

'It gives everyone a chance—thugs, rapists, carjackers,' the taxi driver said. And then, almost to himself, 'Security, security, everything is security. There is no pleasure in life. Life is like a prison. Everyone must carry a weapon for protection, and even then, you are not safe, you must pay attention. That boy probably has a gun. There are laws, but no one here enforces them.'

Stephen was unmoved. Australia's a nanny state, he had reminded Reba. You can't do anything without being penalised—no speeding, no drinking in public places, you can't boo at the footy, you can't ride a bike without a helmet. Carry your licence at all times. You can't even smoke in public. Next, you'll need a passport to enter your own home.

'So, that's why you're here?' Reba had asked.

Yes, that's why he was here, at least in part. He could live like a king.

Stephen paid the driver and got out. His house was located high up in one of the better streets in Camps Bay. A two-storeyed fortress surrounded by a double-brick fence topped with electrified razor wire and CCTV cameras. Cherie had chosen it twelve months earlier and now she had left, which suited him fine, except for the outstanding expenses. He had no idea why she was still so angry with him; he'd done nothing to her.

Still, after tonight he was on a forward path and happy enough with the meeting he'd had with Frost and his new associate, Vadim. Small shipments—the ant trade. Not exactly the start he'd wanted, but the opportunities should flow from there.

Once inside, he turned off the alarm and poured himself a nightcap. He reached for the remote control and switched on the TV. There was footage of the latest killings in Johannesburg. Riot police with bulletproof shields and scenes of looting. It might've been an Xbox cutscene except for the follow-on story about a nine-year-old kid who'd shot and killed the headmaster at a local school. People said things could be shit here, but it wasn't as shit as other parts of Africa, where there were ongoing wars, genocide, even crappier leadership. In Uganda, there were stories of rebel armies who recruited children as young as eight or nine, and if they couldn't get volunteers, they abducted them from their families.

Tessa was mad to go there. When she stopped over in Cape Town she was robbed before they even met: phone, laptop, credit cards, all gone. She couldn't believe it—she said she'd only put her bag down for a moment.

'You left your bag unattended?' He laughed and shook his head in disbelief. He didn't say anything about the bruise on her arm or that he'd seen her try to conceal it. She would do that; she would pretend that everything was okay, she would want to keep it light-hearted, make out that she could cope, and he, as usual, would go along with her—why overreact?

He couldn't resist stirring her though. 'God, Tess, you're such a retard,' he teased later that day—a chance to make fun of her in a way that signalled a return to the old ground between them. It was a longstanding taunt, a carryover from a time when, trekking through the bush on one of their family camping trips, leeches had clung to Tessa's bare legs, their moist bodies growing fat with blood. He could remember looking at them as they began to swell. 'No, don't pull them off,' he told her. 'They'll fall off when they've had enough.' But she yanked them off anyway. 'God, Tess, you're such a retard!' It became a standard line, the mocking winner's call in their endless rounds of one-upmanship.

On the coffee table in front of him was the stone carving she had given him before she left for Gulu; a thank you for helping her to buy a replacement phone and laptop, and for getting her passport sorted out. He picked it up. It was a standard African souvenir made from serpentine stone and sold in just about every street market. A knotted representation of the family—*ukama*, people said here. He put it down again with a clatter. A dozen quips came to mind, a chance to tease and unsettle her, but then something else too, since he saw the risk she was taking. Tessa had always been worth ten of him. 'This decision of yours . . .' he had said, then paused for effect, 'do you have any idea what you're doing?' Only then did he see that she looked worried.

He poured himself another drink and raised his glass to the statue. 'Careful, Tess—the way you're going, it looks like you're one hundred and ten per cent set for a fall.'

11

Garamba, Congo

Looking up with a start, Tessa heard another shout and then saw at least ten men heading towards them.

In seconds the group closed in. They wore green gumboots and an assortment of khaki uniforms. Those at the rear seemed to glide through the tall grass. They all carried rifles.

It was an escort party sent by Kony to take them to where the talks would be held. The youth who appeared to be in charge spoke to the Ugandan general in Acholi. He pronounced Kony as *konj* and when he talked he tilted his head to one side. He wore a red beret and carried an outmoded satellite phone which he answered, lifting the cumbersome device to his neatly shaped ear. He was leaner than the others, with high cheekbones and slightly tapered almond-shaped eyes that were more like an Egyptian pharaoh's eyes than an Acholi's—perhaps like one of the first Arab ivory traders who had come to this part of Africa. He nodded and pointed, then led them further along a steep narrow track.

The sky had cleared to a bright kerosene blue and the

temperature had risen. They headed downhill again and their pace quickened. Tessa focused on the rough ground in front of her and adjusted her pack. An hour later they reached a camp. Situated in an airy glade, it was at once more organised and more elaborate than Tessa had thought it would be. A large tent with plastic chairs inside had been erected and there was a fire pit in a central area from which came the appealing smoky smell of campfire cooking. Armed guards patrolled the boundaries. Their voices rose and fell in what sometimes sounded like a disagreement, at other times a nervous exchange; occasionally there was laughter. About a dozen adolescent soldiers gathered in observant groups—teenage boys and also girls, dressed in a combination of fatigues and ill-fitting street clothes, all carrying weapons, some with heavy bandoliers crossed over their shoulders. Several had tufty hair or dreadlocks, others had sores on their hands and arms.

The soldier in the red beret directed them to where a group of senior rebels lounged in the grass or sat on a low bench seat enjoying the pleasant breeze. Eventually they were greeted by a commander who, like an obliging host, offered them food and water. He nodded in the direction of a young woman, who brought them a platter of fish with accompanying pots of beans and *posho*.

'*Angara*,' said Dominic with some surprise at the bony yet flavoursome river fish. 'How did you get it?'

'What you have in Uganda we also have in Garamba,' the commander said.

'It's good,' Dominic replied and took a second helping.

There was a radio playing in the background. Someone turned it up on the hour when the BBC World News was broadcast, then turned it down again to a mumble when the bulletin had finished. They waited, and continued to wait, although what had begun with a cordial welcome eventually became strained, and then formal and uncomfortable again. Gideon spoke to the general, covering his mouth so the others couldn't hear. Dominic's brow furrowed. He wiped his lips and rubbed the stubble on his chin as armed guards stood in restless groups of twos and threes and watched them. The breeze dropped and the heat returned. There was always the possibility that Kony would not turn up, and some of the delegates, including the Sudanese mediator, began to pace up and down.

'A no-show is the most likely outcome,' Alphington said. There was something of the doomsayer in the way he spoke, and it felt as if he might have the last word, but in the minutes that followed a low whisper passed around that Kony was approaching.

Suddenly the mood in the camp shifted.

'He has come from another camp a long walk away,' the soldier with the almond-shaped eyes said, his voice hurried and excited. There was a hush and a rising sense of expectation, and then, as if he were royalty, Kony entered the clearing flanked by four heavily armed guards. He was not nearly as tall as Tessa expected nor as fine-looking as earlier photographs had suggested. He frowned at them as if to suggest his being called here was an imposition on his time and authority. The soldiers who were with him took over the security of the area, checking again for weapons and phones. They were particularly thorough with the soldiers from the Ugandan army. Tessa was roughly searched, but it was clear that, being a woman and a non-participant, she was treated more reproachfully and deemed less important than the men in the delegation. They patted her down, one of them touching her breasts—perfunctory, if expected, and hardly any different from an airport search—but they missed her phone, which she had already slipped into the inside pocket of her hiking pants. Should she hand it over? She decided not to; there was no reception anyway, there hadn't been any since they crossed the park border. Seldom switching it on since they left Gulu, she had kept it close, mostly for her music, her photos, and the familiar security of it—the smooth, reliable, flat-pebble shape that she thought of as a talisman.

Kony moved to the centre of the clearing and all attention shifted to him. He stepped forward and lifted his arms in an elaborate gesture that seemed at once awkward and staged.

His appearance surprised her. Was this the godly figure? The freedom fighter, the self-styled prophet with mystic appeal? She felt something close to disappointment then incomprehension. Instead of a charismatic leader standing head and shoulders above everyone else, instead of the handsome visionary with beaded cornrows who inspired devotion with his mesmeric speeches, she saw only an ordinary round-shouldered man with a wispy moustache and a chipped front tooth. He didn't wear the crisp military uniform she'd seen in photographs—instead he was dressed in a short-sleeved suit made from some light-coloured polyester. The small paunch exposed by the clinging fabric drew attention to his middle age. His hair was oily and cut short and his mouth was slack, but then one of the soldiers spoke to him, and as he began to laugh, Tessa saw in his eyes, then heard in the commanding sound of his voice, the power of his appeal.

'You come to us and accept our protection? Well then, let it be known that we have been chosen. We are the ones defending the people of Uganda. I am a freedom fighter. I am not a terrorist. A terrorist is not a person like me. But if you pick up an arrow against us and we end up cutting off your hand, who is to blame? If you report us with your mouth and we cut off your lips, who is to blame? It is you.' He might have been on a stage and these his nightly lines. 'The Bible,' he went on, 'says that if your hand, or eye, or mouth is at fault then it should be cut off. What I do is God's will.' As he spoke, he looked around with an expression of triumphant satisfaction. 'But—' and he wagged his finger '—I will remind you that I am a human being like you. I have eyes, I have a brain, I wear clothes also. It is the president of Uganda, it is Museveni, who has lied. He has spoilt our name, saying we are animals, we are *lajok*, the evil ones who practise witchcraft.'

Arms raised, he wheeled around to face those who stood in a semicircle around him. His speech had the rhythmic quality of a repeated sermon and he, the conviction of a high priest. Tessa listened to him. At first she couldn't take her eyes from him, but then she forced herself to scan the faces of the delegates. Dominic looked on with fixed purpose, and the general regarded him suspiciously, although the rebels who followed him listened with rapt attention. When Kony paused, they cheered, and he continued in a manner that suggested he was working himself up as he went along.

'Ah! So you have come here to talk about peace? Let me tell you what name we have for false rumours—*radio kabi*. You have seen the toy radios children make? For the antenna they use *kabi*—the straw of sorghum. It is a game. They tell lies to each other. They whisper false stories. So I ask you, is this more news from *radio kabi*? Or should I believe what you say?'

He spun around, glancing from one delegate to the next. Tessa stepped further into the shade and his gaze swept past her, coming to rest on the Sudanese mediator. He laughed. 'I want peace too! It is Museveni who is the warmonger. Talk with him ends in failure because he engages in further military campaigns! It is Museveni who achieves power through the barrel of a gun. He refuses to admit that he has committed crimes against Ugandans. And now he wants us to apologise to him?' Shaking his head, Kony turned to the Ugandan general with a bemused smile and spoke with authority, as though he was surrounded by schoolchildren who didn't have the sense to understand what he was saying. 'Your army was the first to kill,' he said, raising his finger. 'They destroyed our homesteads. They were the ones who rustled our cattle, who took our children. It is the big shots in the government who now control the roads. They destroy our families and take our property. It is they who have stolen the power they do not deserve.' His eyes flashed. 'We are not fighting the Acholi people—we are fighting Museveni's government and all his supporters, and if there is to be an apology at all, it is for us to demand an apology from Museveni and his party of cronies!'

There were theories, Tessa thought, a list of possible diagnoses. He fitted certain profiles—delusional, paranoid, schizoid. A sociopath. But it was still a shock to witness him in person. What he said was extreme. He was irrational and contradictory. And there was something else that reminded her of what she understood about such personalities; it had to do with the way one always feels ill at ease in their presence, because no matter how charming they are, no matter how clever, other people did not exist for them, except as opportunities.

Kony lifted his chin and clicked his fingers—a signal to his guards—and the delegation was ushered into the tent.

As they turned to go, Alphington glanced at Tessa and pulled a face. *Wish us luck*, it seemed to say.

Tessa watched as they filed into the tent then glanced at the younger rebels under the shade of a large mango tree. Teenagers. All boys now. Some of them wandered off, although those who remained watched her too. She felt isolated and exposed. Now that she was here, the reality of Kony and those he led terrified her.

She thought of the phone in her pocket—the last text from Stephen: *Have tracked down your passport.*

How? she'd replied, but he hadn't responded.

It worried her—there had always been something extreme about Stephen's personality too, and more so now than when they were younger, as if some increasing intensity had taken hold. After she was robbed she thought it was going to be a nightmare to get another passport, but out of the blue he produced it. 'It was handed in,' he said, smirking. He didn't elaborate further, nor did she pursue the matter. The two days she spent in Cape Town were a tangle of red tape: cancelling her credit cards, deactivating her accounts, listening to muzak while she was shunted from one department to another, then the frantic trip to the Apple Store to buy a new computer and a new phone, with Stephen handing over a wad of cash like it was nothing.

Now the phone was out of range and the forest surrounded her. Discarded mango pits, left by a couple of the rebel soldiers, lay on the ground, ants crawling over them as they began to ferment in the warmth of the late afternoon. Tessa tried to still herself. She thought of her work and took in what she could of the camp. Was this home base to these fighters, or were they shunted around from one site to another? Did they train here? It didn't appear to be permanent; the tent where the talks were taking place was the only substantial shelter. She wrote notes in the small notebook she had carried with her. At best, what she could gather would be anecdotal research, but she was aware that she had this one chance to observe, to take in small details, and although such observations might not provide much in the way of validating evidence, they afforded valuable and particularised information. The challenge, of course, was to be objective, to avoid bias, although that seemed an impossible proposition now that she was actually here. Amid the green glow of the forest the world looked different. The heat made her feel flabby, her thinking slowed. She felt a pressing urge to pee. Should she ask where to go? Maybe she would be told to go with a female escort, one of the girls she had glimpsed, but there was a lull; the soldiers who had been sitting nearby had drifted off and she was afraid she would not be able to hang on any longer. She got up and sought a place a little way off where she might go in private.

The bush that surrounded the camp was layered and dense. She found a spot surrounded by shrubs and crouched down, her urine dark and concentrated, its warm release little different from the humid air that surrounded her. When she finished, she straightened and rebalanced, then began to hitch her trousers up, and, a sudden realisation came to her: of course she was still being watched; she would have been watched the whole time. She saw the boy with the gun and her brain jumped awake, but she was unprepared for how he stared at her. Standing silently, he was only a few feet away, one of the younger rebel soldiers, although she hadn't noticed him until now. He was thin and gangly and beneath his eye there was a pink sickle-shaped wound that appeared angry and raw. But more shocking than his appearance was his expression; he looked directly at her, assessing her with hostile, unblinking eyes. He did not move, but stood to attention. The gun that was slung across his shoulder was almost half as big as him, the weight considerable for a child who could be no more than twelve or thirteen.

She felt a fearful chill run through her and, looking down, broke the moment. Quickly, she finished buttoning her pants, then headed back towards the tent where the talks were still taking place. The boy dropped back, but when she glanced over her shoulder he was right behind her.

12

The talks went on for another three hours. The tent flap had been closed and Tessa saw no one else enter or leave. From where she sat, she heard voices rise and fall. She recognised Dominic's voice and wished she could make out what he was saying. Only one word came to her above all others: 'Unity,' she heard him say.

She waited in the same place under the mango tree where the soldiers had rested previously. Dark green leaves filtered the light and, high within their dappled growth, there were new mangoes, some still small and green, some blushing orange. The boy with the rifle watched her from a few feet away. Maybe it had been his job to watch her all along. She studied the wound on his face; there was very little blood, and any ooze that might have seeped from it had been wiped away to reveal a slash of shining pink flesh that gaped like an open cleft.

He looked around restlessly, standing then sitting again. He had thin arms and a narrow waist. After a time, he set his rifle down in front of him and disassembled it into its many parts, then, using the corner of his uniform, he cleaned each piece with infinite care before he put it back together again. It was a slow methodical process and when he finished he slid a small boning knife from the sheath strapped to his leg. There was a series of notches in the rifle's wooden grip: a simple Christian cross and the letter F. Using the point of the knife he deepened the markings in a precise, almost pedantic way before finally lifting the rifle to his lips and kissing it.

The light started to fade and the surrounding bush noises intensified. In the distance chimpanzees pant-hooted, and birdsong rose, a dusk chorus that escalated above the flowering canopy. The scent of the rotting mangoes grew stronger and there were other deep earth smells too: geosmin—the history of rain. Then came the swift darkness and with it the hum and whirr of insects, the croaking of frogs. The firepit the other boys lit with dried moss and tended nonchalantly, glowed, and whenever another log was put onto it sparks flew into the gathering darkness.

The boy who had been watching her moved to sit a little closer.

'What happened to your face?' Tessa asked. She spoke in English and did not expect him to answer, but he shot her a quick knowing look.

'Discipline,' he replied.

'You should clean it,' she said. She reached into her pocket and produced a sachet of antiseptic. 'Here, use this.' She tore open the sachet and handed him the swab. He took it from her and wiped the wound, wincing as he did so, then he looked at the wipe and sniffed it before throwing it into the fire, where it flared. As if hypnotised they watched together as the swab became a brilliant blue flame then curled into a black leaf.

After what seemed like a long time, Tessa asked him his name.

'Francis,' he said.

'How old are you, Francis?'

His mouth moved, but he did not answer.

For the next hour he refused to speak. He scraped his muddy boots with his knife. Occasionally their eyes locked, but when Tessa spoke to him he acted as though he had not heard her. The night closed in, and a further seven or eight youths came and sat in a group nearby. These soldiers would not answer her questions either. Recruited or abducted, it was clear they did not wish to talk to her. Unlike Oraako, they hadn't run away or been rescued like those in the camp at Gulu, and they were not encouraged to speak to her. Instead, they treated her as if she was not to be trusted, or they talked loudly and ignored her altogether.

Francis placed a kerosene lamp on a plastic crate and lit it, then very carefully turned down the flame so it wouldn't smoke. When, finally, he had adjusted it, and the other boys had gathered around, he pulled forward a large ammunition crate. The crate was burnished, and in the light of the lamp, it shone like gold. Unlatching the clips on the sides he opened the lid and took out a battered old game of Monopoly. 'This time we use real money,' he announced, then he turned to Tessa with a broad smile. 'Give me your wallet.'

Tessa looked at him blankly, and when she failed to do as he asked he picked up his rifle and waved it at her. 'You should find it, otherwise I will take it from you.' He grinned.

The other soldiers laughed and Tessa felt her heart quicken. She unzipped her backpack and fumbled for her money belt. She had just on seven thousand shillings, grubby soft notes that barely amounted to two Australian dollars. Francis took the money from her then settled himself down on the ground. The other boys followed suit.

Sitting cross-legged, they began to set up the game. The board was worn—the spine split and the surface badly scratched. When they rummaged in the broken box it was clear that most of the original tokens were missing, except for the metal racing car that Francis insisted was his. Otherwise there were only a few remaining utility cards and a handful of improvised tokens, including several carved stones. One resembled a hippo, another might've been a lion. There was also half a wishbone and a small oddly shaped knucklebone.

As banker, Francis doled out the money—unevenly, Tessa noticed, keeping extra for himself. The other boys began to haggle over who should have which of the remaining tokens. There were no girls among them—the girls had gone to another area of the camp from which the starchy smell of cooking came. Maize meal—*posho*, perhaps—and something else Tessa could not identify. Cinnamon, she thought. She had not eaten since they arrived and it appeared no one would until the talks had finished. Her throat was dry.

She looked on as the Monopoly players spoke across each other, some jostling for a better position around the board. Their voices were shrill and high. Francis was not the oldest, but he seemed to be a leader among them. He blew on his cupped hands and rolled the dice. The others crowded in with intense expressions on their faces but before long it became apparent that they did not know how to play. They made up their own rules, and the rules seemed to change from one player to the next. They laughed, they argued. Most of them could not read the property names, but they had their own codes for them. 'Number one red,' a tall boy with large hands said. Another boy with bad acne tossed him a card—Fleet Street rather than The Strand. The stations were most prized. When the first boy's token landed on Kings Cross, Francis turned to him and threw across a station card with an angry flick. 'Next go, that one will be mine.'

They talked in a mix of languages, and before long there seemed to be more at stake than just a game. It brought to mind Stephen and those endless rounds of Monopoly during school holidays, games that lasted an entire rainy afternoon. Tessa would end up letting Stephen buy every property just to keep the peace. Sitting so close and watching the soldiers play now, Tessa could tell this game had reached that same point. There was a lull, then suddenly the boy who'd landed on Kings Cross threw down the dice and said something to Francis in Ma'di. Francis lunged at him and, seizing him by the throat, pushed him to the ground.

Immediately two or three other soldiers were on their feet. They began to shout over each other and there was a dull thumping. The boy on the ground tried to hit back, but Francis kicked him in the stomach. They grunted, they drew blood, the wound on Francis's face opened up again. Their violence appeared automatic and natural until the first boy drew a handgun from his waistband and pulled the trigger. There was a click, but no shot. He giggled.

From out of the darkness, the soldier with the almond-shaped eyes and the red beret, the one who had first met them in the bush, shouted in their direction and the group fell silent. Apparently the meeting with Kony had finished and an announcement was to be made. Francis put the Monopoly game back in the ammunition crate while the other boys slung their rifles over their shoulders, each of them pocketing the money they had won before they moved away, a couple hand-slapping as they shifted aside.

The tent flap was pushed back and the delegation began to file out. But as soon as they came towards the firelight Tessa could see that something was wrong. Dominic moved stiffly and when he saw her he shook his head and held up his hand as if to prevent her from asking questions. Behind him came the Sudanese mediator and the other delegates, Gideon still wearing his cap with his wraparound sunglasses perched above the visor. Alphington and Berg murmured together with their heads bowed.

When they reached Tessa, Alphington shrugged. 'Kony will not agree,' he said. 'He refuses to sign the peace agreement.' The disappointed twist of his mouth formed deep grooves from nose to chin, which made him seem even more severe. 'It may've worked,' he added, and drove his hands deep into his pockets, 'but . . .'

'But what?' Tessa asked, following his pale eyes as he looked back at the tent.

'But nothing. Kony says it is his right, that he acts according to the limits we have placed on him. He is stalling. Maybe he is hoping for time to regroup his army. He pretends he doesn't understand what the ICC warrants are about.' Then, taking his hands from his pockets, Alphington ran them through his lank grey hair. He rocked back on his heels. 'The West wants neat answers,' he said. 'They set deadlines and expect tyrants to obey them. This is another taste of failure—and who has the courage for more failure?'

Dominic, who had not spoken until now, shook his head. 'We can't negotiate because he believes he is fighting the whole world—cast in the role of guerrilla rebel and labelled a terrorist, that is what he has become.' Anguish crumpled his features and his shoulders slumped so that he seemed another person entirely. Had he broken with the idea of hope he held so dearly? His hands fell to his sides, but then he straightened, and Tessa saw in the way he lifted his eyes that he would try again, he would will himself not to despair. To despair, he might have said, would be self-fulfilling.

Behind them the rebel soldiers began to cheer. On the other side of the fire, Francis jumped to his feet then raised his hand in a fist above his head. Kony exited the tent flanked by his senior commanders. Looking triumphant, he held up his hands. 'This you will remember,' he said. 'We are *dano adana*, human persons like everyone else. We have a right to freedom, and so, if you threaten us, we cannot be expected to keep the ceasefire.'

He looked around, almost spinning in the firelight, and for a brief moment Tessa thought that in another life he might have been a dancer, with his lithe catlike movement, his graceful hands—a Joaquín Cortés, despite his small potbelly and the cheap polyester suit. He raised his voice. 'So you have heard me,' he declared. 'You will not lift the indictments and I will not be handed over to the ICC. And now you can go back and tell everyone that we will continue, and in less than ten years we will win the war!'

Beside her Tessa heard Alphington scoff, as if to say: Kony has been fighting for twenty years without victory, how is he going to win in less than ten?

Kony looked beyond the delegation party and waved his hand dismissively. 'That is enough,' he said. 'You must leave now.'

But they did not leave. It was dark and there was further argument about who would take them back to the park border. Kony departed with his entourage, but no one would escort the delegates this late; they were told they must stay the night and leave first thing in the morning. They were offered the dry *posho* that Tessa had smelt cooking earlier. It was accompanied by a thick salty groundnut sauce. Tessa chewed it and washed it down with weak black tea. As the camp settled, she could still picture the bizarre game of Monopoly and the motley assortment of weapons the boys carried. Dominic had told her it was cheaper to buy a handgun than a mobile phone. A grenade cost even less. Food, guns, children, machetes. How do we live in this world, she wondered, a world where children go to war?

Even the Romans thought that was wrong.

She tried to sleep, but couldn't. She lay awake for a long time going over what she'd seen and heard, snatches of English together with a mix of languages she could not understand, her scrawled notes, and the question of why some people survive better than others. If being mentally healthy required integrating your childhood into your adulthood, how then was it possible if that childhood had been taken from you?

Finally, she slept, dozing fitfully and waking from a strange disjointed dream into the still darkness of the night. She rolled onto her back and listened to the whine of insects and, closer still, the murmuring of voices. After what seemed like another hour, she got up and went to sit by the campfire. No one tended the fire although there were a couple of soldiers patrolling nearby. She heard them whistle softly to each other.

She chewed her bottom lip and tried to roll the stiffness out of her shoulders. She felt for her phone—music to calm her. Carefully pressing an earbud into one ear, she hid the wire under her hair, a schoolgirl trick she had often used in class with her first Discman. She stared into the glowing coals and the music filled her; a choirboy's ethereal voice sang, his tone so exquisite that when Francis appeared before her, it seemed he had stepped out of the music into the light of the fire. He crouched beside her and she noticed the ladder of his spine through his shirt and the small indentation at the nape of his neck. The wound on his face seemed to glisten—a snail's trail, she thought. His eyes were wide, different from his earlier watchfulness, softer, less brooding. He pointed to the earphone wire and she took the phone out of her pocket then offered it to him. His hands were fine-boned but callused, and in them the phone looked more toy-like than functional. The earphones fell to the ground like streamers. She wondered whether he would keep the phone or give it to his commander. Surely that was what was expected of him. Instead, he tapped each app, and she saw that his fingernails were dirty and broken. Clumsily he swiped the calendar, maps, calculator, but it was the photos that pleased him the most.

'Who is this?' he asked.

'My father,' she said. 'And that is my mother.'

'And this one next to you? Who is he? Is he your boyfriend or maybe is he your husband?'

'No.' She laughed. 'That is my brother.'

Francis frowned. 'And this—this is you?'

'Yes.'

He waited.

'It was taken at the university when I got my doctorate.'

'You are a doctor?'

She nodded then shook her head. It seemed too much to explain—the graduation cap and gown. All the ritual and pomp now irrelevant. What good would it do to say she was an academic? Francis did not ask her for any more information; instead he stared at the photograph, his eyes shining as they reflected the screen's blue light.

'Thank you,' Tessa said, and held out her hand to take back the phone, but he refused to return it. Once he understood how to scroll through and enlarge the photos he was like a gambler at a slot machine. She offered to take a photograph of him, but he shook his head. He magnified the photo of her graduation day and stared at it.

'You said this one is your brother but he is not with you now.'

'No.'

'Then who will protect you—your mother, your father? But they are not here either. Where are they?'

'They are in Australia.'

'I don't know Australia.'

'It is a big country, surrounded by the ocean.'

'Bigger than Uganda?'

'Yes, but not as many people.'

'You are not American?' He seemed disappointed.

'No.' She smiled.

'Ah, I am disturbing you?' he added with sudden self-consciousness.

'No, Francis, you are not disturbing me. I am very pleased to talk with you. My country is far away. It is different—the bush, the animals. Have you seen a picture of a kangaroo?'

He stared at her with a blank look. 'A what?' But before she could answer, he said, 'Do you have war in your country?'

Tessa shook her head.

He was silent and she thought he would not speak again, but after a long pause he asked: 'How much does the aeroplane cost?'

It took a moment to understand what he meant, and when she did, she calculated the airfare as best she could. 'About a thousand US dollars.'

He drew in a quick breath. 'Then I will not be going there,' he said in a low voice, and once again his expression took on the same fierce stare with which he had first held her, resolute and older than his years. Then slowly he nodded, and after another long moment, he placed her phone at her feet then got up and walked away.

13

Still some way from the park border, the party of delegates stopped to make a fireless camp. The vegetation was dense and Tessa had to pitch her tent several metres from the others. Returning had been slower than trekking in. There was a dejected mood among them—hardly anyone talked, not even Gideon. They had walked hard all day and were tired, although Tessa could not relax. She thought of Dominic, how depressed he had become since the talks. 'We will have to begin all over again,' he'd said earlier in the day, and then nothing much to anyone since that time. When they were setting up camp she saw him sit down on the ground and clutch his head with his hands. She pictured the rebels she'd encountered, especially the watchful boy, Francis, and how they all fought during the game of Monopoly; the one who drew the handgun, his skin blotchy with angry wheels of acne; and Kony raising his arms when he dismissed them. Images piled, one over the other, until Tessa slipped into a light skimming sleep, only to be woken by a brutal wrench.

Grabbed by the hair, she was dragged from her tent. A wet cloth was forced between her teeth. She couldn't see. It was too dark, although there were several of them. Rebel soldiers? Bandits? Three, maybe four. One man gripped the back of her neck; another pulled her to a standing position. Further back Tessa heard Dominic's voice, an urgent protesting, then nothing. Pushed forward, she slipped and was pulled up again. She felt a pressure at her back, and when she tried to struggle, a stinging clip across the top of her head. Someone ran alongside her. A rifle shot sounded.

Stumbling, her feet scraped against stone. She wore the T-shirt and hiking pants she'd gone to sleep in, but her feet were bare. They forced her to run along the track for about fifty metres, then suddenly they stopped and one of them held the point of a knife to her throat. Tessa felt the blade nick her skin. It was still too dark to see properly, but she was certain it was Francis's voice. 'Here,' he said, 'put these on.'

She reached out and felt the shape of her boots. The gag in her mouth choked back her tongue and made her drool. She tried to speak, but couldn't.

'Hurry,' he said. 'Or they will hurt you.'

They Will Hurt You.

Trembling, she sat down and tried to make her hands work. Her socks were balled inside her boots. She put them on, then pulled her boots on and blindly tied the laces. When she finished, a strong youth bound her hands behind her back then wound the rope around her waist. He pushed her forward and they began to run again. She listened for Francis's voice, but she no longer heard it. They set a fast pace and in the pale moonlight she could hardly see where she was going. Whenever she tripped she felt the rope tighten and another jolt yanked her forward.

At no point could she tell where they were headed, although her captors seemed to know. When the terrain flattened out they pushed the pace, running or jog-walking in the pale blue light of the moon. Once, they stopped to drink at a stream where the water ran swiftly. The gag was released, she drank, and then it was tightened again.

All through the rest of the night the muscular youth who appeared to be in charge pushed them on into the grey-green light of dawn. Her entire body strained, resisted, then finally gave in to the pain until it became a dull noise inside her head. They would have to stop eventually, she kept telling herself, they must have a purpose. At first she believed they were heading back to the camp where the negotiations with Kony had broken down, but then she realised they were going in a different direction altogether. *Think*, Tessa told herself, and try to remember your bearings. She used her family names, *Tess*, *Tessie*, come on, take a breath, slow it down. In the early-morning light, a soft vapour rose from the ground, it reminded her of entering a warm cave. At times, there was the forest's distinct animal scent, musky, vegetative, dung-filled. Chattering noises surrounded her—monkeys, she thought, or nightjars; cries that reflected her own terror.

She clung to the hope that she would see Dominic or John Alphington, maybe one of the other delegates, but there was no sign of them. What had happened? Were they okay? Dominic's cry had sounded as if he'd been hurt, and there'd been gunfire, loud and flat.

When the sun rose, Tessa could see her captors more clearly, four in all, two surly youths in their twenties—the muscular one with short dreadlocks who was their leader, and skinny Francis, at least ten years younger. All with rifles slung across their backs.

They came to a sluggish river and made her cross it. The water was like a thick noodle soup, and she felt minnows worm against her skin. Parasites, her mother had warned. In the murky shallows the fear of crocodiles. The leader shouted and again prodded her with his rifle. She waded out, her hands still tied, her mouth still gagged. She staggered against the current. Her thighs ached.

Struggling to climb the far bank without the use of her hands she almost lost her balance. Pushing herself forward, she looked up and saw Francis. He stood there with his pink facial wound and bony limbs, his rifle slung over his shoulder. His eyes met hers, although this time she thought he smiled and, alarmingly, she had no idea what he meant by it, or if perhaps she had merely imagined it.

Around midday they came upon a camp. It was similar to the one where the delegation had met, but larger and more established. A number of flat paths, trodden in the thick grass, lead to a cluster of mud huts with thatch roofs. Yellow plastic water containers were stacked up against the walls along with a collapsed bag of grain that had the blue-and-white WFP insignia on it.

When they reached the campfire most of the soldiers, including Francis, scattered, but the one who led them made her sit down and untied her hands.

Tessa pulled the gag from her mouth then leaned forward and retched. A thin trail of yellow bile burnt its way up from her stomach to the back of her throat. It was gritty and hot-tasting. Her tongue was swollen, her mouth raw. She felt sweaty, her hair damp against her head. She swayed then dropped her head between her knees. Tinny rap music came from somewhere, then faded out. The soldier offered her a flask, she thanked him and drank greedily, gulping the tepid water, then instantly felt sick again. She coughed, and spat the water out.

An irrational idea persisted that Alphington and perhaps Dominic, along with the others, had been taken ahead of her, although it would be better if they had escaped to the border. That way, Tessa thought, they might be able to get help. For now, she could only hope they were safe and that, somehow, she would be able to get back to them. Her pulse quickened, she could feel it in her throat. She looked for Francis, but he too had disappeared.

The soldier motioned that she should stand up, then walked her across to a small hut. At the entrance, he pushed aside a blanket that served as a screen and ushered her in.

The smell met her first, a sickly scent; salt-copper—meaty. Then came the sound of someone groaning. When her eyes adjusted to the dim light, she saw the shape of a man writhing on the floor. His face was bloated, and as she drew nearer, she realised that he had been wounded in the chest. Blood oozed from him. There was a darkened area where it soaked into the mat that lay beneath him, and around the edges it seeped into the earthen floor.

'You fix,' said the soldier. He stood behind her and Tessa could feel his breath on the back of her neck. She turned and looked at him.

'You?' he said. 'You are the doctor.'

She straightened. Panic filled her. There was a tingling sensation across her scalp and a strange tightening at the back of her throat. *Oh shit.* She looked at the wounded man. This was why they had brought her here; they thought she was a medical doctor. They thought she could help him. The man ceased to moan, his eyes rolled back as he took a breath—a shallow gurgling. He wheezed, lifting his head from the mat, then let it fall back again.

'If you do not help us,' the soldier said, 'we will be forced to take action. Maybe we will shoot you too.'

The injured man moaned again. Tessa struggled to recall what first-aid knowledge she had—very little, she now realised. What would her mother do? She stepped forward and knelt down beside the man. Peeling back his blood-soaked shirt she saw how the flesh opened like a ragged fissure in his chest. He had been shot, not once but twice—twin entry sites that almost merged into one.

She sat back on her heels and only then heard a shuffling movement to her left, followed by a succession of words mumbled in a low singsong voice. An elderly man was crouched against the wall with an assortment of charms set out in front of him—rusty nails, shards of broken glass, bones and snail shells that lay on a tattered leopard skin like a poor hawker's treasure. Her understanding was that the rebels didn't encourage traditional healers, that they trained their own medics, looting hospitals for supplies, but here, methodically mixing what appeared to be a wad of grass and mud in a small clay pot, was an *awjaka*. He looked up at her, although his eyes, like the dull pieces of glass that lay among his collection, did not appear to see her.

Once again the injured man groaned. The sound came from deep within him, and his great body gave a violent thrust forward as though he was trying to get up.

'You fix,' the soldier repeated.

Tessa rubbed the back of her neck. 'I'll try,' she said quietly. 'I'll try my best.'

And she did. Throughout the night she tried everything she could think of. She struggled to staunch the flow of blood. So much—she hadn't thought a body could contain so much. It seeped, and when she applied pressure she felt a rippling pulse beat. There were a few medical supplies in a battered tin; gauze, a tourniquet, bandages and not much else. She attempted to pack the wound and bind it while the man struggled, arching his back with each breath he took. He gasped then coughed, expelling a fetid bloody scent through his mouth. She sat with him through the spasms while the soldier stood by and the *awjaka* continued to mix his potions, chanting softly as he rattled his gourd.

When the injured man defecated, there was blood too, tar-black with a foul smell. The stench was overpowering. Tessa gagged and tried to clean him then covered him again, but he used what energy he had to push the blanket off. Something gurgled in his chest. Occasionally he tried to talk, *Orwo neka*, he said, and Tessa understood that he was thirsty, although when she offered him some water to drink, he brushed her hand away and she felt his warm blood against her own skin. She wiped her hand on a piece of cloth that lay on the floor, and when the man's breathing grew more laboured she began to count the seconds between each breath. Occasionally a whole minute would pass before he would breathe again, and there were times when his breath became so shallow and irregular that she thought he would die, then suddenly he would gasp once more.

At one point he opened his eyes and looked up as if some spirit was beckoning him, some horror he did not wish to follow. He reached out his hand and she thought he wanted to say something. He wanted to survive, she was sure of it, he was fighting for that, but just before dawn the *awjaka* got to his feet and began to sing a tuneless dirge that continued until the man's eyes emptied and it was the shocking depthless vacancy in his eyes that told her he was dead.

Outside rain began to fall in heavy sheets. Thunder rumbled and what little morning light that came made it seem like an extended dawn. Tessa's body ached and her thoughts alternated between a strange delirium and a heightened lucidity. She had never seen someone die, had never seen a corpse—even her grandfather had been hidden away in a casket—and it struck her that the confidence she had in life was rupturing because this was the only truth you could guarantee: ultimately it didn't matter what kind of life you lived, it ended.

She could not stop staring at the dead man. His mouth hung slack, his tongue slightly protruding, the skin across his brow appeared sleek and his lips were grey, almost whitish. Torpid flies had already begun to buzz in a slow loop around his mouth, some coming to rest on the bloody bandages. She waved them away and they lifted lazily before regrouping to form the same insistent pattern. The urge to wash her hands was strong; blood under her fingernails, the thought of AIDS. She used the drinking water the man had refused, pouring it over her hands and into a small bowl.

To the other side of her, the *awjaka* gathered his charms then shuffled out of the hut. The soldier left too, and Tessa was alone with the dead man. She slipped her hand into her pocket, took out her phone and turned it on, but there was still no reception. She turned it off again, and when Francis entered she felt an immense and unreasonable gratitude at the sight of the boy's familiar face. His eyes widened and she smiled, but Francis's expression did not change. The other soldier entered the hut once more and spoke briefly in Acholi to Francis. Tessa listened without understanding very much. She tried to read their body language, but that too seemed unclear. What mistaken idea had allowed her to think she could make some kind of connection with Francis? He stood squaring his shoulders, completely different from the boy who had asked about her family. Focus, she told herself, you need to think clearly, except she felt as though she were in a fog.

'You must come with me,' Francis said and, like a sleepwalker, Tessa got to her feet and followed him out into the rain. He led her to a larger hut on the other side of the compound. The forest was bathed in green shadow and a little way off a red-tailed monkey moved through the trees. Soldiers strolled past, their voices loud; someone laughed—a scene happening in slow motion. Under a frayed tarp, the carcass of some type of bush meat—a small antelope, maybe a kob—hung from a tree, its exsanguinating blood collecting in a plastic bowl beneath it.

Blood. So much of it.

At the hut, Francis gestured for her to enter, and when she hesitated a small flicker of irritation passed across his face. He nodded again, and she went inside.

Two men sat on folding camp chairs. They were speaking together in a conspiratorial huddle—senior rebels, both dressed in decorated military fatigues. The commander closest to her had thick lips and a full moustache. He was particularly well-built. He carried his weight in his back, a roll of fat sat on his neck. His uniform had elaborate gold epaulettes and red-and-yellow braid over one shoulder.

'This is Colonel Kolo,' Francis said, then nodded in the direction of the other man who, although lighter in build and almost birdlike in the way he inclined his head to one side, appeared to have the greater authority. 'And this is our preacher and *lapwony*—Brigadier Obed Lokodo.'

At first glance, Tessa almost mistook the man for Kony, but he was too young, closer to her own age. There was an energy about him; he appeared as Kony might once have looked—the same alarming intensity, only rejuvenated and made new again.

'You can go,' Obed said to Francis.

When the boy had left, he sat back and frowned at Tessa. Around his neck he wore a string of large wooden beads, what looked like a composite version of rosary beads, only the crucifix that would normally hang at the end had been replaced with a postage-sized photograph of Kony. The photograph was plastic-covered, cracked and discoloured as though water-damaged. It was like the devotional scapular Tessa's grandfather had worn—she remembered her grandfather's Catholic reverence, how he would bring it to his lips and whisper, *St Christopher protect us, keep us safe*. A faith she viewed as irrational and pagan even as the allure was recognisable and at times desirable.

The *lapwony*—it meant teacher, she had heard the title used at the centre—reached for the scapular and closed his eyes. His face was fine-boned. He swayed; he might have been meditating. She tried to gauge what to do. She wanted to ask him, 'What will happen now, will you let me go?' Would someone escort her out of here, or was she a liability? Even with his eyes closed Obed was full of authority. *They will harm you.* What was to stop them? She had heard the stories. No, she reminded herself, there would be consequences, reprisals; she had to trust they would fear that.

She glanced around the hut. The roof and walls had been neatly woven from grass and it had an earthen floor, pounded and swept. In the corner was a camp bed with a striped blanket. There was a whiff of body odour, earth, charcoal. The colonel ran his forefinger and thumb in an arc over his moustache while Obed continued to sit with his eyes closed, but then, as if he had been given a silent signal, he slowly opened his eyes again. Tessa felt his scrutiny too. Annoyance crept across his face; a pained smile, she thought.

'The man who died, the esteemed major whom you did not save, will never know peace now, and why? Because of you.' His voice had a marked accent, a type of corrupted colonial English, polite, anachronistic, commanding. Once more he gave her an aggrieved smile then sat forward and clasped the scapular. 'Despite the ceasefire, the government has attacked us. They wounded the major and took out our *dakta*, you know this? Our medic—the one who would have healed the major. So, at great risk, we have brought you here, but you have failed. Is your medicine so weak?'

Colonel Kolo shifted. He was armed, a handgun at his hip, as were the soldiers outside the hut—those Tessa had seen, at least ten of them, carried rifles or pangas.

Her mouth was dry and when she spoke she heard herself as if from a great distance. 'I'm sorry. I'm sorry. I tried, but there was no way I could help him.'

'You lie.'

'No,' she insisted. 'By the time I got here, he'd lost too much blood.'

'And you know this for certain?'

She nodded. 'He stood no chance of surviving,' she said and felt a jag beneath her ribcage, afraid of them and afraid to admit the truth of how little she knew.

Obed waved his hand in the air. He had the manner of a prophet. 'Perhaps you are a fraud? Or a witch? Clearly you do not have the Holy Spirit.' He looked at her as though he pitied her, but then in the next moment, his expression changed to something more conspiratorial—or perhaps he meant to trick her, she couldn't tell. 'Do you know why we are here?' he asked.

Tessa glanced at the colonel's powerful shoulders, squared by his gold epaulettes, then again at the preacher. Despite how fearful she felt, she saw that this might be her best chance. If I make a connection with them, she thought, if I try to cajole them.

'You are part of the rebel army,' she began. 'I respect—'

'No!' Obed declared. 'We are religious fighters—we are infinitely more than you think. Colonel Kolo here is a brave soldier, a soldier of God—as was the major who we must now bury. Whose spirit will come after you and haunt you in the night.'

Her stomach clenched.

'And I am their *lapwony*,' Obed continued. 'I lead, I preach, I spread the Gospel.' He used his hands when he spoke and held his head high.

He's boasting, Tessa realised, bragging—he wants to be admired. She felt dizzy. She hadn't slept for more than twenty-four hours, had drunk only the stale water they'd offered her, eaten nothing.

'You spread the Gospel,' she repeated. 'That is good.' She needed to keep him on side, but a part of her recalled the things she had learnt about the war here—hands, lips cut, the destruction of entire villages, *war crimes*, *atrocities*, children raped, shot in their classrooms.

'Yes.' He smiled. 'The Gospel is good. The Gospel as passed through Kony. We are trying to bring God's law.' He spoke without irony, his long fingers pointed towards the scapular he wore around his neck. 'But there are others who do not want God's message. It is Kony who wants peace.'

'And yet he has just refused to sign the agreement,' Tessa said before she could stop herself. It was an error, a mistake, blurted out.

Obed fixed his eyes on her and lowered his voice: 'Why do you say this? Why do you fool yourself? If Kony accepts the indictment by the ICC, he will be exhibited in the West and a spectacle will be made of him.' He tilted his head to one side in his birdlike way and looked at her as if she were some shiny object. 'It is the West who do not want peace,' he added coldly. 'It is they who are corrupt, because it is in their interest to keep us shackled. But Kony,' he said softly, '*Konj* has the Spirit. We know this because what he has predicted has already come true. Soon—' he raised his hand '—the Silent World will come and then everyone will know.'

Dominic had spoken of the Silent World. Kony had predicted that there would come a time when all the guns fell silent and only those who knew how to use weapons like machetes would prevail against their enemies. It was madness, crazy talk.

Obed nodded as if he expected her to respond, the look on his face suggesting he knew something she did not. Tessa pressed her lips together. She would do well to keep quiet, or better still agree with him and gain his confidence. 'Yes,' she said. 'You are wise.' It was the sort of thing she'd espoused in her thesis—a positive interviewing technique—but what had looked good on paper failed her now. She needed to engage with him, compliment and encourage him to talk. 'But,' she said quietly, 'I don't understand. Can you tell me how this Silent World can happen?'

'That is what we believe!' Obed replied confidently. 'It is faith.' He laughed. 'Your problem is that you do not understand because you are removed from God.' Then he frowned and made an expansive gesture with his hands. 'We in the Lord's Resistance Army are guided by the Holy Spirit and so we fight a virtuous war, while those like you and those in the government have no faith. You are the ones who bring death. *You* are the problem.'

She had to be careful, had to work out how to get out of here. Back down, she told herself, although she felt unhinged; it was as though she were drunk. She had seen the way Francis had kissed his rifle, had seen Dominic's expression when he came out of the failed peace talks, and the rejection of Oraako from his village; *they do not want him, he is damaged.* The major's bloody death played over in her mind, the smell of it and the terrible sound of his gurgling breath filled her. Her heart thumped and a spike of anger rose inside her. *I have spoken to your soldiers*, she might've said, *to those children who have fled your ranks, and I have heard from some of them what you do.* But she dug her nails into the soft flesh of her palms and kept quiet.

There were voices outside the hut and the rising smell of wood smoke. Colonel Kolo got up and went to the entrance, where he gave orders to one of the soldiers to cut down the meat and cook it. When he came back he stepped past Tessa then sat heavily in the folding chair and once again looked at Obed, who continued sweeping his hand in a grand gesture as though he was enjoying the discussion. As though it was his mission to enlighten her. 'The Kingdom of God calls for everyone. Jesus Christ says, "Go and be a catcher of men", and so that is what we do.'

He laughed casually and Tessa tried to laugh with him, but something other than her own need for safety surged in her. 'But that is not what you do,' she replied incredulously. 'What you do is abduct children.'

He smiled again, impatiently, then shook his head as though he must explain something to someone infinitely less intelligent than himself. 'That means abducted; Jesus Christ instructs us to go and teach. Go and abduct!'

Tessa's eyes widened. 'He said, *Go and abduct*?' I don't remember that being in the Bible, she wanted to add, but held her tongue.

'Yes, Jesus Christ said, "You are no longer going to be fishermen, but you are going to catch people instead of fish."' Then stretching out his arms again, Obed turned his palms upwards and added: 'We are instruments of God.' He nodded and continued to study her with his curious birdlike expression that was both piercing and strangely hypnotic, and despite herself Tessa was pulled in by his words. 'This is a violent country, the dead fall like leaves. Do you forget the British? They were the ones who classified our tribes according to the Englishmen's hierarchy. They set us on the path to civil war. Divide and conquer. Do you forget Idi Amin? You say stop what we do, but there is no end.'

Just then a girl entered the hut and sat down against the wall. She wore a brightly coloured *khanga* and had an infant strapped to her back. Deftly she unwrapped the binding and moved the baby around to her lap.

'This is Colonel Kolo's wife,' announced Obed, and lifted his chin in the girl's direction. 'She has given him another son. Is that also abducting?'

The colonel drew his shoulders back with pride, while the girl, who was maybe fifteen or sixteen, looked on with a calm, self-contained expression even as the tiny infant squirmed in her arms and began to cry.

'Hush it up now,' Colonel Kolo told her, and she adjusted

her position to allow the infant to feed. Looking back at Tessa, he added, 'When she is finished, you will go with her and help the other women work.' There was a pause before he continued, 'Like Joseph Kony, I have more than one wife. This year I have three wives and many strong children. Like the *lapwony* says: Love is built. This is what you do not know. You see my wife here, Mildred, she was abducted, as I too was abducted. Now we create a new generation.'

Mildred bent forward and very gently stroked the side of her baby's face. She wore a pink plastic butterfly clip in her hair and as the infant continued to suckle the clip slipped forward. She pushed it back. '*Chiki, chiki, chi-ki*,' she crooned and rocked, cradling the dark softness of her baby's head so that it blended into the outline of her own body.

'Yes, so you see,' Obed added, sitting back and presiding over the scene like a proud and boastful brother. 'We punish with death, but our message is love.'

'Love,' Tessa repeated.

'Yes, love.' He smiled. 'We have God; we preach love. Together we are the LRA. We are a family.'

14

Mildred handed Tessa a plastic plate with strips of meat. '*Apwoyo*,' Tessa mumbled—thank you—then quickly gulped down the charred stringy flesh. It'd been nearly two days since she'd last eaten, and although a vegetarian, she ate, hungry for more, not even knowing exactly what it was she ate—gazelle or tiang or kob, she had little idea. It had not taken all that long to break with the belief she once held so self-righteously. She remembered Stephen laughing at her earnestness in a Greek restaurant one night. 'So what's this? Because you don't eat meat, you think you're better than everyone else?'

Before long, the carcass was stripped to the bone.

Obed and Colonel Kolo sat alongside one another like incongruous siblings. Kolo ate heartily, his lips glistening with grease, while Obed ate in an almost delicate way, picking out small morsels of meat with his fingers and taking neat bites as though he was at some sort of formal high tea. Across the campfire, a group of soldiers was seated together on a makeshift bench seat while others came and went. Tessa scanned their faces until she saw Francis. Yes, she thought with some relief, he was there among them. She had been waiting for the right moment—she felt that because they had spoken, and because he had seen the photographs of her family on her phone, they had a fledgling bond. However nascent and insubstantial it might be, he was her best chance of an ally. She was trying to think of some way to get his attention when he gave her the slightest nod before looking away again and draping his arm around another soldier.

She watched him and realised she would have to continue to wait, at least until he was on his own, but the night wore on and the chance did not come.

The next morning she sat curled in one of the camp chairs with her T-shirt tugged down over her trousered knees. She had barely slept in the hut they allocated her, thinking all night of the dead major whose haunting Obed had taunted her with and wondering what she should do now. She needed to get away from here or at least find a place where she might pick up reception on her phone—a higher elevation. She needed a strategy, a plan. Perhaps she could get to talk to Francis, who seemed to have a better grasp of English than Mildred or the other soldiers under Kolo and Obed, but could she trust him? And how might she get him to trust her? She had begun cramping, and so badly now that she thought her period might have come early. She felt a spasm in her lower back, and a wave of nausea passed through her while birds glutted on insects, their small *wheeping* calls like a distressing song.

She closed her eyes against the dizziness she felt and when she opened them again she saw Colonel Kolo walking across the compound towards her. He was carrying a small portable microphone and wore a green beret with his jacket buttoned to his throat. He stopped before her and held out the microphone. 'Do you know how to repair this?' he asked, then after a pause he added, 'What is wrong with you, are you sick?'

'No, I'm all right,' Tessa lied. It would not help if he thought she was sick; better if he thought she could be useful to them.

'Good,' he said. 'Because now you will come. We are holding a funeral for the major. He must be buried in the proper way. Do you know this? If a body isn't interred correctly, bad things will happen,' and he waved his hand as if to indicate the air around him. 'We shall rightly honour him.'

Kolo put the microphone in Tessa's lap. She had seen the same type used in lecture theatres—a small strap-on speaker and a headset. There was nothing wrong with it that she could see except that it had dirt in it, which she blew out, and one of the batteries had been put in the wrong way. Lucky for her, she thought as she turned it around. Perhaps she would now be as seen as an asset. She could only hope.

The colonel tested it: 'Hello, hello,' he said, then nodded his approval. How old was he? She guessed he was in his thirties, although he acted in a way that suggested he was middle-aged or older. 'Come,' he said.

Tessa followed him a short distance beyond the camp to a gap in the forest where the air was lighter and the sunlight more intense. A barbed-wire fence enclosed a triangular vegetable garden. In the loamy soil grew mounds of sweet potato and cassava—a mass of green hand-shaped leaves that shone in the sun. Steam rose from the red earth. *At nightfall, if you plant your walking-staff in the ground, by morning it will have sprouted*—it was one of the local sayings, a favourite of Dominic's. Tessa wondered where Dominic and John Alphington were now, and where the other delegates—Berg, Gideon with his wry humour, the argumentative Ugandan general—might be. What if they had been injured, or worse? She recalled the major's gun-blasted chest and the warmth of his blood soaking through the bandages. It's my fault that we were attacked, she thought. But she needed to stop tormenting herself, that would not help anyone. She tried to push back the feelings of self-recrimination, but the reproaches kept coming.

Her stomach roiled. She placed her hand on her belly and pressed down. Maybe it was something she'd eaten.

Kolo was leading her through a clearing that appeared to be a training area. In the middle, there was a life-sized target in the shape of a man. It had been assembled out of dry branches and old jerry cans and wore the remnants of an Allied Democratic Forces uniform. On the rusty kerosene tin that served as its head, a cartoonish face had been painted in blue, its mouth like a wide O. As they walked past, Tessa saw it'd been shot through numerous times, bullet holes to the heart, the crutch, the head—a great number were already oxidised while others glinted as if lit from within.

Towards the end of the clearing there were several camp chairs and a few plastic crates arranged around an open grave. Kolo motioned that Tessa should stand at a distance while he and several other soldiers sat on the seats. The *awjaka* crouched nearby. He wore his leopard skin over one shoulder and began a low guttural chant. His dirge stopped when, from the direction of the camp, came a sound that was neither a cheer nor a lament but a weird mix—voices rising and falling as the major's corpse was slowly carried forward on a stretcher. About fifteen soldiers marched behind the corpse-bearers, among them Francis, with his watchful eyes and split face. When they came to where Kolo and the others were sitting they set the stretcher down on the ground beside the grave then stood in silence.

In the time since the major had died his body had stiffened and bloated. He no longer wore the uniform he'd been shot in—someone had washed his face and dressed him in clean fatigues. It would have been an intimate undertaking, and Tessa thought that whoever had attended to him must have done so with care. He lay with his eyes closed and his arms at his sides. A piece of black cloth had been strapped around his chin to keep his mouth closed.

The sky was very blue, almost lurid. Against it, large grey plantain-eaters hopped among the branches of an ironwood tree at the edge of the clearing. In the stillness, they made their alarming *cow-cow* calls and preened themselves with their bright yellow beaks. The soldier who had force-marched Tessa through the bush now wore a red headband around his dreadlocks and began to play a small barrel-shaped drum with the flats of his hands. At the sound of his drumming the plantain-eaters flew into the sky. From the edge of the clearing Obed Lokodo, in every sense the high priest now, came forward. Thin, straight-backed, princely. He was dressed in a white robe and a finely brocaded stole with his scapular placed over the top. As he came towards them, the soldiers held up their guns. Their shadows flickered across his robes as he passed them.

He moved with solemn purpose, and when he stopped in front of the stretcher he raised his face to the sky. His eyes rose and dipped. The drumming ceased and again there was silence.

Tessa watched transfixed. She saw how he held the Bible in his right hand, although he did not read from it. With ceremonial dignity, Kolo stepped towards him and placed the headset on his head like a crown. When it was turned on there was a whine of feedback that wailed then cut out. Obed began to pray, his voice amplified through the speaker, 'Come, the Lord has prepared the way for you . . .'

The *awjaka* started to chant again, his bracelets rattling as he shook his arms. He had his array of trinkets, eggshells and glass—things of the earth, blood, water, bone. He held up a hornbill feather, his voice reedy without the magic of the microphone.

'We do not want violation!' Obed declared over him. 'We do not want death! We are here to protect, but we have been betrayed, and so there will be retribution. Take strength from the Lord: Moses was sent to kill on his mission and so must we. That is justice! And without justice we have no respect.' As he spoke it was as though he grew in size. He was more effective than Kony, Tessa thought; whether his pupil or his rival, he had surpassed him. The sun reflected off the light fabric of his robe and broke apart as he raised his hands and lifted his voice in hymn. Tessa did not recognise the melody or understand the words, but the beauty of his singing was astonishing—a cappella, resonant, percussive. He sang solo then once again the drumming started and the soldiers joined in, becoming a chorus as they moved in closer, arranging themselves in a crescent shape around the grave. Sweat glistened on their skin, and on the breeze was the heady sourness of their body odour, a stark reminder of their vigour and youthful energy.

Tessa's vision blurred. Beads of gold glimmered off Obed's brocaded stole as he sprinkled water on the dead major, then on the soldiers who stood on either side of him. 'Protection from harm, protection from bullets,' he announced, as if they were preparing for battle rather than conducting a funeral. 'We will not let our brother's death go unpunished!' His voice reverberated through the microphone.

Tessa felt a chill panic, her mind reeling as the cramping worsened. She was going to be sick. First she was hot, then cold. Forgotten images came to her—a man she had kissed and made love to, but who did not love her. Her stomach spasmed again. She needed to sit down. Kolo was opposite her with his arms folded; his gold epaulettes dazzled, great whirls of colour blared. She brought her gaze back to rest on the major's body, but when she did, she saw that his hands and legs had begun to ooze a clear serous fluid. It was seeping through the thick fabric of his trousers and leaking onto the stretcher, and again she saw the terrible fear that had been in his eyes. She saw it as he fought for his last breath and, in that moment, it rose from him and entered her.

She stumbled towards the shade then crouched down and rested her forehead against the tree's corky bark. It would pass, she told herself. But she heaved, and in one burst she expelled the meat she had eaten. It was still recognisable—the half-chewed contents of what she'd devoured splattered onto the ground at her feet in an acid soup of vomit. For a moment, she felt a sense of relief, but then the nausea quickly built again. She tried to stand but could only remain on her knees while the sermon continued. She could hear Obed's magnified voice boom from the microphone and carry through the thick air as the soldiers slowly lowered the major's body into the ground.

She tried to steady herself. She wiped her hand across her mouth and looked at Francis, who stood staring into the grave. He glanced back at her, his eyes flickering in her direction and away again as the drumming increased and the overwhelming need to vomit took hold of her once more.

15

It was dark when Tessa opened her eyes. She lay in the corner of the hut, not far from where the major had bled to death, and continued to vomit into a plastic bowl. Each time she felt herself improving, the pain in her head grew worse and the spasms took hold again.

Outside, thunder rumbled and lightning lit the space around her in momentary flares. Rain fell. She heard water dripping off the thatch and fell asleep only to wake once more in her own clammy heat, or later chilled, she curled herself into a ball and shivered, the pain at the very base of her spine. It was better to sleep, she told herself; it was better to sink back into oblivion. Voices came and went outside the hut, part of the strange dreams that drifted through her mind. She was inhabiting the dead major's world, moving through the forest gloom, mud, blood, an army of vengeful *cen* with their pointed teeth and shining eyes. Just before dawn a shape detached itself from the wall of the hut. She thought it would come for her and take her by the throat, but in the next moment she recognised

Francis in the dim light. He crouched by her side and offered her a gourd half filled with tepid water. Holding her head, he said, 'Here, you can drink this.'

She took a sip and thanked him, her voice thick with gratitude. She tried to sit forward, and when she felt his hand brush the hair from her mouth she made a small gulping sound at his childlike helpfulness.

Francis's voice was low. 'I could do better for you. I would be better for you.'

'Better?' she asked, groggy and confused.

'Yes. Better than your brother, better than your father—I am a soldier.'

She smiled weakly.

'You might die here. You need protection. You do not want to die,' he added with sudden hostility, then he sat back and punched himself in the chest. 'I do not want to die.' He crouched beside her silently and did not move.

She dreamt again, this time of what she knew—for one brilliant moment she saw the sweeping coastline of her summers; she was swimming in the ocean where the water was deep and cold, then lying on the warm sand, her striped beach towel salty and dried crisp. Homesickness broke inside her. Her mother placed a cool hand on her forehead. 'Come on now, sweetheart, try to get up.'

Okay, okay. Dawn, daylight, dusk. She caught the reek of her own sour breath. If she didn't do something she might lie here and get worse. Francis was no longer in the hut. She was alone now and from the open door she could smell the post-storm earth. She struggled to her feet and rinsed her mouth, which helped, then she made her way outside. Her ribs hurt. She found a place where she could empty the plastic bowl she had vomited into, scouring it with wet grass then washing her hands and face in the same way she had seen the soldiers do.

A tall soldier she did not recognise indicated that she should go back towards the centre of the camp. He pointed his rifle and nodded. Walking, she felt a little better. Smoke rose from a small cookfire and birds called. Grey clouds drifted across the sky as the evening meal was being prepared. She sat down on an upturned kerosene tin and watched the scene unfold before her. There was the sound of chopping, voices talking excitedly. She noticed a vigorous soldier stacking firewood alongside the wall of a hut; another darted across in front her. It reminded her of a strange version of Robin Hood's hideaway camp, a band of outlaws with guns and machetes rather than bows and arrows slung over their shoulders.

Colonel Kolo's girl-wife, Mildred, bent over a large cast-iron pot of maize meal, her baby strapped to her back, and stirred the soupy mix while steam rose. When she had finished, she put the stick aside and went to sit beside Kolo. The sleeping baby lay with its head to the side and its mouth open, a thin sticky trail of mucus running from its nose into its mouth. Mildred moved closer to the colonel and nuzzled her cheek against his shirtsleeve. Without looking, Kolo reached across and stroked her hair. His muscled arm flexed through his tight fatigues as he drew her in. It was a gesture at once personal and tender, and Tessa could almost feel the gentle pressure of his fingertips, as if they stroked her own head—a precise knowledge of the sensation embedded in her memory, she felt it in the roots of her hair, a lover's touch.

To be part of a family, even here. Especially here.

Tessa scanned the camp for Francis, but he had disappeared. She thought about approaching Obed or perhaps speaking to Kolo and wondered which of them made the decisions. Or did their instructions come from someone higher up the chain, maybe Kony himself? Satellite phones, notes left in trees. Robin Hood and his band of children.

Mildred stood up and tightened her *khanga*, securing the infant on her back. She scooped a portion of *ugali* into a bowl and handed it to Kolo, then nodded in Tessa's direction before passing her a bowl too. If I'm sick again, Tessa thought, and shook her head, but the girl insisted, lifting her chin. She wore the same proud expression on her face as when the colonel introduced her. How in this place had she managed such assurance? *You can get used to anything*, John Alphington had said when they drove past the internal displacement camp. A comment made with his usual world-weariness, but she could tell he meant it.

Tessa took the bowl. She smiled apologetically, then put the bowl to one side and lifted her arms to gather her hair. Twisting the mass of it into a knot she lifted it off the nape of her neck. For a moment relief—the breeze cooled her—but again she felt the nausea return.

Kolo glanced at her. 'You had better eat,' he said. 'You had better look after yourself, learn how to get on. You will probably be here for a long time.'

16

Melbourne

Neil used a screwdriver to loosen the upper hinge on the back door then wedged in a shim and tightened it. The door needed to be planed, but his makeshift repair would have to do, at least until he got the right tools for the job.

The phone rang again and he went inside.

'Mr Lowell?'

'Yes,' he replied, his voice faltering as he recognised the East African accent. He looked through the window to where the ivy on the side of the garage glowed a deep crimson. Something was wrong. Tessa.

'My name is Dominic Oculi,' the man said. 'I work at the rehabilitation centre here in Gulu.' There was a pause. 'I'm calling about your daughter. About Tessa.'

Neil pulled the door towards himself and shut it with a bang. He felt his heart constrict. His mouth was gluey. 'What's happened?' he asked and forced his tongue to unstick.

'I'm afraid I have troubling news.'

The connection sounded as if it might cut out. Neil pressed

the phone closer and kept his eyes focused on the ivy; the way the light shone made it seem metallic.

The man's voice echoed. 'Your daughter has been abducted,' Neil heard him say. 'I thought it would be better if I phoned rather than you hearing first from the Department of Foreign Affairs. You can contact them yourself of course.'

Neil closed his eyes and opened them again. 'I don't understand. Maybe there's been a mistake.'

'No, sir, there's been no mistake. It happened three days ago. I was with her.'

'She was taken from the centre?'

'No, not from the centre. We were across the border, more than a day's drive away. We tried to go after those who took her—rebel soldiers. But they know the bush too well.'

'Rebels? You're talking about the LRA?'

There was the sound of a keyboard clicking. 'Yes.' And as he listened, Neil kept thinking, Oh shit, Oh shit, but the man was talking again. 'We were hoping to have heard more by now, but I'm afraid there's been no word.'

'There must be something,' Neil stammered. 'Do you know anything else? Was Tessa hurt?'

But Dominic Oculi didn't know, and when Neil asked if anyone else was taken, he replied, 'It was just your daughter they abducted.'

Neil looked for his reading glasses, which he failed to find, then searched for a pen in the cluttered drawer by the phone and began to scrawl notes on the back of an envelope. 'Who else have you notified?'

Dominic paused. 'We have contacted the Allied Democratic

Forces here in Uganda, but I think you should notify the Australian embassy. Unfortunately, there's only a consulate branch in Kampala. If you want representation from the embassy itself, that is based in Kenya.'

Fuck, what a mess.

'Do you have the name of the consul general?' Neil asked.

'There have been some changes recently. I'm not sure who is in charge now.'

Neil's jaw clenched. Everything was moving faster than he could process. He gripped the phone in one hand, writing names, scrawling question marks on the back of the envelope with the other. There was a tightening in his chest, a pressure that seemed to worsen and extend up into the back of his head and down his arm. Fear gripped him. He spoke in a loud voice and kept asking, *How? What? When?*

'Where were you exactly?'

'In the Congo. Garamba. We were travelling back from talks when it happened.'

'Talks?'

Neil was certain that this Dominic Oculi was not telling him everything. He felt a rush of indignation. 'Why on earth did you let her go with you in the first place?'

'Let her go, sir? She insisted. I told her I could not guarantee her safety, but she came anyway.'

Neil closed his eyes. Yes, insistent, headstrong girl. What an idiot. Oh, Jesus, Tess.

'Once she made up her mind she was determined,' Dominic Oculi continued. 'She said she wanted to see where the children she had been interviewing came from.'

'If only you'd stopped her.'

Neil heard Dominic take an inward breath. 'And how would you have had me do that, Mr Lowell? Lock her up? She herself is not a child.'

'Yes, of course, I'm sorry. *I* should have stopped her.'

But what was the point in making such declarations now? He knew Tess would have gone no matter what anyone said. He recalled the hand-painted placard, OUT OF IRAQ!, and the photograph of her holding it above her head on the front page of the newspaper when she was an undergraduate. The fierce expression on her face as they chanted, *Impeach the murderer!* Her desire to address what was wrong in the world, the force in her that wanted to effect change—that declared *I will go, I will march*. She was an idealist who, like him, was also impatient.

Their conversation continued, but it didn't make things any clearer.

Neil's immediate impulse was to get on a plane straight away; he wanted to go and find his daughter. In his mind he was already there. The connection faltered and Dominic's voice began to break up. He said he would ring if he heard anything else, but Neil knew he couldn't wait for that. A vision came to him of Tessa; he pictured her being brutally assaulted, her throat slit, and he tried to shut it out, tried to think of solutions, of how to protect her. How could he? From the day he found out he was to be a father he'd been humbled by the task ahead. You try to prepare yourself, you believe that you'll have the insight, if and when the time comes—that you'll cope. But that was so far from what he felt he was doing now.

'I'll call you back if I hear anything at this end,' he said, and hung up. A surge of adrenaline ran through him. He tried to focus. He needed to prioritise. But all the things he understood seemed to slip away, as if any knowledge he had was like smoke.

He called Leigh's number. The words piled up in his mouth. He listened to the ring tone and waited for her to answer. The call ran to her message service. 'Leigh, it's—listen, I have to speak to you. It's urgent. Just ring me as soon as you get this.' He hung up, then looked at the information he had scrawled on the back of the envelope, although he could barely read his own handwriting. His breath caught in his throat. His left hand felt numb and the pain in his chest, which had started as a tight centralised knot, bloomed. Dropping the phone, he crashed to the floor.

In the white space of the emergency room Neil opened his eyes. He could hear Leigh talking to the other doctors in the medical language that was their own. The clipped formal sound of Leigh's voice rose above him as her fingers found their way back to his wrist so she could check his pulse. He had no idea how he'd got here; a vague memory of a stretcher, a door closing. Maybe the side door of the ambulance. But now, under the bright lights, he tried to bring himself back as if from an alcohol-induced sleep.

Above him Leigh's face appeared slightly misshapen. She smiled uncertainly, her eyes wide. Everything was moving very slowly, and yet Neil felt as if he were hurtling towards an accident on the freeway, the same kind of frame-by-frame action in which each second lagged, until the inevitable moment of impact when he would crash and know, irrefutably, that everything had spun out of control.

'Neil. Darling, can you hear me? Are you okay?' Leigh asked.

'It's not me,' he said, trying to sit up. 'There's something—it's Tess.'

Later they argued. 'The rebels have her,' Neil repeated, and it sounded as if his voice were not his own. 'I have to go. I have to do something.'

Leigh was incredulous. 'How can you go? It's out of the question; you've just had a major heart scare.'

'I blacked out. It's not that serious. But this isn't even about me. Leigh, you read the papers, you watch the news—you've seen how these things escalate! We've no way of knowing what might happen. We don't even know if Tess is hurt. These people . . . shit, they kill indiscriminately. What's to stop them from harming her, or worse? I need to go there.'

'And what if you arrive and collapse again?'

'There are a million what-ifs.'

Neil glanced at the doorway. Six hours in casualty, and now shunted into a room on the cardiac ward. He looked at Leigh, then at the cannula in the back of his hand. It was connected to an intravenous line that ran up to a small chamber. Clear fluid dripped into it from the bag above. Another machine monitored him. There were whole years, he thought, when very little changed, and then out of the blue something happened that altered everything and then you needed to know exactly what to do and how to do it. He closed his eyes. He'd had an echocardiogram and an ultrasound of his heart, but he had been told that he needed more tests. 'We suspect it might be stress-induced,' the cardiologist had said. 'A syndrome known as takotsubo where the ballooning of the heart resembles the Japanese octopus pots it's named after.' A fanciful name, but temporary, not as serious as it sounds, he was told, but it still meant he would have to stay in hospital at least overnight, maybe for another day. 'We have to be convinced beyond reasonable doubt,' the cardiologist had insisted.

Leigh pressed her lips together. 'Let's wait. For all we know Tess might already be safe.' She spoke without conviction and looked at him as though she could no longer trust herself, or him, and in that moment his perception of them changed. His body tensed and his breathing became tight again.

'We have no idea if she's all right,' he said. 'No information that gives us the slightest confidence. We have to do something.'

Two hours passed before they got through to DFAT, and then there was more red tape—calls that involved being shunted from one official to another. At last Leigh got to speak to a senior politician in Canberra. They had their policies. I'll stay on the phone, Leigh insisted. The politician said he'd look into it, but it would take time. Leigh walked around the room. First she was rational, then angry; she couldn't make any further headway. Neil made simultaneous calls, tried the embassy in Kenya. An eight-hour time difference meant it was still the middle of the night in East Africa. They would need to wait.

Leigh held the phone and looked at Neil. Tears brimmed in her eyes. 'Who else can help us?' she asked the official on the other end of the line, then quickly wrote their names and numbers down on a piece of paper. Neil contacted everyone else he could think of, all the people he'd worked with in Johannesburg and anyone he thought might have some influence; people from ten, fifteen years ago. Mostly they were pessimistic. One colleague said: 'Roadside attacks, civil war—shit, Neil, the place is a hell-hole, especially in the north. It's a mess.'

Another advised him to hire a kidnap specialist. 'Get on to one of the security firms that advertise themselves under "international risk mitigation".'

International risk mitigation, Neil thought. Christ, what sort of world have we made for ourselves? 'There isn't time,' he said, thinking frantically that if he didn't go himself he'd regret it or go mad first.

'Doesn't Stephen have connections?' a producer friend in Johannesburg asked. 'Can't he arrange some sort of private service?'

'What sort of private service?' Neil asked. And who exactly was his son mixing with? There were things he didn't know, things he could only guess at. The producer from Joburg wouldn't say any more, even when Neil tried to pressure him into providing details.

At that moment, a young nurse wheeled in a trolley. She applied a tourniquet and tapped his arm; his vein came up like a blue worm. She swabbed his skin then slid the needle into his vein, and with a vacuum gush his blood was sucked up into the labelled vial.

Tests, treatments—all he wanted to do was to get himself discharged and get on a plane.

He couldn't get through to Stephen. He'd left messages, but there had been no reply. Maybe he was asleep or in a bar somewhere. He would have to ring him back. There were other obstacles too, other delays. The Australian authorities said he would have to wait for the Ugandan representative in Kenya to contact them. Tomorrow or the day after; it was Africa, after all.

'We've heard nothing from the rebels,' another official told him. 'If they demand a ransom, then negotiations could take place.'

'But they haven't demanded a ransom.'

'No, but if they did, then there would be a chance to make contact. The thing is, we don't know where your daughter is or what they'll do.'

Leigh wanted to phone Dominic Oculi again.

'No, we've already grilled him for as much information as we can,' Neil said, pinching the skin at his throat. 'What more can he tell us? He said he'd ring if there was any news and he's promised to keep trying to get help from anyone who might be able to communicate with the rebels. Meanwhile, we have to do something ourselves. We need to act. There isn't time for anything else. Besides, we have no idea how Tessa's coping.'

Leigh winced. That much was true; who knew how Tessa would react? She had been a sensitive child, a difficult adolescent; all those anxieties, not sleeping, a course of anti-depressants. Her study had saved her, or so they had hoped.

Neil clicked on the TV above the bed. Tessa's story was already on the news except they had misspelt her name, Lowell with one 'l'. The report stated that she was an aid worker employed in Sudan. What else had they got wrong? And what did it matter to the wider world anyway? In less than twenty-four hours her story would be knocked off by Mitsubishi's closures or Beyoncé's wedding rumours.

The infusion pump beeped, a high-pitched pinging. Leigh flicked a switch to silence it.

'We have to contact Stephen,' Neil insisted. 'I don't care what time it is over there, we need him and his business connections. He knows people—he can fly to Gulu and then, when these tests are finished, I'll join him.'

Leigh shook her head. 'What if something happens to him too?'

Neil sat forward. 'Lu, please. Stephen can get there in a couple of hours, but even without this—' he nodded in the direction of the monitoring equipment '—it will take us at least two, maybe three days. Anything could happen in that time.'

There was an obstinate quality in his voice and Leigh knew that it didn't matter whether she agreed with him or not. He'd decided. He needed to act and he would do so alone if he had to. She pushed her hair back from her face then turned to the window. Suburban streets panned out below. Large family homes. For a while she was silent. 'I'm not sure that Stephen will go. And if he does, I'm not sure he won't do something reckless in the process,' she said. 'He's too—I don't know. I have a bad feeling about asking him to help.'

Neil shook his head. 'No, Stephen can do this.'

He rolled his shoulders. Now that he had settled on a course of action, he felt a fierce, irrational certainty that Stephen must go, and that his going was the only answer. 'He's smarter, maybe better than you think.'

Leigh sat on the bed next to him. He let his arm fall around her and felt her shoulders slump against his chest. He could smell the faint scent of her shampoo.

He sighed. 'We need him to do this.'

Leigh sat back. 'It's complete madness. What do you expect him to do?'

'At this stage, a hell of a lot more than we can.'

'Why not wait—at least until we hear more. What about the people you know?'

Neil shook his head. 'That's not going to work. Even if they agree to help, there'll be a delay and we can't afford that. Trust me on this. Please. We can't pass it on to someone else, we can't sit by and do nothing.'

'So we contact Stephen, get him to go to Uganda—and then what? You want him to try to find her?'

'Yes. He's her brother.'

'And what if it goes wrong?'

Neil rubbed the back of his neck. 'What other choice do we have? Besides, it won't. Stephen's too savvy. I know him, he'll look after himself.'

'You know him? Oh, Neil, come on.'

They teetered on the brink of a new argument. Leigh took a breath and felt the heat rush through her. She resisted the urge to say something she might regret. Instead, she slipped her hand into his. 'All right, but let me be the one to arrange the flights—for both of us.'

He nodded.

'And I'll speak to Stephen. Okay?'

The lines in her face deepened. Neil squeezed her hand. He nodded again. Okay.

17

Cape Town

Stephen recognised the thugs standing around him as small-time dealers from one of the townships out near the airport. One of them sprang forward with a knife and held it against his throat as he watched Cherie drive off in his car. He felt the blade nick his skin. His eyes opened, and it was as if he was both inside the dream and outside of it. He reached for his neck and the phone rang, or rang again.

'Hello? Stephen, is that you?'

He groaned and drew his hand away from his throat, a little surprised that there was no blood. His voice was groggy. 'Hey Mum, listen—'

'No, wait. Please, *you* need to listen to me. I wouldn't be ringing if it wasn't important . . .' He heard her hesitate for a moment and started to cut in, but she began to talk over him. His father was in hospital.

'A heart attack?'

'No, he collapsed. A heart scare—temporary,' his mother said. 'Thank God, it's not serious. I think he'll be okay, but that's not the reason I'm calling.'

Stephen switched on the bedside lamp and sat up. He checked the time on his watch, the hands at a perfect ninety-degree angle: 3 am.

'It's about Tessa—I'm ringing because Tessa's been abducted.'

'What?'

'Tessa's been abducted,' his mother repeated. She spoke quickly. He wasn't sure what she said next. Information tumbled out in shorthand. They were desperate, he heard her say; they didn't know anything, except that Tessa had gone along with a delegation to some peace talks across the border. 'She wanted to visit one of the camps.'

'Where?' he demanded.

'In the Congo. Garamba National Park.'

'And?'

'And the rebels took her the following night.'

There was a long silence.

'Fuck,' Stephen said. 'I warned her. But does she get it? No, she thinks she knows everything. And now? What now?'

'You're in Africa. Your father and I think you should go up there.'

Stephen made a sound at the back of his throat. Would he say 'no'?

'Don't you get it?' his mother said when he didn't answer. 'We're terrified for her.' Her voice broke. '*Please*,' she added in the same urgent tone. 'I wouldn't ask this of you if there was another option. We need you to go and see what you can find out.'

'Great, and what is it you think I can find out?'

'Anything that might help. You must have some idea of how the system works over there.'

'Mum, I'm more than four thousand kilometres from where Tessa is.'

'*Please*, we need you to do this for us. Your father's contacts are reluctant and the government's fobbed us off. The amount of red tape is incredible. For Christ's sake, Steve, she's your sister.'

'I know she's my sister.'

'Well?'

'Okay, but you have to calm down. If you want me to go down that path, then you need to be one hundred per cent certain of what you're asking.'

'Steve . . .' his mother said, and he thought she might be crying.

'Look, maybe you're jumping to conclusions,' he offered. 'It could be a mistake—they might have found her already.'

'In that case you won't have to go. But as it stands . . . we'd do anything, don't you understand that?'

There was a silence in which neither of them spoke. He heard her exhale. He shifted forward and looked up. The security sensor blinked frantically and went off again. 'All right then,' he said, 'if you want me to do this, then let me do it. But you have to remember that things are different over here, okay? And you might not be comfortable with that.'

'I'm not comfortable with them now. I want you to do whatever you can. Do you understand me?'

'You know what you're asking, right?'

'Yes, I know. Do what it takes,' his mother repeated, and for a moment the gulf between them closed—a Faustian pact.

She had just played her only card and given him her backing; whatever she might have disapproved of she must overlook now, and allow him to do what he thought was necessary to bring Tessa back.

'All right then, I'll go up there. I'll text you if I can,' he replied and hung up.

Stephen got up and, pulling his boxer shorts on, went into the living room. There he poured himself a Scotch and switched on the TV. He muted the sound then leant forward on the couch and twirled the glass in his hand. The first shot he sculled calmed him. The second had the opposite effect. His mother's request blasted through his brain. Did she really believe he could go to Uganda or the DRC or wherever the fuck Tessa had ended up? Did she honestly think he would find her and that, even if he did, he'd be able to bring her back?

His lie evaporated. If the rebels had Tessa, then she was in deep shit. He knew that, he knew how it worked.

The glass clattered on the tabletop. He looked down at his hands, at his nails cut short, then picked up the stone carving of the knotted nuclear family. Tessa had made some comment when she gave it to him about wishing things were not so difficult between them. The catch in her voice revealed what he knew anyway: that there had always been a tension between them, and that despite the ease with which he could pull rank—he was older, an authority who better understood the world, while she would always remain his little sister—the underlying truth was that she saw him for the rich white boy he was. A currency of sorts, for who knew you better than a sibling? Certainly no friend or girlfriend that he'd ever had.

He balanced the carving in his palm and for a moment ran his thumb over the serpentine stone. Then he pitched it across the room.

18

Melbourne

'It's the middle of the night there,' Leigh said. 'I woke him, and now I don't know—maybe I've made things worse by asking him to go . . . Dogs don't chase cars anymore, have you noticed? They've forgotten they're dogs.'

Neil looked at his wife quizzically. She had begun rummaging in her handbag, looking for something that obviously wasn't there, her hands busy as she spilt the contents onto the bed. Neither of them was coping.

'But he's agreed,' she added. 'He said he'd go.'

Neil ran his hand across the grey stubble that sandpapered his chin. He wanted to get up. He wanted to shave and put on his normal street clothes. Most of all he wanted to fix what had gone wrong. There was a terrifying impulse in him that was violent and domestic. It had its origin in his instinct to protect, in the simple belief that he could keep himself and those he cared about safe, but where was that confidence now? Where was that family, the wriggling lightweight children he'd carried on his shoulders? Stephen, Tessa.

The thing he could not believe was how quickly the years had fled. First Stephen, then Tess. They were toddlers, and then they were at school, then suddenly they had grown up and were at university, Stephen getting drunk and denting the car, Tessa heartbroken over some boy. He waited for them to come home at night. Some nights Stephen didn't come home at all; he never rang, never gave an explanation. He needs his own place, Neil had told Leigh. He needs to move out.

He had a distant, shameful memory of striking Stephen when he was a teenager. Whenever Neil thought about it, the violence was still there, and even though he had forgotten what they'd argued about, the rift between them remained. The look Stephen had given him, and the accusation that Neil was only a half-time father. 'What would you know about anything other than your boring old documentaries? You're never fucking here,' Stephen said coldly before walking out of the room.

Leigh glanced at Neil's phone on the locker beside the bed. 'Have you heard anything else?' she asked.

He shook his head. 'No,' he replied and watched her hands fumble with old receipts, sunglasses, a tube of lipstick. She was a person who kept diaries, organised other people, wrote lists. 'No one's children tell them everything,' she said, still searching in her handbag for whatever it was she was looking for. She pushed the bag aside. 'I can't think straight,' she confessed. 'I'm worried now about what's going to happen when he gets there.'

'Lu, he's travelled in that kind of country before,' Neil replied. 'We have to trust him. Until we can get there ourselves, we can't do anything else. Any other option—well, let's face it, they're just dead ends.'

'You're right, I suppose. It's just that since Cherie, there has been something more worrying about him.'

'What do you mean?'

'Tessa told me that when she was in Cape Town, Cherie said he treated her badly. Not physically, but emotionally, I think.'

'We don't have his side of the story.'

'No, but there's a certain kind of intelligence that refuses to do damage to someone else.'

'Oh, Leigh, this isn't helping. We don't know.'

'Yes, but when he was with her there was something more to him, he was less reckless. At least I thought so.'

Neil leant against the plasticised pillow. It crackled as it gave way. The linen was cold on the back of his head but he still felt hot. Leigh would not sleep well, he knew that; she would be up half the night. He saw her in their house alone, her old grey cardigan flung on to keep her warm.

He felt a lump in his throat. He knew he was being dismissive and saw Leigh react to that. She gathered the contents of her bag and stood up to leave.

If only he could tell her what he meant, but there was the same old problem, her ease with words, sometimes saying too much, against his lack of them. Words stumped him. Photographs, he thought; give him a camera and a lens any day. An image. Leigh had first contacted him because of a single black-and-white photograph and when he thought of her, he pictured her on their favourite beach, standing there on the soft sand in her bare feet and rocking gently from side to side.

He knew he should hold her now, he knew they both needed it, but he felt a strange distance between them, the gap widening as much from her side as his own.

19

Cape Town

As soon as Stephen entered the departure area he saw Matt Reba sitting in a coin-operated massage chair, his eyes closed, his fingertips drumming the armrest. He wore good-quality hiking boots and khaki trousers. Good, Stephen thought, he'll need them. The best thing about Matt was that he was up for just about anything. Stephen could ring him at 5 am and say, *Want to go on a joy flight?* and he'd be there. Suggest a spur-of-the-moment safari or a slog through rough country and he would jump at the challenge.

'Let's go,' Stephen said and Reba got up, shoving his headphones and car keys into his knapsack, and followed him to the booking desk.

The woman behind the counter nodded as they approached. She had the paperwork ready and handed it over with a pen. Stephen ran through it: a business jet, big enough to get them as far as Entebbe without refuelling. The lease was through Frost, who'd arranged for a Gulfstream G200, a model that'd been around since the late 1990s—not Stephen's favourite, but at least it was serviceable.

'It's already fuelled,' the woman behind the desk said. 'I'll let traffic control know you're here.'

Stephen signed the forms and she put his credit card through, then he and Reba left the concourse to prep. Outside, one of the ground-service workers, a Xhosa man with a flat high-bridged nose, helped them to load their packs then turned and spoke to another worker, switching back to the complicated soft clicking sounds of his own language.

Stephen checked the engine then came around to the cockpit. Reba had already unblocked the wheels and climbed into his seat. They ticked off the instrument check.

'All right, so where are we headed?' Reba asked.

Stephen took a piece of gum from a pack and began to chew it. He had good teeth, straightened by one of the best orthodontists in Melbourne and whitened at SuperSmiles on Kloof Street. 'Uganda,' he said, and gave a wry smile.

Matt scoffed. 'What the fuck? Come on, man, you're joking.'

'It's no joke. Gulu, Uganda, then the Congo.'

'Shit. Are you mad?'

'Not me. But Tessa probably is.' Stephen clipped his seatbelt and adjusted the tiller. 'She went off on some peacekeeping mission and now she's missing. Abducted by the LRA.'

'Hang on, she's—'

Stephen gave a dismissive wave of his hand. 'Wait, hear me out. The plan is we fly to Entebbe first, then north. From there we rely on coordinates.'

'Jesus,' Matt said. 'Have you got someone else to back us up? Security, the army?'

'That would only waste time. And money. Besides, I don't want to rely on anyone else.'

'Good for you, but I'd rather not die.'

Stephen shrugged. He had already started the engines and was taxiing into the wind, easing a little so as not to ride the brakes. He turned towards the runway and waited for clearance. There was hardly any early-morning haze—a clear sky, indigo and cloudless, and along the horizon a brilliant crimson line that looked as if it had been painted there. He tightened his grip on the throttle and watched as the sun began to rise. The stars were disappearing and the dawn light stretched across the tarmac, giving the surface a black liquid appearance. The engines sounded in his ears and for a moment he wondered if he would be able to find Tessa. The idea came to him that he might not—there were a million things that could go wrong, and they were just the ones he was beginning to anticipate.

Matt began to jiggle his knee. 'Steve, come on, your sister's with a rebel group? What the hell?'

'Yeah, right, let's not go into it. You're lucky you're an only child. Firstborns get all the responsibility and none of the pandering. But it turns out, we're the ones who end up with most of the advantages. Money, attention, brains apparently—it all falls our way.' He grinned for effect and when they got the go-ahead he released the brakes then applied full power.

The plane sped down the runway, juddering as the wheels lifted. Once airborne, they went into a steady climb. Stephen felt the adrenaline kick in, something to do with the speed and the pure energy of that. He never tired of flying or the thrill he felt at take-off. As they reached altitude the engines buzzed softly and beneath them the rapidly diminishing landscape panned out. Table Mountain, purple-headed in the early-morning light and free of the cloud that usually draped it stood below. It loomed—a great impenetrable wall that cast its shadow over the city and the mass of sprawling shanty towns that radiated from its sides. In the distance, the vivid blue of the Cape.

He arced around and flew to the north, where the country had been cleared and parts of it mined. From this height it was easy to understand why things went the way they did. Simple logic was how he saw it. Africa equalled land, and land was the primary resource, which meant profit—the scrabbling for ivory, for diamonds, minerals, oil or any other trophy the market might demand. A continent filled with resources so extensive that everyone thought they could have a piece—and there were a great many who did, only some more than others.

At school, Stephen knew little of Africa. If someone had asked him, he would've thought that tigers lurked there. It was only later, when he took notice of his father's films for National Geographic, that Africa began to enter his imagination. When he met Matt Reba, the new exchange student from Cape Town, it became real for him. Later, he saw the potential, but what he hadn't anticipated was just how far-reaching that potential was. Everything here was wilder, bigger, without limit. He felt at home—more at home than he'd ever been in Australia; there was something too restrictive, too regulated about his own country. 'Shit, man, this place is boring,' Matt Reba had said when he first arrived in Melbourne, and Stephen found himself agreeing. 'You said it, the ultimate house of correction.'

Not so in Africa—even now the relaxed aviation regulations meant he could keep to a low altitude. Beneath them the landscape was map-sized. It was like putting himself into a video game; he could make out each landmark, at times follow the plane's shadow as it glided across the earth's surface. They flew north over the dry scrubland of the Kalahari Desert, rivers of sand that led to the Okavango Delta, a herd of zebra scattered below them, then west over Zambia, where the vegetation thickened and it was like viewing another of his father's documentaries; he could make out the jungle, the green pulsing maze of it. *An Eden from which two thousand generations ago*, a British-sounding voice-over might say, *all humankind arose*.

Beside him Reba was busy opening a packet of beef jerky and pouring coffee from a thermos. Steam rose and the wake-up smell filled the cabin. Reba talked with his mouth full. 'What I still want to know is: how come Tessa went there in the first place?'

Stephen shrugged. 'Beats me. Maybe she thinks she's saving the children. She wants to change the world. Remember her when we were at school—involved in just about every do-gooder cause? Well, now she's in deep shit. Apparently, she's been missing for four days.'

'Oh, great, and what makes you think you're going find her when no one else can?'

Stephen rolled his shoulders.

'Come on, Steve, didn't you see that show on BBC *Newsnight*?

The closest the army have ever got to capturing Kony has been seizing one of his suits. No one can find him. They say he's a fucking wizard. He lures people on then disappears back into the bush.'

Stephen spat his gum into a spare paper cup and took a sip of coffee. 'I don't intend to stop anyone. I just aim to get in there and get Tessa out.'

'Yeah, right.'

'I've got a GPS location.'

'How?'

Stephen shrugged. 'Tessa had her phone swiped in Cape Town, and when she got a new one, I jailbroke it and put FlexiSPY™ on it.'

'What?'

'It's this new monitoring software. It's supposed to be pretty accurate.'

Matt pushed back his cap and scratched his head. 'Why would you do that? I thought you wanted to get away from your family.'

'I do, but then maybe I pretty much counted on Tess getting caught up in some kind of shit storm—anyway, it seems to have worked.'

'What, in the Congo? You can tell where she is?'

'There must be a tower somewhere. International mining companies, who knows what else—fucking technology, hey? Anyway, I'm not getting anything from her phone now; the last location had her smack in the middle of Garamba National Park.'

'And when we get there?'

'I guess the world has a way of offering up people like Tessa.'

'Man, you say that so lightly. Have you thought about what can go wrong?'

'No.' Stephen glanced across at Reba and smirked, then finished his coffee and handed the cup back to him. 'So don't tell me the odds, okay? That would ruin everything.'

Five hours later they flew over the Serengeti, where great tracts of dry grassland stretched to the horizon and smoke from dozens of spot fires rose like thin wraiths into the sky. A burning world, once trodden by fierce warriors, only to be exploited by Arab slavers and, after that, Portuguese, German and British colonists—a theatre for the massive wildebeest migrations that now encouraged an entire tourist industry, the tourists themselves a caravan of movement.

They veered further north then began their descent, decreasing altitude as they crossed the vast expanse of a choppy Lake Victoria, before finally touching down in Entebbe. There they had their paperwork checked and took on more fuel.

After an hour on the runway, with stuttering static from air-traffic control, they set off again. Rain was predicted, although the sky was still clear, and as they tracked the silver trail of the Nile, the landscape became greener. Below them, equatorial rainforests and valleys threaded with a glistening network of tributaries, coffee and tea plantations panning out from virgin forests that led to the fabled Mountains of the Moon, now snow-capped and swathed in a light mist.

Stephen pushed his sunglasses up the bridge of his nose.

'Uganda: The Pearl of Africa,' he said. 'You know who christened it that?'

Reba shrugged.

'Churchill. The English, of course. They loved those kinds of pet names—they had them for all their colonies, all their precious jewels. Look at any early twentieth century map and you can see them strategically dotted all over the world.'

'All bar Australia,' Reba mocked. 'That was never a jewel; more like a dumping ground.'

'Maybe,' Stephen replied, 'except that convicts make the best survivors. You've heard the stories—Alexander Pearce?'

'Your cannibals?'

'Sure. Africa hasn't got the monopoly, you know.'

Reba laughed. 'You're such a tosser. Is that what you're saying? That you'd survive at any cost?'

'Sure,' Stephen replied. 'We're all like that, aren't we? Under certain circumstances we are all capable of being complete arseholes. I know I am. I'm sure you are.'

'Right, except you're an expat arsehole.'

'*Yebo*, and you're a gun-happy *umlungu*,' Stephen said, putting on a South African accent.

Reba drew his handgun from the holster on his hip and aimed it with a sharpshooter's flourish, then spun it deftly before re-holstering it with a satisfying click as it re-engaged. '*Ja*,' he said. 'Whatever.'

Ahead of them, storm clouds rimmed with black banked up and lightning lit the sky. Stephen nodded as another lightning strike flared. 'Looks like we're in for a ride,' he said and began flipping switches.

As the storm gathered, he reverted to manual flight mode, flying them higher to avoid the oncoming turbulence, but within moments the main updraft out-climbed them. Clouds billowed and before they could get above the storm they were met with the full force of its fury.

A radio voice cut in, then failed.

The lights in the cockpit went out and flickered back on. The console flashed.

'Shit,' Reba said. 'The instrument panel—' But his hand froze.

Stephen adjusted and aimed for the weakest spot in the storm. The plane dipped and levelled out again. Seconds, but it seemed much longer.

'Yo!' he shouted as they flew through the squall—a total hoodrush, then he glanced across at Reba. 'What the?' he said, when he saw Reba's pale face. 'Hey, I didn't think you'd spook so easily.'

'Are you mad? That was crazy, man,' Reba said, tapping his fist against his upper lip.

'Chillout,' Stephen laughed and, looking ahead, flew them on through the rain.

Half an hour later they began their descent. There was still heavy cloud, low-lying and swirling. It was only when they were within metres of the ground that they could see Gulu's single-strip airport. A high wire fence ran around the boundary, although in places it appeared to be damaged. Despite the recent NGO traffic the runway hadn't been upgraded since it was laid in the early 1960s. It was badly cracked. Grass grew in some parts, and where it didn't, rainwater evaporated off the tarmac. On touchdown, the wheels slewed and the entire aircraft shook until Stephen slowed, and bringing the plane around, taxied back towards a small half-built terminal.

Taking their packs, they disembarked and locked the plane.

'Is it going to be safe here?' Reba asked.

Stephen ran his hands through his hair and gave a slight shrug. 'It's insured,' he said 'Come on.'

They crossed the tarmac to the terminal, where a solemn man with an Elastoplast bandage on his forehead came forward to meet them. 'Hello,' he said formally. 'I'm Dominic Oculi.' There appeared to be dried blood—or it might just have been iodine—on the bandage. His right eyelid was slightly swollen, which made his good eye seem somewhat higher than the other. 'I am from the rehabilitation centre where your sister has been working,' he said. 'Your father let me know you were coming.'

Stephen nodded and offered his hand. They shook warily.

'If you'll come this way,' Dominic said and directed them towards a battered four-wheel drive. 'So now you have arrived, Mr Lowell, and yet I am afraid we do not know any more about your sister other than what I already told your father on the phone.'

'Well, I guess I'll have to work with that,' Stephen replied. Then, more testily, 'So tell me again what it is you do know.'

Dominic straightened then moved his head as if his neck was stiff. 'There was an ambush, it happened very quickly. The rebels came in the early hours of the morning. There was a struggle.' He indicated the bandage on his head. 'They must have had specific orders, because they didn't target anyone else from our party. They took your sister and fled.'

'And you didn't go after them?'

Dominic brushed one palm across the other as if he was pushing something away and looked steadily at Stephen. 'We did. We followed them that night, but we lost them. One of the soldiers who was with us was wounded; thankfully he is all right now. It might have been worse. Another delegate, an American, fractured his ankle running after your sister.'

Stephen raised an eyebrow. 'And since then?'

'Since then, we have tried to get more information. We are still trying, but we haven't been able to trace them or make any contact. The army may know more by nightfall. For now, I can take you to the centre where your sister was doing her research. Maybe we will hear something then.'

They loaded their packs and climbed into the four-wheel drive. Dominic started the engine and drove them through the township where stallholders were hawking their wares under bowed awnings and children played or carried heavy loads on their heads. Stephen watched. Horns blew. Motorbikes and bicycle-taxis wove past. Most of the buildings in the town centre were old single-storey shops built by the colonialists and now in need of repair. Further on there were lean-tos assembled out of corrugated sheets, or small bungalows built from concrete and secured with metal doors. Everywhere grilles, shutters, wooden boards. Occasionally, there was a new building surrounded by weathered scaffolding or a hand-painted sign: NOAH'S TAKEAWAY—TWO-FOR-ONE; PATIENCE PAYS—HIGHEST QUALITY HAIR ADDITIONS; BELIEVE IN JESUS

AND BE SAVED. But for the most part the town appeared to live on the street; people clustered in groups or sat by the sides of the muddy red-earth roads, waving to them as they drove past.

It began to rain again, drops that came down in fat splotches and splattered onto the windscreen. The wipers scraped and the mud made a wet sticking sound as it sprayed up under the chassis.

People sheltered under banana leaves or plastic bags and stared out, slowly chewing on sticks of sugar cane. If there was a difference between South Africa and Uganda, Stephen thought, it was that Uganda was smaller and poorer—although right now, it might have had more to do with the cloying heat and steady rain. 'Suffocating,' Stephen mumbled under his breath. He looked at his watch; it would be dark in less than an hour. He could not afford to waste time, he had to make plans. He had packed enough supplies for an arduous trek, but he would need a vehicle, preferably a four-wheel drive. He would also have to work out who he was dealing with. That was the key to knowing where he stood. He began to question Dominic Oculi, this big pious man with his gold crucifix. What did he think the rebels wanted?

Dominic shrugged. 'I don't know what they want with your sister. As for their overall intentions, it is difficult to say. Independence, autonomy. I'm not sure if they know anymore. War here has become normal. Still, there is a chance—we are trying to find security again. We must hold on to that.'

'Except the peace talks you just went to failed. And people still go missing. What kind of security is that?'

'Yes, so it continues,' Dominic replied. 'Problems erupt. I am afraid there will have to be many more peace talks. War stories do not have endings, Mr Lowell. Although sometimes I dream they might.'

When they reached the entrance to the rehabilitation centre, about ten or fifteen children who'd been playing nearby ran to greet them. The place was bigger than Stephen had anticipated. Under a torn plastic tarp, a large generator ran like an overtaxed tractor. The exposed engine, with its oil-pressure gauge and drain hoses, looked like it had been soldered together out of cast-offs. It made a thumping sound and gave off a whiff of diesel. Recycling at its most resourceful. High mesh fences surrounded the centre, which included a muddy playing field and an assortment of low concrete buildings, some with metal doors, others with shards of glass set like pointed teeth on the top of window ledges.

Dominic said he had some work to attend to and that he would come back and speak to them later. Reba rummaged in his pack while Stephen strode around with his hands in his pockets. The place unsettled him—the red mud, the children's constant coughing. The rain had stopped, but with dusk, the insects returned. His skin itched and when he looked at his forearms he saw they were already blotched with small swollen bites.

'I need something to eat,' he said, 'and I need a drink.'

The girl who served them at the centre's cafeteria had stubs for hands and tight shiny scars where her ears and lips had been cut. She might have been beautiful once, but now she looked like a doll that had been thrown into a fire.

Stephen ate the cassava and beans she served, although its tastelessness formed a wad in his mouth. He pulled his hipflask out and took a swig.

'So now what?' Reba asked.

'We drive as far as we can, then we go on foot.'

Reba grunted and stirred sugar into his coffee, and even after the sugar had dissolved, he kept stirring. The table rattled and he might have been going to say something, but before he could, Dominic Oculi came across to where they were sitting and lit a kerosene lamp, then took a relief map from his shirt pocket and opened it out in front of them.

'There,' he said, pointing. 'That is where she was taken.'

Stephen bit the ragged side of his thumbnail. 'Okay, that's doable. Except I'll need to borrow your four-wheel drive, and these,' he said, indicating the maps.

Dominic frowned. 'I must warn you not to go on your own, Mr Lowell. There are problems. Some of the local people support this conflict, and there are those across the border who are also with the LRA. Tensions are high.'

Stephen picked up the map. 'I don't expect you to come. In fact, I'd rather you didn't.'

Dominic sat back and shook his head. 'Ah,' he said. 'Just like your sister—you have already made up your mind, so I must ask myself, what is the point of arguing with you?' He made a soft exasperated sound, then added: 'And yet you are a stranger here, so I feel obliged to take you as far as the border. But I must warn you, even if you find your way after that, you ought to have backup. If you wait until tomorrow or the next day, I can arrange for someone from the Ugandan army to accompany you.'

'There isn't time,' Stephen replied. 'We've already taken a day to get here, and it'll take another two days to get to Garamba. That's if nothing else goes wrong. I can afford a few hours' sleep, but I can't wait for an army escort.'

Dominic shrugged. 'The road is not mine-free, nor is it bandit-free. Also, you must be prepared to pay any soldiers you come across along the way.'

'I figured as much,' Stephen replied, thinking if there was one rule it was: Avoid authority. At all costs avoid the army, avoid the police. 'Thanks for your trouble, Mr Oculi,' he said, 'but you've already done enough. How much to hire the jeep? I'll make it worth your while.'

20

They set out before daybreak and drove all morning, following the route the delegation had taken. Matt did most of the driving, napping when Stephen took over, but mostly it was Stephen who slept or followed their progress on Dominic's map. His GPS worked intermittently, losing its signal east of the Nile then blinking on again. The roads were rutted and partly washed out—a spidery network of dirt trails that cut away into the bush like an intricate labyrinth. Even so, they made good time and by mid-morning they came to the overgrown track where Dominic said they could avoid a checkpoint at the border.

It clouded over but the rain held off and they drove for the next five hours, crossing rickety wooden bridges and bumping along narrow village roads that led through forested areas dotted with subsistence farming. Clusters of mud-and-thatch huts were grouped amid sparse crops of plantain, maize and sugar cane. They passed people on the side of the road and occasionally had to swerve around a scattering of goats or pigs.

Finally, they came to a small village on the edge of Garamba, where Stephen told the park ranger they were surveyors.

'You've had some of us come through the park before? We are looking for poachers.'

The man nodded. It was enough to satisfy him. He appeared thin and tired and was happy with American dollars. Happier still with the P38 Stephen handed him.

'You can take this, and in exchange will you look after the jeep?'

Again, the man nodded. 'There is trouble in the bush . . .' he said, and Stephen handed him some extra ammunition along with the gun.

Locking the jeep, Matt pocketed the keys. They shouldered their packs and trekked across the grassy savannah into dense forest with the last of the day's light. When darkness fell, they set up a fireless camp and ate beef jerky and tinned sardines. Afterwards, Stephen offered Reba a drink from the flask of whisky he carried. There was still a camaraderie between them, although the undercurrent of tension had thickened. Matt repeatedly checked his equipment and kept his handgun, a Glock, close beside him.

'What is it?' Stephen asked. 'Don't tell me you're nervous?'

Matt rolled his shoulders.

'You are,' Stephen scoffed.

'Fuck, Steve, what's the matter with you? Don't you see how dangerous this is?'

Stephen grinned. 'What do you want?' he asked, 'a foot massage before we set off?'

Reba shook his head. 'This isn't the first time you've got us in over our heads. I'm telling you, man, I don't like our chances. Either we get into deep shit over this or we're going to need more than luck.'

Stephen put the flask down and began to pack their provisions. The extended safaris and combat-style shooting expeditions they'd gone on had been little more than entertainment, chancy at times, but this was something else entirely. He knew it, Matt knew it, except there was no point in going on about the risks. If Matt had come this far—tagging along or maybe even thinking he'd be bailed out of his financial woes in exchange for his help—then it was his fault if he felt duped. Happens when you're not so smart.

Matt sat forward; he was looking at the ordinance map. 'We might find your sister,' he said. 'But then how do we get out? Have you thought about that?'

Stephen felt his jaw harden. 'Calm down,' he said. 'If you start to freak out, it feeds on itself. We stay in control, right?'

'Oh, great, so you think you're in control?'

'At least one of us is.'

The next morning they pushed deeper into the forest, trekking in silence. They scaled a ridge to a high point, where Stephen watched for some time, focusing on what he thought was a plume of blue smoke. Reba said they should head further west, where the understorey was thickest, but Stephen insisted it would be quicker if they went in a direct line.

As they made their way down into the valley, the air became heavy. They continued, cutting aside the vegetation that blocked their way and pushing through where there were no paths except for the occasional crisscrossing of animal tracks. After some time, they reached a small clearing with the remains of a camp and rising, as if from the ground itself, the scent of burnt meat. The whole site was deserted except for a speckled jackal that was making a snuffling sound as it clawed at something in the campfire. As they came upon it, the jackal looked up then slunk away into the grass, although it didn't go very far before it turned back to watch them.

The campfire was still smouldering and insects, or perhaps it was a bird, started up in the tree above them, making a rapid clicking noise. Stephen glanced up and the noise stopped. In the stillness, he moved closer to the campfire, walking to within a few feet of it before he realised that what lay among the coals was the badly charred body of a man. Swollen and split, with pieces of clothing melted into flesh, the skull cracked open like a broken cup. The stench released the memory of a burning corpse he had once seen on a funeral pyre in Bali—the stink of scorched hair, a flaming boat being towed out to sea. But here there was no ceremony, no distance, only the immediate proximity to violence. Was this what the park ranger had tried to warn them about? Stephen's stomach roiled. All right, so he'd underrated what he was up against and Reba's fear was clearly justified, but it wasn't as though he hadn't thought about the risks, only that he hadn't really imagined what he was dealing with. He figured a quick exchange was necessary and he would be able to pull that off, but now he saw that this was a closed world, and that Dominic Oculi was right: for more than twenty years these people had adapted to a merciless civil war and there was probably little else that mattered to them beyond their need to survive.

Just then the jackal loped back, more confident than before, and began to nose again at the remains in the fire. It snuffled close to the man's skull. Stephen had never seen a human brain before and its wormy greyness shocked him. Somehow he'd expected something more majestic, less ordinary. A breeze picked up and the swales of high grass rustled. Matt appeared to be looking for something he'd lost. He was pacing up and down, slowly kicking over the rifle cartridges that lay scattered on the ground as if he was trying to figure out what they were used for rather than something he sold on a daily basis.

'Come on,' Stephen repeated. 'This hasn't got anything to do with us.'

'Bullshit,' Matt replied. His mouth was hard. 'This has got everything to do with us. If you want to keep going, fine, but I'm heading back. I'll wait with the jeep. Twenty-four hours, then I'm gone.'

21

Tessa had stopped vomiting but her mind still raced. She was of no use to them now. If a ransom was negotiated she might have a chance, but why would they do that when it could risk outsiders knowing of their whereabouts? Studies showed that hostages without value were more likely to be abandoned or harmed in some way. Gruesome images filled her mind—would she end up in a ditch somewhere, or starve to death? There were certainly reports of such atrocities; she had heard of a woman in Gulu who'd had her eye scooped out with a spoon. Stop, she told herself. Think, try to think clearly, and look for a way to get out of here.

She had seen several narrow paths that radiated out from the camp like wheel spokes and disappeared into the tangle of green foliage, but she had no idea where any of them led or where she was. The gloom confused her, the position of the sun was obscured in a thickly clouded sky, and there was the feeling that she was being watched, and not just by the guards who patrolled the camp; it was as if a watching, waiting presence hovered within the forest itself. The fear of the spirit world filled her. *Cen*—it was alive to her now, no longer a fable. She thought of the buttressed tree roots and the papyrus swamps as if they were alive and knew she was being illogical, that she had to try to concentrate on something else. First, how she might gain another opportunity to speak to Obed Lokodo or Colonel Kolo. And then what? Maybe she would be able to reason with them. She would need to keep her cool. Be pragmatic. Other studies showed that the relationship between hostage and captor could produce a bond, sometimes empathy. Stockholm syndrome, Tessa thought dryly.

She made her way to the centre of the camp, where she could see the swirling pattern of the *khanga* worn by Mildred. Amid the drab huts and the green light, the shock of bright yellow looked like a striking emblem. The colonel's child-wife was bent over a cookfire with the sleeping baby tied to her back.

'Mildred,' Tessa said softly. The girl looked up, then cast her a warning glance. Clearly, she had no wish to talk. Tessa ran through what Acholi phrases she had learnt by heart, but before she could say anything the colonel approached. His head had been recently shaved, revealing the powerful shape of his skull, and he moved with a purposeful gait, the image of an impeccable soldier in his flawlessly arranged uniform which, although worn in places, was surprisingly clean. Presumably Mildred washed it for him, sewing on buttons and reattaching the shoulder epaulettes which added further prestige. His square shoulders and proud face gave him a regal look; Lion-man, they called him, Colonel Kolo. He came to stand beside Mildred then put his hand on her head in a proprietorial gesture.

Tessa nodded in his direction.

'You see how we live?' he said.

'Yes,' Tessa replied. 'You run a well-organised camp,' she added in an attempt to flatter him, although it was true; the camp had the structure of a working village, a daily routine around food, repairs and chores.

The colonel nodded. He appeared relaxed and Tessa felt her confidence return. She straightened. 'I can see I am of no use to you, Colonel. Perhaps it would be better if you directed me to the park border. I could make my own way out from there and not trouble you anymore.'

Kolo gave a short derisive snort and shook his head, then raised his eyebrows and looked at her as if she, too, were a child.

'There are people who will be worried about me,' she added. 'My work colleagues in Australia, my family, they will be looking for me. They—'

'Enough,' Kolo said. 'Do not bother me now. When we are ready we will let you go. Not now. Now it is too dangerous for us. We have other matters more important than your welfare.'

Tessa went to speak, but Kolo held up his hand. 'It is our safety we are concerned about. Not yours. It is only the security of the Lord's Resistance Army that matters.' His teeth were surprisingly small, one or two along the bottom were missing, and when he spoke his tongue moved pinkly in his mouth. He leant forward. 'Do not make demands of us,' he added softly. 'That would be unwise.'

Tessa nodded. 'I understand. Although if you let me go, I can assure you there will be no recriminations—'

'*Recriminations?* Ah yes, you want me to hear your educated words, but what authority do you think you have? You come here, you *patronise* us,' he said, emphasising his own vocabulary. 'Do you think we are powerless? Do you think we are unable to help ourselves? You are not the first person to arrive with your self-important talk.' And then, as if something more relevant had occurred to him, he changed tack. Smiling, he said, 'Tell me, what do you think you are here to do? Hmm? What is it you think your Western influence has to offer?'

Tessa hesitated. 'Nothing, I didn't mean to . . .' she stammered. 'But if the priest, Obed . . .'

'Obed Lokodo believes you are a witch.'

'What?' Her mouth had gone dry.

'Stop! He flatters you. I do not think you are so powerful. What I see is just another outsider trying to bargain with us. Another *muzungu*, isn't that right? A dizzy tourist who thinks they can make things happen because that is what they've always known. The only error we've made is to think you were better than you are. But you cannot help us. You are not even a proper doctor.'

His critical stare bore into her, and as if to verify what he had just said, he made an airy gesture with his hand. 'People like you make out they know everything, but they only ever talk about negative things—civil war, humanitarian crises, famine. Your gossip is designed to pour scorn on Africa. You like to say you are the peacemakers, but look at your own corruption; you are not so smart.' His expression was scornful and Tessa felt her face burn. 'You do not understand because you *cannot* understand,' he said dismissively, then he reached forward and closed his hand around her throat. It felt clammy and heavy, and now that he was so close, she could smell the sour scent of his breath. His teeth were rotten. 'Do not think you have any say here,' he said. 'For you do not.' His words were spoken slowly and the pressure of his grip hurt.

Behind him Mildred called out and he spun around, striking the girl, a powerful blow that made her fall. She landed heavily on her side.

'*Dawe!* No! You do not intrude,' he said. Then, without looking back, he walked away.

Mildred pulled herself to her knees and positioned the crying baby at her breast. The baby latched on and began to suckle; milk—opaque, almost blue—bubbled around its lips and as it quietened, Mildred moved her fingers in a small semicircle over its close-set ear.

Tessa knelt beside her. '*I tye nining?* Are you all right?'

But Mildred did not seem to hear her. She was concerned only for her baby. Her first instinct was not to look after herself but to comfort her child—and she had done so, spontaneously and effectively, this girl of maybe only fifteen who was already an accomplished mother.

Tessa pictured the people who mattered to her—her friends, her family—and recalled something her own mother had once said: that the most important thing a person could do was to care for another. To nurture. What drove that? Was it love alone, or did responsibility and family come first? The crucial thing about family—you could not survive so well without them.

*

The soldiers who patrolled the camp looked bored and restless. Some had their rifles slung over their shoulders, while others leant on their pangas. Tessa heard them call to one another, lanky teenage boys who wandered around as if they were looking for something to do. One youth spent half an hour bent over his foot trying to remove a splinter from under his skin. He used a small stick that he'd whittled to a sharp point with his knife. The whole procedure involved the meticulous precision of a surgeon and was executed with the same diligent patience. When at last he removed the splinter, he jumped up and danced in a small circle, laughing as he held the offending thorn between his thumb and forefinger. Others strolled around or talked in groups. Sometimes they were boisterous, they wrestled or put their arms around each other and looked at magazines that had machine guns on the front cover. Many had become familiar to her. She listened for their names: Caleb, Nangila, Moses. Amos, whose wrists were thin and who was blind in one eye, and Lambert, whose laugh echoed. But it was Francis she was searching for. She remembered his concern when she was sick and wondered if it had been an illusion, some part of the fever that now left her feeling vague and unsure of what he had said.

As the day wore on and the heat increased, Tessa watched the movements in the camp. She had thought that such bush hideouts were temporary, hastily set up only to be abandoned, but this site was more like one of the communities she had visited. It reminded her of Oraako's village, where they had gone for the cleansing ritual. There were similar clusters of mud-walled huts with thatched roofs, a toilet pit, even the well-tended *shamba* in the clearing where cassava was grown. She counted twenty-three soldiers, plus Mildred and her baby and several other girls, although she wasn't sure if this was everyone. She had noticed a steady stream of movement between campsites and was beginning to think that Francis might have left and gone somewhere else. It was possible he was a messenger. Satellite phones run the risk of detection, Alphington had told her, but soldiers who know the bush well can be relied upon to carry notes from one location to another. On the trek here, Francis had shown that kind of skill; she had seen him look for markers on certain trees and once scale a steep rocky crag as if it were a staircase before reappearing and nodding in the direction they were to go.

She kept looking for him. The other soldiers were less vigilant about watching her now—presumably they knew she had no hope of finding her way out and that she would be better to stay where she was. She was put to work with Mildred and three other girls, collecting water and washing clothes in a stream that flowed away from the camp towards what appeared to be a submerged grassy swamp. She wondered where it led. This country of braided waterways, with the great Congo River basin at its heart. They used worn cakes of yellow soap—the lemony smell reminded her of her grandmother's kitchen—and beat the clothes on rocks then left them on the banks to dry. The girls talked and laughed, but did not include her. They watched her suspiciously and treated her with mild derision. Mildred turned away whenever Tessa tried to speak to her. Maybe the days would go on like this, Tessa thought, and if she did not do something soon, her chances of being released and getting back to safety would slip further from reach.

When they returned to camp just before dusk, she caught a glimpse of Francis's angular frame skirting one of the grass huts in the direction of the clearing where the major had been buried. There was a commotion near the campfire; someone had spilt a pot of maize and several voices erupted loudly into an argument. In the confusion, Tessa took the chance to follow Francis. Keeping her distance, she trailed him to the edge of the clearing, where she stopped and cautiously stood in the shadows.

Francis knelt on the ground beside the grave and made the sign of the cross, then bent his head and began to move his lips. He was praying in a solemn manner, not secretive exactly, but in a private way that was serious and intent.

Until now, Tessa had not understood the depth of his faith, but it was clear, watching him pray, that religion was deeply ingrained in him. She imagined that he heard the spirit voices in the forest and believed they were infused with an irrefutable power, yet maybe something else too, for perhaps what also possessed him was the version of Christianity she'd heard in the preacher's words, and before that in Kony's sermon. The two strands of belief merged to become one.

Francis swayed, as though his body was weighted from the hips, then closed his eyes and bent forward as if offering himself in some way—Isaac to be sacrificed. But what seemed more important than a belief in God was survival, or perhaps it was that survival and religion were the same thing. How else could he feel safe? Suddenly, he raised his head and said loudly, 'For

I am called upon through the word of our Lord Jesus Christ.' Once more he made the sign of the cross, then he brought his hand to his mouth and kissed the tips of his fingers. Alone in the clearing he had the face of a boy—soft, a little rounded. It was only the scar that hardened it, gummed now with a thin trail of yellow pus. Tessa drew a deep breath. What weapon had been used to peel back his cheek, and who had done this to him? Discipline, he had said, but Tessa had no idea how or why; nor did she know why he'd come at this hour to kneel by the major's grave.

She remained in the shadows, a voyeur, but suddenly, as if given a signal, Francis stood up and looked in her direction with a scowl. 'What are you doing?' he demanded. 'Why have you followed me here?' It sounded like a threat.

Tessa hesitated. 'I need to ask you something.'

'Ah, yes,' he almost jeered. 'You want help—but I cannot help you. There is nothing I can do.' He picked up the rifle that was lying next to him.

'Please, Francis.' He flinched at his name. 'I need to leave here. I need to speak to the preacher—to Obed, the *lapwony*. Just tell me where I can find him.'

'No,' Francis replied. 'You would be better to stay away from him. I will not help you. I owe you nothing.'

22

By nightfall Francis had changed out of his army uniform into a tight, sleeveless T-shirt. Around his neck he wore a string of blue beads. It was a mixture of styles—American rapper, South African gangster—possibly modelled from one of the tattered magazines they liked to look through, although Tessa wondered how Francis had got such an outfit, whether looted in a raid or bartered from one of the other rebels. She noticed the way he'd knotted the T-shirt at the back so the fabric clung to him, accentuating his shoulders and highlighting his narrow waist. He sat across from her on a plastic chair wearing his worn but carefully polished boots, his feet set apart and his rifle across his knees. Frogs croaked and the night sky was star-massed above them. In the foreground, there was a small smokeless cookfire whose hot coals glowed.

From behind them someone called. It was Lambert in his red beret, and when Francis heard him call again he joined the group of older boys. They welcomed him with loud cries, Lambert cheering and slapping him on the back. Clearly

Francis was one of them, these boy-men whom he'd eaten with and fought with. They were his friends, his family. They joked and laughed together, one of them farted and the usual hilarity followed, a fraternity that was reminiscent of Stephen and his friends when they were at school or mucking around in the backyard. But there was something else, something more potent and binding, and it was evident in the way they sought Francis's attention—he was a leader among them. He stayed for a while, drinking from the plastic sachets she understood had been looted in a recent raid, then he stretched and strolled back to where she was sitting.

'You are popular,' Tessa ventured. 'The other soldiers like you.'

Francis smiled and shook his head. 'No, they are just being soldiers,' he replied. 'They are rebels. That is how we are.'

'But they respect you.'

'*Respect?*'

'They think you are smart—they do what you say.'

'Yes.' He nodded. 'If you keep up the raids you get more food, and you get more *respect.*' He said the word slowly, as if its meaning had just become clear to him, and in a way that he might attach it to himself. 'And if you abduct others, you are given a higher rank. I am strong like that. I can protect myself,' he boasted. 'I can protect even you.'

'How?' Tessa asked, but he refused to answer.

She was hungry after the day's physical work, carrying water and pounding clothes in the river, and could now smell beans and *ugali* cooking, the aroma a little like salty popcorn. When Mildred came to the campfire and began serving heaped platefuls from the pot, Francis put his rifle on the ground beside him, then sat back with his steaming plate and, looking at Tessa, spoke with his mouth full. 'For a long time, I followed you and you didn't even notice I was there.' He laughed—sheepishly, she thought—as if taking pleasure in the skill he was revealing. 'You could never be a soldier,' he stated. 'You do not know silence.' He put his plate down and began tapping the side of the chair. After a time, he brought his hands in front of him and looked at them, then he shook his head. The muscles in his biceps flexed to form a bulge, yet when he lifted his arm above his head, his armpit was smooth and hairless. Mildred ladled a portion of *ugali* onto a plastic plate and handed it to Tessa. Tessa took it from her, saying, '*Apwoyo*,' thank you, and began to eat. About half-a-dozen more soldiers had come up and Mildred served them too, scraping out what was left in the pot. Music played somewhere—the same hip-hop beat on a continual loop.

Tessa used her fingers to scoop the *ugali* into her mouth and chewed each mouthful slowly. The food was warm and filling. She was no longer surprised that she'd started to accept this basic mode of survival. What consumed her now was what else she might get to eat and if she might be given some water to drink; where, afterwards, she might go to relieve herself; if she would sleep. There was no sign of the colonel and she still hadn't seen Obed.

The other soldiers had wandered off again and Tessa looked at Francis. 'You knew the major well, the one who died?'

Francis licked the food from his fingers and cast her a quick glance.

'He was important to you?' she asked, then nodded when she saw how his lips moved as though he wanted to speak. Should she press him further? The thing was to gain his trust, but how? She sat a little way forward as if to mirror his body language. 'Yes?' she prompted.

'Yes,' he said proudly. 'When I came to the bush the major picked me out. He asked me did I attend school. I said I did. To what level? Primary five, I told him. After that he asked, can I listen to the BBC? I said, I can listen. He turned on the radio, and asked me to listen to what is being said and then to tell him. After I told him, he gave me praise. *When the opportunity comes, I will send for you*. That is how it was with him.'

It was a simple fact—some people were cleverer than others. Francis was clever, he must have been bright at school, he had learnt English. The major had seen that and known how to use him and it was something that Francis understood—a transaction which, if not his whole story, was vital to it.

She watched the way he looked into the forest. The slash across his cheek moved as he chewed. Another tier of night noises had begun; bats replacing birds as if to shift from one level to the next, nature's self-appointed clock. A dance, her father might have said—certain animals favour the same hour each night.

'When I saw you earlier, what were you praying for?' Tessa asked cautiously.

Francis pinched his bottom lip, then in a softer, more circumspect voice—the voice he had used when she was sick—he said, 'I was asking for protection. I prayed, *Lord God the Father, in the name of Jesus Christ, I ask for your protection and because you give it to me. I thank you for keeping me safe.* Those were my words.'

A light breeze blew through the canopy and the top branches swayed. Tessa looked at Francis's face, which appeared older in the glow of the campfire. 'And does God answer your prayers?' she whispered.

'Yes,' he replied. 'God answers me, that is how I find my treasure.' Then the smile went from his face. He folded his arms. 'God is here. But why do you ask when Obed says you do not believe?'

Tessa hesitated. She could hear the other soldiers talking. 'Maybe if you explain your God to me,' she said carefully, 'if you were to tell me how He speaks to you and what you do in His name, I might understand better.'

Francis gave a nonchalant shrug, but apparently it was only for show, since in the next moment he hunched forward, wrapping his long arms around his legs. 'God shows me not to be afraid.' He paused, then looked directly at her. 'When the rebels came,' he said quietly, 'I was nine years old. In school, I went ahead of everyone, and when I became a soldier—again, I went ahead of everyone. That is because the major taught me: *If you do not kill, you die.*' He looked around then lowered his voice further. 'But when the major was dying I felt it too.'

'You felt it?'

'The pain in my heart,' he said and tapped his chest. 'It was his pain. *Cen* came, and now I have the pain of his life in my skin.'

'And you are afraid?'

'No—not afraid; if you are afraid, you die. I made myself strong. I am one of the strong ones.' He looked at her for a long moment then made a slight motion with his hand. 'Before the rebels came, I did not need to pray for protection. I did not know death. But they attacked my village and made me go with them. They took all the children who were big enough—the girls as well as the boys. If you were chosen, you were made to come. They used sticks. They forced us to run for a very long time. My feet got cut and the cuts began to swell up. If you had shoes, you were better off. Afterwards, I got the boots of another boy.' He drew breath. 'I got them and then I could run over the hard ground.'

Tessa glanced at his boots. They were unlike the green gumboots most of the other soldiers wore. Deeply creased across the top, they were a worn pair of combat boots, but she had seen how he cared for them, oiling them regularly as he did his rifle.

'They are good boots,' she said.

He nodded.

Amos, with his blind eye that looked like a strange sealed pod, came over and handed Francis a plastic sachet that had already been cut open then drifted off again. Francis drank from the sachet and offered it to Tessa. She shook her head. Still speaking softly, she asked: 'How did you get those boots from the other boy? Did he give them to you?'

But Francis ignored her question. 'We had to cut through the bush,' he said. 'Everywhere it was tangled, it was like swimming through green mud, we had to keep going like this, and this, and this,' and he used his hand to make a brisk chopping motion. 'After a few more days the land became dry again and we were made to run faster. I did that. I did what I was told. It was better that way.'

On the other side of the campfire, four of the other soldiers were playing music on a portable CD player and talking loudly. One of them let out a loud whoop and there was laughter, but when they called to Francis, he dismissed them with a wave of his hand. It was a military gesture. Tessa had seen them exchange similar signals as they patrolled the camp. Another language, their shorthand code—brief, functional, almost hostile.

'We were followed by a pack of wild dogs. You know these? They are called painted wolves. They are very smart. Five of them came after us. I saw them sniff the air. For three nights, they followed us. Those dogs live by hunting together, and when they eat they make a chirping sound—*chirrup, chirrup*,' he mimicked. 'They are a team. People say they are not in Uganda anymore, but we saw them just across the border in Sudan. I wanted them to follow us. I thought about how it would be good to have one of those dogs to protect me, but I knew they were distrustful of people. You cannot train a painted wolf. That is why they call them wild.' He looked at her and his voice dropped further; he was speaking now in a soft conspiratorial hush. 'But I have been trained,' he said. 'Boys like me are trained to be soldiers and we understand why we must fight. We fight for our motherland, against all the bad things Museveni is doing. We kill those in the army. We do not argue. If you want to live, you must do as you are told. Yes? You must be *obedient*.' He pronounced the word with extreme care, rolling it on his tongue. 'We use guns, but we are also taught to use knives and machetes—pangas that cut real quick. Guns are good, but if we have no bullets, we use what we have. Knives work, sometimes they are better; they are silent.'

Now that Francis had begun to talk, he was like an informer; he spoke with the urgency of someone who is compelled to confess, and with the alarming quickness of a gifted kid. Occasionally he looked over his shoulder, but the words kept coming. 'If you do not do as you are told, the commanders will beat you with sticks, they will cut you. Maybe take out your eye. I did as I was ordered. I forgot everything else. One day I forgot my family, I could not even remember my mother's face. You find a place to leave—you go out of your body. Your brain opens a door and you go through it. But I remember those painted dogs and how they looked at me. Watchful eyes like a true soldier's eyes, and there is power in them because they know God.' He lifted his head and stared at her. Tessa nodded. He was a survivor, a fighter, and that too made him different.

'I have been purified,' he said, and he smiled, stretching the ugly wound on his face. 'I have been marked with shea-nut oil by Kony so I am *his* soldier. Before an attack we are sprinkled with holy water and sometimes the colonel will make a cut mark on our skin then put brown powder underneath to keep us strong. Each time I pray. I pray for the Spirit.'

'And is that how you kill? With this spirit?'

'Yes, I have the Spirit. I kill,' he replied, and then added with a gust of enthusiasm, 'Death comes to those who do not obey the law of the Ten Commandments.'

It was a complete contradiction and yet he believed it. Tessa stared at his hands, at the dirt under his nails. He was a murderer.

'You have to make sure the skull is crushed.'

'But what if one of those commandments is *Thou shalt not kill*?' she whispered.

He frowned. 'You do not understand. We are told to follow instructions and no harm will come to us. We are doing God's work.'

He began to knead the flesh on his forearm, pinching the skin and twisting it in tight bunches. Tessa reached across and rested the weight of her hand on his, something her mother might have done. He stopped, and quickly pulled away from her. She had urged him to tell her his story—and it was shocking. Beyond belief, she thought; beyond understanding. Her face burnt and a surge of anguish tore at her chest. She felt a tremendous responsibility which she was ill-equipped to handle; he had lived with different rules and there was little place for the mild, kind psychology she espoused. The knowledge behind his eyes terrified her.

She noticed that he nodded his head in a strange way, stiffly and as if to shut out some internal voice. After some time, he stopped nodding and slowly shook his head, then, as if to check that the blue beads he wore around his neck were still there, he touched them and murmured something that Tessa did not catch. When he spoke again it was like he was talking to himself. 'I do not have pity for the ones I killed,' he said. 'I follow orders.' His manner had become very calm. 'I am a soldier. A not-so-smart soldier cannot be useful to the LRA. They will die, but I will not die.'

He exhaled and looked around the camp, then touched the blue beads again. 'But sometimes at night the ones I kill come back.' His mouth was dry, and as he spoke, his voice suddenly thickened—a mix of anger and resentment and something else, Tessa thought: fear, or perhaps the desire to reveal something more. 'They come out of the dark and move inside me. I feel them wrap themselves around my bones. Their blood is in me. It is then I cannot forget. It is then I am a painted dog and I feel myself killing again. Guns and knives and sticks.'

'Who are you killing?' Tessa whispered.

'The first ones. Later on, I do not remember them.'

'You mean, you kill the boy whose boots you wear—you kill him again?'

'Yes, he was the first. If another abductee escaped, we were forced to chop them. I was told to beat him with a stick, and when he fell to the ground I was made to hack him or I would be killed. On the way to Sudan if you did not keep up, you were punished. The weak ones were beaten in front of everyone else and then they were killed. From this you gain courage. That is what the commanders tell us is important. *Courage*. You know this word?'

She nodded, even though it felt misplaced.

'Yes, courage. You have to know what to do—the commanders watch your face for signs of strength, and if you do not show that you are strong, they punish you too. This happens from the very start.'

'So the first boy you killed was from your village?'

'He was my brother!' Francis said violently.

He lifted his head and blinked back tears. His eyelashes clumped and glistened. He swallowed. 'But he was weak,' he said. 'He was not strong enough to keep up. They ordered me to, so I hacked him until he was dead. We do what we are told: we stamp on them until they die and because of this we survive. Afterwards I ate without washing my hands and now I can eat anything, anything you give me. But his *cen* comes to me. At night, the demons come. That is why I pray. I pray for protection.'

Tessa took in a breath and covered her mouth, watching as Francis tugged at the beads around his neck. 'You see these?' he said. 'If I take them off I am lost. Kony has blessed them. On the day I became a soldier, he put them on me and now I am safe.'

For a moment Tessa imagined the weight of the beads around his neck. She dropped her hands to her lap. 'So you will always wear them?' she asked.

'Yes.' He laughed. 'Every day. That is my life.'

'Oh, Francis, *your* life.' She took a deep breath. She would comfort him if she knew how, find the right words, put her arm around him, although she felt certain he would shrug her off again. 'Do you know you can take amnesty? *Timokeca?*'

Francis's brows drew together.

'Do you know what I'm saying? Amnesty means you will not be punished. If you take amnesty, you can return home.'

'Home?' He smiled. 'What is that? There is no home left for me.'

'You don't know that for sure. There have been other soldiers like yourself—soldiers who have been reunited with their families.' She recalled Oraako and the uncle who did not want him, then quickly pushed the thought from her mind. She wanted Francis to believe there would be a place for him to return to, even if that meant lying to him now.

But Francis shook his head. 'No, it is not so. On the night they came to my village they set it on fire.'

'The rest of your family might have escaped,' Tessa offered. 'They might have hidden.'

He scoffed. 'You do not understand. It is too dangerous. If I try to leave they will kill me, and they will kill you too. They are just waiting for the right time. It will be easy for them. They will make it look like an accident, or they will make it look like a lesson.' Abruptly, he changed the subject. 'Show me your phone again.'

Tessa reached for her phone and turned it on. He took it from her, scrolling through the photographs, and after a while she showed him how to listen to music. He had not known he could do that, and suddenly he was greedy for it. She watched him, his eyes closed, earbuds pressed into his ears, his arms stretched out as his hands danced above him. He looked like he was drunk, maybe from whatever was in the plastic sachets or maybe from the music alone—the song she'd left on repeat—and she saw how it pleased him. A haunting mix of the secular and the religious, with its fractured 'Hallelujahs', and only when the battery went flat did he give the phone back to her.

'It's no good now,' he said, looking at her with a sullen expression.

'No, it is still good,' Tessa replied. 'It is only because of the battery.'

'We are always looking for batteries,' he said. 'In some camps, there are generators with petrol.'

'With this,' Tessa added, holding up the phone, 'you have to put it on a charger. Do you know about chargers?'

He didn't, but when she explained he nodded, comprehending.

'Like magic,' he said.

'Yes,' she replied. 'Like magic.'

He stood then and walked away, the side of his face lit by the light of the kerosene lamp that he held at arm's length. Tessa felt a wave of pity for him and suspicion too; it struck her that he might trick her somehow, that he was unpredictable. Still half child, he had told her only some of his story, yet the full horror of it ran beneath. He had been forced to murder his own brother. How could he not be ill-adjusted in such an unhinged world?

She waited in the dark. He was not gone for very long, perhaps only fifteen minutes, but there had been a shift of some kind. When he came back, he sat down close beside her—no longer the boastful youth or the watchful boy, more like one of the shy returnees from the rehabilitation centre. Oraako again. After a little while he asked for her phone, which he took discreetly and put into his pocket. His skin was dry and surprisingly soft, and for a time he sat next to her in a childlike way until, in the dark, she felt the cold metal of the handgun he placed in her palm.

'When you try to escape, they will come after you,' he said. 'If they catch you, that is the end of your life. This is your protection.' Then he got up and strolled off to be with the others.

23

Melbourne

Leigh woke to the full force of her body's radiating heat. Damp with sweat, she thought it should be morning, but it was still the middle of the night.

She had dreamt in colour. Vivid, in the way dreams had blared when she was young, it came clear and informed, like occupying two minds or losing one sense of herself and gaining another. Green tendrils unfurled and red flowers bloomed then darted like tropical fish and there was Tessa with her faun-like features—her small triangular face and snub nose, her maddening determination. But something was wrong—not wrong in the way dream spaces warp, but dreadfully, morally wrong. She knew this as an irrefutable fact and, as the full force of it came to her, the surrounding landscape dissolved and a large grey she-wolf appeared out of the shadows and stood between them. It had been running, and the energy in its body was still apparent, majestic and territorial, yellow-eyed. It raised its head and panted. Leigh felt her own body tense; she could see right into the wolf's corrugated mouth and along its flank to the rise and fall of its ribs. It was lean and scarred and as it lifted its head its eyes held her.

She pushed the doona off as if it were a great weight and reached for her phone. There were no messages, except for the last from Neil: *Try to sleep, try to rest. xo.*

She could not stop the feeling of panic. She got to her feet and went downstairs, where she turned on all the lights. She felt crazy, committable.

Their tickets to Entebbe were on the kitchen bench.

Her older sister had said, 'Why go? What good will it do? Why not wait until you hear something further? Ever since they were small you've done this. You and Neil go in and try to fix everything.'

'Is that so unusual?'

'Unusual?'

'Yes, unusual. Is it so unusual to want to protect your child?'

Leigh rinsed her mouth and splashed water over her face and throat. She thought of Neil, the awful pallor of his face. The events of the past twenty-four hours felt like a rehearsal for what life might be like without him. A warning, a threat. She wanted desperately to speak to him, but what could they say to each other?

In the hospital she had searched for answers that did not come. Worse, his assurances irritated her—the violent irrational certainty that Stephen must be the one to find Tessa, and that he would succeed. She was surprised by her own lack of faith, her furious need to blame someone—to blame Neil for Tessa's stubborn insistence. A prickling sensation ran across the top of her head and she found it hard to breathe.

Perhaps her concerns about Stephen were out of proportion, but then a fury of self-righteousness returned to her. She did not need a dream to tell her there were things in this world worse than death.

She tried to picture Tessa, where she was now, and what might have happened.

How long does it take for a person's life to change—ten minutes, five? Even less.

Another hot flush ran through her then, chilled, she shivered. She went to the laundry and got a pair of Neil's socks, which she put on before sitting down at the computer. She read what she could. The list of kidnappings ran to countries she hardly knew, news that had slid over her at the time it happened—tourists, foreign aid officials, humanitarian workers. She skipped between sites. *Exercise extreme caution. Avoid travel in the north . . . the longest-running African conflict—a civil war, ethnic-based, one of divide and rule . . . President Museveni has likened the Acholi people to grasshoppers in a bottle, saying, 'They will eat each other before they find their way out.'* There were articles about guerrilla warfare, rebel atrocities and Kony, no longer a man but a monster, the former altar boy who had become a bloodthirsty zealot.

She closed the computer, her eyes blurred. It was so far outside the scope of what she thought she could deal with, yet Tessa had taken them into the midst of it and now they were like frogs in a pot of water that was slowly being brought to the boil. She looked at the familiar living room. Her life, her home, the things she had arranged for their comfort—scented candles, the state-of-the-art entertainment system, a gleaming

Boca do Lobo sideboard; her expensive tastes that accused her of her own self-absorption.

'How far away do you have to be from something for it not to matter?' Tessa had asked. 'At what point do you begin to care?' She could hear her daughter's reasoning: one Australian life is worth how many Africans? Six hundred, six thousand?

'I'm not sure why I'm going, but I need to,' Tessa had said, and in one stroke she had made up her mind.

'Are you mad?' Stephen challenged her on their last family Skype call. 'You can't go crashing around there like some self-styled Angelina Jolie.' Tessa had only shrugged and walked out of the room. 'What's the point?' he called after her. 'Is it so you can come back and boast about all the suffering you've seen?'

'They don't see the boundaries we did—it's a generational thing,' her sister, with her teacher's scrutiny had said when she and Leigh spoke about such things. 'Children—you make room for them. From the very beginning the body swells, allowing them to grow, then it goes on remembering them there beneath the fading stretchmarks. And, love, there's no "off" switch! No guarantees, only a perpetual force that carries you forward. It's embedded in the idea of family—or is it just DNA? The need to survive, to protect—at every turn to be propelled by the constant fear that you might not do enough.'

If Leigh had learnt anything, it was that to parent was, for the most part, an illusion. You could not live their lives, you could not shield them from all they would face. They would go their own way and it would be a shock to see how much they discovered without you, and then beyond you, how much more of the world they still wanted.

'You're wrong to say I shouldn't do this,' Tessa had asserted—a declaration Leigh might have flung at her own parents.

'Let her go,' Neil had said. It was what he always said. What he insisted on for himself.

Leigh considered pouring herself a glass of wine—or, better still, a whisky—and then thought better of it; she needed to focus. She crossed the hall and flicked on the light in what had once been Tessa's bedroom. The thumping noise of a possum echoed outside as it ran across the roof, and when it receded she heard the distant slewing of traffic on the highway. She stood, looking at Tessa's uninhabited room. It still spoke of her childhood and adolescence; of the years before she moved out of home, the once necessary belongings left like forgotten relics—a chunky CD player, the world globe on the windowsill that looked as if it were suspended in the night sky, and on the bookshelves Neil had built, a children's book of myths and legends with a shimmering Pegasus on the cover. Hybrid creatures, legendary chimeras—a collection of fantastic amalgamated beings alongside an ingenious Swiss music box that played 'Edelweiss' and was still full of glitter make-up.

'We do not have proof of life,' one of the people from DFAT had said. 'At this stage, we must wait.' *You* must wait.

Leigh lay down on Tessa's bed, overcome by the faint smell—citrusy on top of something a little sweeter. It was intimate and familiar. She curled onto her side and, bringing the doona to her nose, breathed in. The globe on the windowsill was lit from within—Australia in its isolation. Africa, the great shape of a single wingspread. She focused on the blue distance between the two continents and recalled the way Neil's face had glazed over in the hospital. He had turned inwards, turned away from her completely. He could do that, fold into himself like a pocketknife, although it was not their separateness she thought of now, but rather the way in which they had merged. Together they had created Tessa, she was a part of them, just as Stephen was a part of them. Scientists spoke of *microchimerism*, where a few cells from one individual might be found in the brain of another, the idea that during pregnancy they travel from the foetus to the mother's brain and persist into adult life. Her children were part of her. She wrapped her arms around herself, feeling the warm soft skin of her belly beneath her T-shirt.

She closed her eyes and opened them again. She knew she should go back to her own room and try to sleep, but instead she remained lying on her daughter's bed, waiting until the last hours of darkness slowly gave way to the first light of morning.

24

When Leigh entered the room, Neil sat forward. 'Have you heard anything?' he asked. 'Has Stephen phoned yet?'

Leigh shook her head. There was a persistent buzzing, almost a hissing, which she thought must have something to do with the equipment that surrounded the bed—perhaps the oxygen outlet had been left on. She adjusted the flowmeter, then realised the sound seemed to be coming from within her, from inside her head.

'It feels like we're running out of time,' she said. 'I can't get any more information. It doesn't seem to matter who I speak to—DFAT, the police, the so-called private security services, especially the one in Sydney that claims they have people in East Africa—no one will tell me anything. Besides, it's the Easter break, everything's on hold.'

Neil waved his hand, a gesture that begged her to stop. 'The cardiologist said he would discharge me as soon as you got here. We'll go, see what we can do.'

'It's six days, Neil. Tessa's been gone for six whole days now.'

Neil took a deep breath and began changing into the clothes Leigh had brought in. He pulled on the clean T-shirt and jeans, then sat on the chair beside the bed to put on his socks and shoes. Should he tell Leigh what he feared? Christ, had he blinded himself to what he did not wish to see? Had he missed something vital? Or because he had committed himself to his children, and because that commitment tended to intensify whenever they made a mistake or did something wrong, had he simply refused to acknowledge what was going on?

Birds identify colours that humans cannot, fish react to vibrations in the water.

He looked at Leigh. 'I heard from Thompson last night, the bloke from the BBC. Do you remember him?'

Leigh looked puzzled.

'I worked with him on that story about illicit trafficking. Money laundering in South Africa. You remember? Skimming credit cards, hacking into people's bank accounts.'

Neil sounded as though he was rambling. Was he confused? Leigh reached for his wrist, checked his pupils, then shook her head.

'Anyway, he got back to me last night. He rang from Cape Town.'

Leigh frowned. 'What are you saying?'

'I don't know. It's just that it might've been a mistake to contact Stephen.'

'But I thought you said Stephen was our best chance of finding Tessa?'

'I did.'

Neil cleared his throat, a sound so familiar that Leigh didn't know if it was a comfort or an annoyance. She studied him. 'You said we had to take a leap here, we had to trust him.'

'I think he has other things on his mind.'

'What things? Is it money, the cost of going?'

'I'm not sure. I might be jumping to conclusions.'

Already he regretted beginning the conversation. He'd had an impulse to voice his doubts about his son—doubts that were little more than gut instinct—but now he had an awful feeling he'd said too much.

'But you know something else?' Leigh urged. 'What did this what's-his-name, Thompson, tell you?'

Neil shook his head. 'I don't know the whole story.'

'Well, what *do* you know? What is it? Are you saying Stephen shouldn't have gone, or do you know something else?'

Neil looked away. He would close off now and hold back what information he had.

'Can't you trust him, is that it?' Leigh persisted.

'I'm not sure. I'm not sure about anything except that we have to go.' He stood up. 'What time's the flight?'

Leigh checked her watch. 'We need to be at the airport in an hour. We can go from here, I've already packed.'

'Good.' And for a moment he moved his hand up and down her back as though she had just fallen over and needed consoling. He reached for her hand, but she shook her head and pulled away.

'Neil, I don't get it. First you say Stephen should go, now there's something you won't tell me. But Stephen agreed, he's probably already there.' Leigh straightened. She was afraid of her own anger now, and the damage it might do, but in the next instant she didn't care. 'God, I wish you'd never funded Stephen in that business venture with Matt Reba or encouraged Tessa to go to Africa in the first place. You set this in motion. *If you want to succeed, then you should move away, go beyond Australia.* Your advice, right?'

Neil felt the sting of her accusation. He knew she held him responsible; the reproach in her voice was clear. She thought he was too indulgent, trying to make up for the fact that he'd spent so much time away from home when they were growing up. She was right, of course, but he raged against the judgement. Resented it. He threw his hands up. 'What the hell is that supposed to mean? Christ, Leigh, what would you have me do? Try to run Stephen's life? Stop Tessa from doing something she believes in? They're adults!'

'Yes, they're adults now,' Leigh cried. She had got to her feet and was glaring at him, red-faced with fury.

Something happened then: in all their years of marriage they had covered most territories, but not this. Neil's face hardened. 'So you're saying this is all my fault? I know what you think, but if you're going to blame me, you ought to remember your part too. You favour Stephen, you always have; surely you can't think that doesn't make for problems.'

Tears welled in Leigh's eyes. Neil saw them—he saw her hurt, but he didn't want to acknowledge it. The need to attribute blame was too potent. 'You're just as indulgent,' he went on without stopping himself. 'More so. Fuck it, Lu, don't you think I get that?'

'I'm sure you do,' Leigh said, her voice choked, for the terrible truth was that he was right. There were the alliances—a confidential look, a Facebook post or a text message that she would keep from him, even if she did not intend to. The clemencies, because they were her children and she missed them, relentlessly feared she was losing them.

A phone rang out in the corridor. It rang and rang.

Leigh looked at her mobile. There were no messages.

The phone at the nurses' station stopped; then rang again.

'Jesus, would someone answer the damn phone?' Her hands itched. The phone stopped again. 'What?' Leigh said when she saw the expression on Neil's face.

'Don't,' Neil cautioned her. 'We're stronger than this.'

'Are we?' she demanded. 'Are we really stronger? You might think we are, but I don't know how we're going to get through it. I keep thinking, what do we tell ourselves if Stephen doesn't find Tessa? If we don't find her? What then?'

Neil looked at her. He knew he should reassure her, put his arms around her and hold her close, but he couldn't. The blame took up all the space between them.

25

Garamba

The gun warmed in Tessa's hand. She had barely looked at it, but she let the pad of her thumb trace the crosshatchings on the grip. Her fingertip moved along the smooth round shape of the trigger then across to the safety clip that seemed to pulse faintly with even the slightest pressure. It might have been a bird she had put in her pocket, its heartbeat there, and when she moved, she could feel the dangerous weight of it knock softly against her leg.

The day had passed with menial work, mostly gathering kindling, bending, lifting, stacking, then walking back into the forest to repeat the task. She had worked with Mildred, who had her baby strapped to her back, and the other girls from the day before. There was the same impenetrable distance between them, and every time Tessa tried to talk they laughed or shook their heads. Patrol soldiers watched her, but she had not seen Francis since his horrifying confession of the night before. She now sat near the campfire, where Colonel Kolo had joined the main group of soldiers. She took her hand from her pocket. Her split nails irritated her. She bit them, tasting the grit that lay beneath. She had been in a state of high, thrumming expectation, fearful too for her safety, especially at night, but she was beginning to grow accustomed to the threat and wondered if it was the same for the rebel soldiers; had they also acclimatised to a constant level of tension, forever alert while at the same time accepting that this was how it must be?

Another flash of blue lightning lit the sky and then came a low rumble of thunder. Static came in bursts from the satellite phone Kolo kept in his top pocket. Every now and then he pulled it out and checked it. He was hunched opposite her, picking his teeth with a twig. From time to time he gave orders.

An hour earlier he'd approached his soldiers as if seeking company. He sat on one of the crude wooden bench seats and swayed a little. At first, he was in good humour; he drank, swigging *waragi* from the gourd they produced at night, and joked with the other soldiers. But now he had grown argumentative. Alcohol was supposedly forbidden among them, although clearly the ban was not enforced. Home-brew was made in the camp and other supplies, like the plastic sachets they had last night, were looted on raids and drunk by most of the soldiers. Kolo passed the gourd to Lambert then took out the satellite phone and waved it in Tessa's direction. 'I have had word that your countrymen have been trying to contact us, but we do not do business with them.'

Tessa was cautious. 'Maybe you should speak with them,' she said, nodding and trying to sound agreeable. 'It would be better—'

'It would be better for you!' He laughed. 'But I know what they would have me do—they would insist that we take you back to safety, and then you would betray us. You would tell them where we are.'

Tessa shook her head. There was still no sign of Francis, and she hadn't seen Mildred since the last meal was served. She imagined the girl was in one of the huts nearby, tending her baby, but she was afraid that Francis may have been sent to another camp. There had been a shift in the mood of the camp that even she could sense. A restlessness, as if they were waiting, perhaps preparing for something.

'Maybe if I speak with Obed, your *lapwony*—the brigadier.'

'He does not trust you,' the colonel said with a fixed smile. 'You say you want to make things better, but you whites, with your "sir", your "master", your *bazungu*—you think you know best, yet what do you know? You have never been hungry in the way we know hunger. You do not know danger—or war.' He sneered. 'You blame Kony for abducting children and transforming them into killers, *kadogos*?' He raised his chin. 'Child soldiers are everywhere! Did you not think about this? Museveni has also used children to gain power. They strengthened his hand. Yes, Museveni—who must be stopped, because he is the one who is corrupt.

'But you try to tell us about our country,' Kolo went on. 'Our immoral rebellion—our religion! You, who have no religion, isn't that right?' He was drunk now, slurring, and she knew it was best to agree with him; she must keep him on side. He began to describe the magic that could kill, but fell quiet when some of the other soldiers stood up and looked towards the forest; a flicker of confusion, or perhaps fear, crossed his face. He reached for his rifle then put it down again.

At that moment Obed emerged from the shadows carrying a kerosene lantern. A soft halo of light preceded him. He was striking, with his high forehead and sculptured cheekbones, his straight back. He sat down next to Kolo and, placing the lantern on the ground, he leant in and clasped his slender hands together. The firelight made his eyes shine and in the orange glow his shabby uniform became impressive, almost dazzling. He spoke in Acholi to Kolo, who chuckled. There was a gleam of perspiration on his forehead and small droplets of sweat in the crevices of his neck. He brought his hand to the scapular he wore around his neck and twirled the laminated photograph between his thumb and forefinger. It was a gesture that somehow made the picture of Kony seem luminous.

Intermittently one or other of the boys patrolling the perimeter of the camp called a point check. Flying ants circled the lantern and a spotted dragonfly attached itself to the glass. For a moment it feathered its stiff cellophane wings before it froze like a mesmerised child at a Christmas window.

The fire burnt low.

Finally, Obed addressed her. 'You are a young woman schooled in the West?'

Tessa nodded. Obed flared his nostrils and smiled at her, and she noticed for the first time a crumpled scar on his otherwise perfect forearm. He caught her looking, and when she glanced back at him there passed between them an unspoken forewarning, an understanding perhaps that she had offended him and should be more careful. He pushed his sleeve down and closed his eyes then opened them again. 'I speak seven languages,' he said. 'One for every day of the week. I understand men and I understand God.'

He crossed his legs and lifted the collar of his shirt in a pedantic way. 'I hear you have been asking to see me. Huh? In this country, your education makes you foolish. And do you know why?' His hands were circling in a slow way as he spoke. 'It is because you have no self-restraint. Here, your knowledge is ignorance and that ignorance is death. Wanting, wanting and still not getting, that is your problem. But if you do what I say, you will be better off.' He arched his eyebrows and gave a melancholy smile. 'Do you understand? It is lack of faith which brings death to people such as you. To survive, you must see things our way.'

The air had become heavier and the first drops of rain began to fall. Tessa felt them on her arms and through the fabric of her shirt. Kolo sat back, swaying a little, his face in shadow—he might have been dozing—but Obed kept staring at her and what she saw in his eyes disturbed her. Francis had warned her, *You would be better to stay away from him.* She wrapped her arms around her knees as if to protect herself. The dragonfly trembled against the glass of the kerosene lamp. Its wings rustled and settled. She had thought it was dead, that the heat had scorched it, but it quivered again, intoxicated by the light.

'We've had other people like you who come here—*muzungu* who complain about our ways. Why come? I ask. Why come tying knots in the devil's tail? You insist you will help, but instead you do more harm. If God meant us to be at peace, we would be at peace.' He cocked his head to the side in his birdlike way. 'You are a foolish *muzungu*,' he added, and gave her an affronted look, aggrieved, almost sulky. 'Yes?'

Kolo opened his eyes and laughed softly, and for a moment Obed glanced at him with an expression Tessa had seen on other occasions—brief, almost pining. And it occurred to her that if Obed had feelings for the colonel he must have to suppress a great deal, or himself be punished here. He scratched his ear and turned to her, a look of irritation crossing his face.

Now she knew to be afraid.

He would deal with her, whether ordered by someone higher up the chain or because he wanted to anyway. She thought of the scar on his forearm and the way he'd covered it with his shirtsleeve. How long had he been with the rebel army? Had he too been distorted by all he had seen and done? How could he not be?

Tessa's throat constricted. It was as though every fibre of her being was refusing him. If she could distract him somehow. She forced herself to smile. Her breath jammed. 'I—'

'Get up!' he said, and picking up the kerosene lantern, with the dragonfly still attached, he pushed her ahead of him.

If she could keep him talking she might have a chance, she reasoned. But once inside the hut he put the kerosene lamp on a small table and shoved her towards the back wall, where there was a single woven mat on the dirt floor. He pushed her again, a sharp jab to her sternum that was a confident gesture, and she sensed what would follow. *No, don't.*

She heard Kolo, outside by the fire, suddenly laugh again, and when she looked at Obed another hot blast of fear ran through her. 'Please,' she said in a desperate voice. 'You're a leader, a wise man.' She knew she had to make the most of the first few moments, when her chances were the best. When he might not be totally in control. She must outsmart him. Trust her instincts. If one tactic wasn't working, try another. The problem was she wasn't in control either. She felt the live weight of the gun in her pocket and had an impulse to reach for it. The desire was so intense that her fingers curled. But he was stronger than her, and if she was caught with the gun, it would only make things worse.

He grabbed her by the collar of her shirt. She felt the fabric stretch and pull tight across the back of her neck, then he drew her closer and pressed his mouth over hers. In her mind, an adjustment took place, as swift as it was complete: don't struggle. Let him—or it will be worse. And then there was the insistent pressure of his body as he pushed her down onto the mat. He yanked at her trousers and wrenched off one of her boots then forced her legs apart. She could smell him, the sweaty scent of his body odour. He made an urgent sound and she feared that what he wanted most was to hurt her—that her pain was proof of his power. His breathing came fast and there was an angry impatience in the way he forced himself into her. Her vertebrae clicked under his weight. Time slowed and the pungent smell of him increased. She tried to make her body passive while her gaze stayed fixed on the dragonfly clinging to the lamp, but then he thrust again and another spasm passed through him. He groaned and she fought to wrench herself out from under him. Suddenly she had a powerful urge to bite, to scratch. But as if he recognised this, he pressed down on her throat. She tried to claw her way free and managed to scream, but he forced her down again, his hand gripping tighter. Her eyes rolled back in her head, yet she continued to struggle, finding enough strength to push him aside and roll out from under him just as someone else entered the hut. She thought it must be Kolo, that now it was his turn. A beam of light flashed across her face. A man's silhouette materialised.

'Move! Get out!' She knew the voice. She knew it as well as she knew her own voice.

She reached for her throat and coughed, trying to make her mind work as Stephen was punched, buckled and fell to the ground. She tugged her trousers on and, scrabbling for the handgun, she released the safety catch and pulled the trigger. There was a flash. The sound of the gunshot blasted, the recoil reverberating through her hand into her shoulder. Blood sprayed across her face and in an adrenaline-slowed moment she saw Obed's blasted face in the light of the kerosene lamp.

Beside her Stephen scrambled to his feet. 'Shit, Tess! Come on, don't just stand there—move!' And he turned towards the entrance where Francis stood holding the torch and gestured for them to run.

Suddenly the night came alive. There were soldiers everywhere. Torch beams flickered and shouts came, gunfire, confusion. Tessa ran, stumbled, and ran again. Her muscles strained as she pushed on, heading blindly in the direction she believed Francis and Stephen had fled.

26

About twenty minutes on, Francis made a shrill bird call then, in the near darkness, folded himself into a half-crouching position and motioned for Tessa to do the same. She noticed how he made himself small, but it was the stillness of his body that surprised her. No doubt he had hidden this way before and knew how to avoid detection, just as he knew how to outflank and confuse his pursuers. Following his lead, Tessa dropped to her knees and tried to imitate him.

She could just make out Stephen. He had found cover nearby, and when Francis signalled to him, he responded with a sharp flick of his hand. Sitting on his heels, Francis cocked his head and listened, then a small smile crept across his face as the pursuing party overtook them. It was terrifying, a crazy feeling, but thrilling too, a kind of hide-and-seek outmanoeuvring. Stephen looked about him, then nodded at her and, with a flick of his chin, punched the air—something he did whenever he was pleased with himself. Tessa's breath caught. How had he got here, how had he found her? Suddenly the two sides of her life collided, each magnifying the other.

When they could no longer hear the pursuing party, Francis waved to Stephen and nudged Tessa in the back. She got to her feet and they set off in the opposite direction, moving quickly despite the darkness, and together picked up their pace with Francis again taking the lead.

Another hour passed; occasionally they slowed but they did not stop. Tessa followed Francis, who now and again called to Stephen as though he was a fellow soldier, and Stephen replied easily and naturally as they fell into a rhythm.

They did not hear the rebels' voices again, although the threat of pursuit remained.

'They'll come after us,' Tessa said.

'Maybe,' Stephen replied.

'Maybe not,' Francis added. 'They will think there are more of you. They don't know that she is the one who had the gun.'

It was the first time they had really spoken. Stephen's voice was edgy, but Francis sounded confident. He flashed the torch on briefly then pointed again, urging them on. Tessa didn't know how Francis had come to be with Stephen. She felt as if she had missed something, as if she had come to after passing out.

A little further on, an almost-full moon appeared from behind a band of clouds, and as it rose higher, they made better time, moving swiftly in the blue shadows. Eventually they scrambled downhill. Slipping, falling and getting up again. Tessa had dropped the gun when it discharged, but she could still feel the recoil that had repeated through her shoulder. The sound was in her head and the astonishment she had felt when she pulled the trigger. She wished she still had the gun; it would be something to focus on, or at least give her security. Protection, she thought. She dug her fingernails into her palms and kept moving.

They came to a river that smelt of swampy grasses and mud, a rank odour that was almost sulphurous. In the moonlight, it glowed like quicksilver. Francis moved with agility, following its course downstream. Surefooted, he rock-hopped from one slippery stone to the next. At one point Tessa tripped near the water's edge, but caught an overhanging branch and righted herself again. When they came to a natural ford they crossed. Water eddied around her thighs. She waded through, letting it wash between her legs, the pain in her bruised groin smarting then easing. She allowed her eyes to close and saw Obed's bloodied face in the moment after she shot him. 'Don't,' she told herself. 'Don't think. Don't stop moving.'

She reached the other side and was climbing the bank when her foot slipped and she fell back. Stephen offered her his hand. She took it and he hoisted her up the steep incline. She could feel the strength in his grasp. For a moment, they stood facing each other, then he leant towards her and gripped her by the shoulders. The sight of him made her heart rise, then sink again. 'How did you find me?' she asked in a testing voice, but he shook his head and released his grip. She felt desperate. Everything was off-centre. People talk about the bond between siblings; sisters, brothers. She recognised something of herself in him. Did he know what had happened to her? She was sure he did. Even if he hadn't found her in the hut with Obed, he would have known. But the thing with Stephen was he could shift his attention elsewhere.

Again, he told Francis the name of the village where he'd left the jeep, and Francis said, 'Yes, this way.' They moved fluidly without doubling back, except for one point when Francis faltered, but even then only long enough for him to climb a tree. He scaled to where the crown rose above the canopy, then slid down again and, dropping to the ground, waved his arm in a forward gesture. 'I know now,' he said. 'Hurry.'

When he turned, Tessa noticed the deep vertical groove in the back of his neck. It was that vulnerable point just beneath where his hair grew tight and dense—the nuchal valley, her mother had called it, as though it were an endangered place. He was half their age, but he led them as an experienced guide might lead them and they followed him, trusting him, as he moved at a resolute jog, his rifle strapped to his back.

A steady rain began to fall, producing the faint arc of an opaque moonbow. It shone iridescent, if diluted, but when the moon went behind a cloud its extraordinary beauty was lost and the night became a vast black ocean. They found a sheltered place and stopped to rest, drinking rainwater from the waxy drip-tips of broad leaves and waiting for what had become a downpour to ease. In the dark Francis spoke softly, telling them things about killing and forgetting, but it was as if he was talking to himself. When the rain lessened they continued.

Again, Francis took the lead with the same determined pace. Whenever he switched the torch on, shadows leapt. At one point they saw a long-legged okapi, a strange, shy relative of the giraffe. It stood in the beam of light like a statue, dark-bodied, banded legs, before suddenly springing to life and crashing through the foliage.

By early morning the rain had ceased. All around them bird calls intensified, a noise that seemed to be there always but was building now to a crescendo. Francis lifted his face to the layered forest. 'Hello, birds,' he said in a surprisingly light-hearted voice. Tessa looked at him with his head raised to the branches. He had been swept into this world so far from his home, trained and indoctrinated, and now he was here, fleeing with them. She wondered if he still believed in Kony or if there had been the desire to escape the rebels all along, and that her coming, perhaps Stephen's too, had given him that chance. Others had escaped, pursuing the hope of returning to their families.

He moved forward and they followed him, climbing for another hour, this time above the tree line at the top of a ridge, where they sat down to rest with their backs against the cool rock.

Francis sat next to Stephen. 'Here, show us your rifle,' Stephen said, and almost reverently Francis complied. Lifting it, he turned it over and allowed it to glint in the morning sun.

'Ah, a Russian. A Kalash. They are the best,' Stephen said. 'They are the most reliable. This one has a radius of three hundred and fifty metres.'

Francis nodded. He allowed Stephen to look at it closely, but refused to let him hold the rifle outright. The sling-strap was an old seatbelt that had been tied at the butt and clipped to the wire loop on the handguard. Stephen pointed out how Francis could shorten it, which he did, proudly showing Stephen the carved notches; the F and the cross, in the polished wood, his eager young face looking to Stephen as if seeking approval.

'Where is your gun?' Francis asked, and glanced at the empty holster Stephen wore. 'Has Colonel Kolo got it now?' His scar, which had begun to heal, stretched as he grinned, and laughter came to both of them. 'Because you made a deal?' Francis teased knowingly, and in that moment they were easy with each other, as if their differences were not such a big thing—brothers, who had always known these kinds of bantering exchanges. *What deal?* Tessa thought. She recognised the confidence in Stephen's smile and tried to figure out what Francis might know. Stephen nodded again, indicating Francis's rifle with casual authority. 'Like yours: gas-operated, clip-fed—good for automatic fire.'

Tessa listened to Stephen. When had he become such an expert on weapons? There were his business interests, of course, but she had chosen to look away from them, just as she had chosen to ignore his gung-ho swagger. Suburban shooting ranges like the one he dragged her to as a 'birthday surprise', or his bragging about hunting trips to one or other of the state's game reserves—rabbits, foxes, kangaroos. Pest animals, he had teased. His obsession with guns. With shooting.

She put the flat of her palm to her bruised shoulder; she could still hear the blast ringing in her ears. The priest was dead. Would he haunt her, like the major; would his *cen* not let her rest?

Across the valley the sun was lifting, its golden warmth lighting the forest. There was no wind. A low purple cloud hung close along the horizon and in the distance the mountain peaks looked like a child had drawn them.

'Reba should be down there,' Stephen said. 'He's with the jeep.'

'Matt Reba?'

'Yeah, remember him?'

Tessa nodded. 'Sure, I remember him—your South African school friend, your business partner, right? Was that how you got here—with Matt?'

Stephen nodded.

'But how did you know where to find me?' she asked.

Stephen looked at her and shrugged his shoulders. 'Someone called Oculi rang.'

'Dominic Oculi rang you?'

Stephen twisted the leather band he wore on his wrist, then slowly wiped the back of his hand across his mouth. 'He rang Dad.'

'What?' She could tell there were things Stephen wasn't telling her. He kept fidgeting, his expression guarded.

'Steve?'

'Yeah—look, Dad wanted to come himself. You know how he is—the fixer, the adventurer. Harrison Ford.' Stephen rolled his eyes and pulled a knowing face. 'Except he couldn't.' He shook his hipflask but it was empty. He unscrewed the lid anyway, sniffed, then screwed the lid back on and shoved the flask back into his pocket. 'He's had some kind of heart scare. Stress, according to Mum—not serious. She asked me to find you. She said she wouldn't forgive me if I didn't.' He winked.

You would be better off if you didn't ask so many questions, Stephen thought, although he was finding it difficult to recognise his sister. It was only when she pushed her hair behind her ear—an old habit—that he was convinced. Her transformation, in just a couple of months, was startling. Her face was harshly tanned, her hair matted, and when she turned away he saw the ugly purple bruises on her neck. There were tiny wrinkles across her forehead and others at the corners of mouth. Her clothes were filthy, the front of her shirt bloodstained, and when she spoke there was something a little crazed about her.

'You look like shit,' he said.

Tessa registered his tone from when they were younger. 'Yeah, well you look worse,' she quipped, and gave him a wry smile. He flashed a quick smile back and his face suddenly softened.

'I didn't think anyone would come. I didn't think you'd come.'

'Who else was going to find you?' He raised his eyebrows, and she knew that gesture too. She could recall a summer's day at the beach when they were teenagers—a big group of them, forty degrees, the sand burning hot. No one had been thinking straight except for Stephen. She had gone out too far and got caught in a rip. He swam out and brought her back. Laughed when she thanked him.

Stephen tilted his head back and looked at the sky, then glanced at Francis. 'Come on,' he said and stood, but before he could move off Tessa put her hand on his forearm.

'How did you do it?' she asked. 'How did you get past the guards?'

He looked at her hand. 'Let's go,' he said. 'We're wasting time.' Then he joined Francis, who had already picked up his rifle and slung it across his shoulder, one hand gripping the trigger guard as he pointed it in the direction he wanted them to go.

27

Standing by the jeep, Matt Reba, signalled for them to hurry. They opened the doors and clambered in. Tessa scrambled into the back seat and, looking down, became aware of the blood on her shirt. It astonished her to see how much there was. It had seeped through her bra and congealed against her skin. Corporeal, already rotting. There was a plastic bag in the seat pocket which she used to try to wipe the blood away, but it only seemed to spread it, the heat from her body setting it further into the fabric.

Francis got in beside her and Stephen hoisted himself into the front passenger's seat. 'Let's go,' he said.

Reba started the engine and revved the four-wheel drive to life. Tessa folded her arms against her chest. A trembling pulsed through her. If she could just keep it together. But like a series of doors opening, she remembered what had happened—her body remembered and her mind played over the details. She saw again the moment when the light went from the major's eyes, then came the violence of Obed forcing himself into her and the strange almost pathetic sound he made as he ejaculated. She recalled such things as if she were hallucinating—she saw the actual bullets as she fired, and when the gun was empty, she heard again the *click, click, click*—things that made her even less certain of who she thought she was. There had been a kind of euphoria when they escaped, but now the truth of what she'd done shocked her to the core.

They drove fast, Matt changing gears and swerving to avoid the worst potholes, the four-wheel drive shaking as Stephen took out his mobile phone. Reba told him there wasn't any reception. After a pause he added, 'You know, I thought you'd had it. I told myself another five minutes and I was out of there. Lucky you showed up when you did.'

Stephen made a dismissive sound, but Reba was serious. It surprised Tessa—she had always remembered Matt Reba as being the blasé one, careless and a bit offhand; the exchange student Stephen had befriended at school, the one from *South Efrica*, as Stephen would say with a grin. 'His father owns a gun shop. *Give me six good guns, and six good dogs . . .*' And there'd been other jokes about the store doing discounts at Christmas and having a Father's Day special.

Reba was looking at Stephen. 'Did anyone come after you?' he asked.

'Watch the road,' Stephen replied, then fiddled with the CD player. When that didn't work, they drove on in silence.

Francis sat close to the door, behind Matt. Occasionally Tessa noticed his eyes flicker across to Stephen, but mostly he stared out the window, one hand gripping the doorframe, the other tight on the barrel of his rifle. The window was closed, but he seemed to sniff the air. Ahead of them dark clouds had built up, and once again it began to rain—slowly at first, then in great heavy sheets. The windscreen wipers beat backwards and forwards, but with little effect: the blades had perished and appeared to be set too far from the glass. Once they got onto the bitumen Reba accelerated and shifted into fifth gear. The engine thrummed as the windscreen wipers laboured with a thwack-thwacking sound. Leaning against the doorframe, Tessa listened to the incessant rhythm. Her breathing was shallow, her body ached. She watched the rain. She wanted to shut it out. She wanted to shut everything out—what she had seen, what she had done.

She closed her eyes and let sleep overtake her.

Adjusting the sun-visor's mirror, Stephen glanced at his sister sleeping with her mouth open. She slept in the back seat of the car in the same way she had when they were kids, the motion of a moving vehicle as good as a drug.

A large mosquito hovered then came to land on her cheek just near her earlobe. He swivelled around and crushed it between his thumb and forefinger. His touch woke her and she jerked back as if she had been struck. 'Hey, don't!' she said in an unrecognisable voice.

'Okay! Take it easy,' Stephen replied and, wiping the blood from the mosquito onto the seat, he turned around to face the road.

The rain stopped and for a time the sky cleared, transforming the greyness into a lush green glow. They crossed the border, passing through several villages where long lines of people were walking by the side of the road. Women dressed in colourful *busuti* blouses with short puff sleeves, church doors wide open. It was Easter Sunday, Tessa realised. Some groups walked with their arms around each other while others were singing and swaying or waving branches of the *olwedo* tree. Watching them, Tessa felt a tug of envy for their faith and sense of community; it was so different from her own secular understanding. Did it help to have that kind of structure? Feeling as she did now, she imagined it might; something to cling to and measure herself by.

Just before dusk they reached the rehabilitation centre. Reba sounded the horn and the gates swung open. They drove through, then stopped and got out. Francis walked around to stand in the front of the four-wheel drive, his rifle slung over his shoulder. He appeared smaller than he had in the bush, although he had a purposeful manner, as if someone had ordered him to stand to attention. A few curious youths began to mill around him. One or two spoke in Acholi and Tessa gathered that their questions were about people who had disappeared or were still in the bush. Francis looked at them with a wary expression then back at Stephen, who shrugged as if some understanding had passed between them. It was a brief moment and Tess sensed that she had failed to grasp it or perhaps had misread it altogether.

The rain clouds had moved further east and it was muggy again. Puddles dotted the compound and a few chickens scratched in the soft earth looking for food. Dominic came out of his office and walked towards them accompanied by

Beatrice who, despite the cloying heat, wore a knitted scarf around her neck. As they came closer, Dominic's eyes widened and he shot a curious look in Stephen's direction. He waved off the youths who had gathered around, telling them they could meet the new arrivals later, and they ran off. When Dominic's eyes came to rest on the blood on Tessa's shirt, a lump formed in her throat.

'Are you hurt?' Dominic asked. 'Do you need to see a doctor?'

Tessa shook her head. 'No, thank you, I'm okay,' she lied. Beatrice stepped towards her. She raised her hands in the air, then took Tessa by the arms and squeezed her. '*Bin kany!* Come here!' she said. She stared at Francis, then glanced at Matt and Stephen, and back at Tessa again. 'Are you all right? How did you escape?' Tessa felt the warmth of Beatrice's hands, her strong reassuring pressure, and wanted to melt into her arms. She faltered. 'We got away. The boy, Francis here, and my brother—No, no, it's not my blood,' she said, noticing how Beatrice's hand fell away from her shirt. The trembling started again. Tessa felt it under her breastbone and in the tips of her fingers, but mostly along her bottom lip. She tried to steady herself.

'You need to go to the medical clinic,' Dominic said. 'And afterwards you must come to my office. I will need to make a report.' Tessa saw that he was trying his best to manage the situation and admired him for it. He wanted solutions. He looked at Francis and the line between his brows deepened.

'This is Francis,' Tessa repeated with renewed incredulity at the way Francis stood with such attention and stillness. 'He helped us find our way out of the bush.'

Dominic nodded and held out his hand. '*Apwoyo bino*, Francis,' he said. '*I tye nining?*'

'I am okay,' Francis replied in English. He looked at Dominic's hand but did not accept it.

Dominic let his hand drop to his side. 'My name is Dominic Oculi,' Dominic said. 'You are in a safe place now and for that reason I must ask you to hand over your rifle. We do not allow guns here—we do not have weapons of any sort.'

Francis pulled his rifle close to his chest and held it there. The gesture was childish, although his defiance was anything but. His eyes shone. 'It is mine,' he said quietly.

'I understand,' Dominic replied. 'But if you are to stay here, then I am afraid you must give it up.'

Dominic held out his hand to take the rifle, but Francis stepped back then glared at Tessa as though his predicament was entirely her fault. 'You told me I would be free,' he said accusingly.

'And you will be,' Tessa replied. 'That is why you do not need your rifle.'

'Francis, you have been gone for a long time—' Dominic began, but before he could continue, Francis spun around and said to him: 'No. I have been gone for four years, plus three months and eight days. That is how long I have been with Kony's army, so you cannot tell me I will not need a gun.'

Stephen, who had come forward to stand beside Francis, raised an eyebrow. Tessa knew that look, knew Stephen's cockiness, how he flaunted his capacity to break the rules. Perhaps Francis caught it too; did he nod? Was this another an exchange between them? It might've been—Francis didn't miss much.

'Now that you are here, things will begin to get better,' Dominic said to Francis.

'You do not know that,' Francis replied. 'Do you know what has happened to my village? Or my family?' He looked around the centre and Dominic followed his gaze.

'We will help you to find out,' Dominic promised. 'But first I wish to welcome you. There is a place for you here.' After that he spoke in Acholi again, using phrases like *ciiro peko*, which Tessa understood meant 'overcoming problems', while Beatrice talked effusively, using her hands and nodding her head.

Francis answered in English and Dominic, following his lead, switched back too, his voice soft but with the same persuasive authority Tessa remembered from other occasions. 'Everyone here has been a former abductee. I promise you, Francis, there are people who will look after you. If you hand over your rifle, we can begin something new.'

At last Francis reluctantly handed over his rifle. Dominic took the weapon in one hand, and placed his other hand on Francis's shoulder. 'Everything you need can be found here,' he said. 'Food, shelter and, God willing, a chance to be reconnected with your family.' It was a conversation that ended in directions: where the canteen was, where Francis could go and wash himself, where he might sleep, as night was coming.

Francis reached for the beads around his neck, which he had slipped under the collar of his khaki shirt. As he pulled them out, Tessa saw that he also wore the talisman the preacher Obed had worn. In those moments after she had fired the gun, and Francis had signalled to her and Stephen to run, he must have slipped back into the hut where the priest lay and taken the scapular.

He knew the drill; it would have been quick—second nature, *you kill, you take.* Now, squaring his shoulders, Francis lifted the picture of Kony to his mouth and kissed the plastic-coated image. Tessa couldn't hear what he said, although his lips formed a sequence of words that she felt were familiar to him—a prayer repeated in a strange mix of English and Acholi. He was intent although, as he continued to pray, his breathing became rapid and Beatrice, seeing him pant, stepped across and gently took him by the arm and led him towards the dormitories.

'I need to eat,' Reba said. 'I need a shower, and I need a beer. After that, I need a decent bed.'

Stephen stood with his hands in his pockets and rocked on the balls of his feet. 'Then why don't you go back into Gulu and find us a hotel. That's if there is one. In the meantime, I need to use the internet . . . And pay in cash!' he called, as Matt Reba walked back to the jeep.

Scratching his ear, Stephen turned Tessa. 'You've got snot on your sleeve,' he said, half joking. They might have been kids. Was he trying to make her feel better? 'You know, you'd probably be dead if I hadn't found you,' he went on. 'Or, who knows, if you'd had enough bullets you might've shot everyone in that shithole of a camp.' He lifted his eyebrows, the old ready-to-stir grin. 'You surprised me, though,' he added in a more serious tone. 'I guess I didn't think you had it in you.'

Tessa touched her lips; they were cracked and dry. She thought of the damage she had done, irreversible damage. The burnished light held the last of the day's colour and the air was warm with the putrid peppery scent of her body. She wanted to shower, and yes, she should seek medical advice for possible exposure to HIV or other STDs, but she couldn't stop her mind from whirring. 'How'd you get into the rebel camp?' she asked.

Stephen looked away to where a few scrawny chickens scratched in the dirt.

'Steve? How the hell did you get past their patrol without getting caught?'

He shrugged. 'I did get caught,' he said.

'Then how—'

'I had an intelligent conversation.'

'With who?

'With your friend Colonel Kolo.'

'My friend?'

But that was enough. Stephen wouldn't say any more. He turned and looked across the recreation area that separated the main office from the school. Several youths ran between the various concrete buildings; they were calling to each other, playing a game of tag.

'What did you offer him?' Tessa persisted. 'He must have wanted something.'

'Forget it,' Stephen replied. 'Go and have a shower, get some rest.' And he made his way towards Dominic's office, where he would be able to use the computer. Even if it was slow, there was still a chance of a connection. There were things he needed to check, and from this distance he would have to arrange them as best he could.

28

Under the shower, Tessa scrubbed her body and washed her hair, rinsing, lathering and rinsing again. The pressure was weak, but the water came needle-sharp from the small fixed shower head. She used a flannel to wash her arms and breasts and between her legs. There were purple bruises on her shoulders and along her thighs, and she washed those as well as the pustulating insect bites. Some, especially those on the back of her neck, had swelled and grown as hard as dried coffee beans, others were inflamed and had raised her skin in hideous red welts.

There was no hot water at the centre so she washed herself in cold. It cooled her itching skin but did not slow her mind or stop the images that kept coming. Slowly she banged her head against the concrete wall in front of her. The blood had washed away from under her nails, although she could still smell it. She saw the rebel camp again, dark green folds of forest and clouds that filled the lower valleys, Obed's face in the light of the kerosene lamp and the gleam of his teeth, and more vivid still, the bloated body of the major. An endless loop, on and on.

She groaned and cursed herself. *Oh God, how insanely stupid, why did you*—but it was Francis's story that kept returning to her, and other things he had told her when they sheltered from the rain on their way out of Garamba, the shrewd expression on his face as he said: 'When you kill for the first time, you change. You are made to change.'

She had come to the showers when no one else was there, although in her mind she could still hear the voices of the girls from the centre, their laugher and talk, the reassurance of their togetherness. She yearned for that, someone who might understand, for Beatrice or her mother, just to feel their arms around her. But when again, she thought of what had happened, self-recrimination and shame filled her.

She dried herself and put on clean clothes, a soft T-shirt and loose pants. She wound a bandana around her head. In the mirror, she looked ugly, worse. She turned away from her reflection and went outside.

As she crossed the compound, children came up to her. 'Hello, hello,' they said, and she replied, 'Hello, hello,' avoiding them and hurrying on. She didn't know where Francis was, whether he had gone to the dormitory with Beatrice or another counsellor, or maybe with some of the other returnees from the centre. When he was with the rebels he had survived beatings and that had impressed his commanders. 'A capable boy.' About killing, he had said only one other thing: *It is the same as a dream. That is how I remember it. That is how I forget it.* And, cupping his hands to the rain, he watched it gather, then splashed it over his face.

In Dominic's office, Tessa filled out a report, the sequence of events already jumbled in her mind. 'There are many recollections after these violent encounters,' Dominic had said, looking down at the pen Tessa held in her hand. 'Things will come back to you. You may want to add more later.' Tessa nodded. Dominic's voice sounded remote and there was a ringing in her ears as she pushed the half-completed form back across the desk towards him. At the clinic, before her shower, the nurse had spoken softly. 'You may change your mind about your reluctance to report this to the police, and even if you say you do not want the sleeping tablets, I can give them to you anyway. You must try and get some rest.' Tessa had nodded, a surge of alarm sweeping through her as she watched the nurse invert then shake the vial that contained her blood. There was talk of her going home or even to Kampala, but she wanted to get back to work. Work, she thought, would give her purpose even as she doubted her ability.

Back in her room, and truly alone for the first time since leaving the centre with the delegation, she lit a candle. It took several tries using wax matches that had softened. The weak orange flame sputtered then glowed. She dragged her notebook in under the mosquito net, but she couldn't concentrate. When she tried to read, the words ran together. Mosquitoes keened and when she looked up there were three geckos on the ceiling. They were pale, almost translucent, with small pointed faces. She watched them take up their positions then wait with infinite patience before darting from the shadows to catch their insect prey with absolute precision.

'They might have killed you, but you are alive,' Francis had said when they crossed the border.

'Aren't you afraid the LRA will come after us?' she had whispered.

He had looked at her with suspicion. 'No. That is a weakness. Your fear.' Then he had shrugged. 'They have more important things to do.'

She woke in the middle of the night to the sound of rain on the roof and tried to get back to sleep. She dreamed, a waking dream. Obed was not dead, but pinned down in a type of cage. He looked at her with open hatred. The photograph of Kony still hung around his neck, and his chest, slick with sweat, rose and fell. She felt his mouth on hers. Her hand gripped the gun, her finger locked on the trigger, but the next thing she knew the gun was not in her hand—what she held was a greasy rag. She pushed it over his face so that it covered his nose and mouth and then, straining to smother him, she drove the pressure of her entire body through her wrist until her hand caught fire and burnt. His eyes were open but fixed, his body limp, she brought her hand to her mouth and blew on it—woke with her heart pounding.

When you kill for the first time, you change. You are made to change.

The hours passed and early-morning light came in through the thatch, making a golden pattern on the wall. Outside a rooster crowed. Tessa remembered her first few weeks, when everything was new and she thought her research might make a difference. A time when she believed she knew what she was doing, that she would find answers to her questions, collaborate with others whose work aimed to improve people's lives. Instead, she had taken a life. 'Self-defence—you should be proud,' Stephen had said. But there was a riptide of guilt. A gap between who she actually was and who she had once believed herself to be. It left her feeling as if the world was not real but breaking apart, a widening distance separating her from where she needed to be—for no matter how hard she tried she could not reconcile what she had done.

You must stop, she thought, remembering what Francis had said: 'You need to be strong so you can live. Not just once, but every day.' He was thirteen, fourteen years old, and he knew this one thing. He knew how to survive.

29

'You don't have to come,' Tessa insisted. 'I'm fine—I'll *be* fine.'

It was a bad connection with a faint echo each way. The poor reception meant the picture had failed, although Tessa would've turned it off anyway. She didn't think she would be able to look at her mother on the screen, both of them able to read too much in each other's faces.

The computer in Dominic's office was outdated, the keyboard grubby and cracked. Her mother's voice came and went as if she was speaking through a fog. 'We're in Dubai, we'll be boarding again in ten minutes.'

'And Dad?'

'He's okay. Really, he's all right. It's *you* we're worried about. Tess?'

Tessa could hear the distress in her mother's voice and with it the familiar whirr of parental concern that had been set in motion. 'You don't have to come,' she repeated.

'We don't,' her mother said. 'But, sweetheart, we need to come. We're already on our way.' There was a pause and then she said, 'We heard about the shooting.'

It was instinct her mother ran on. A maternal sensitivity that could gauge what was wrong before Tessa barely understood herself. 'Tessie, listen—'

'Mum, I can handle this.'

The door opened and Stephen entered the office. Tessa nodded at the computer screen, but Stephen shook his head.

'We'll be in Entebbe in about six hours—after that it's just a short connecting flight. Can you hear me, Tess?'

Tessa chewed her bottom lip. She was aware of Stephen standing behind her and the hairs on the back of her neck rose. She struggled to regain the feeling she'd had earlier—that she must focus on one small thing at a time. If she was going to cope, let alone get through this, she needed to hold on to that.

'Okay, I'll see you soon,' she said with a mixture of resignation and relief. Maybe it would help to have her parents' support, someone there to say, *You got in over your head, you're not the first and you won't be the last. Now you must be strong and take responsibility for your actions.* The kind of advice and family loyalty that might stop her from indulging in the sort of negative self-recrimination that fed on itself.

'Thanks, Mum,' she said, adding, 'I love you.' The call ended.

She turned to face Stephen.

'What?' he asked.

'Why won't you speak to them?'

Stephen shrugged. Fresh from the hotel, he now wore a pair of clean jeans and a pink linen shirt with the sleeves rolled up. He was perfectly proportioned, his arms tanned and muscular, a leather strap and chunky silver watch on his left wrist. Clean-shaven, his hair still damp, he had a pair of aviator sunglasses perched on top of his head.

'I guess it'll be enough when they show up,' he said.

Tessa pushed the chair back from the desk. 'They know I shot the preacher.'

Her eyes were shining and there was an edge to her voice that Stephen recognised—he had heard it when he found her. He noticed how she scratched her arms and chewed her bottom lip. A couple of years ago, she had almost gone off the rails, she had been so wound up about failing something, and there had been a relationship with some bloke that hadn't worked out; he could hardly remember now. She was all right afterwards, but that was with a whole lot more working in her favour.

'What else did they say?' he asked.

'Do you mean, do they know I was raped? Do they know that I killed him? I'm not sure. Maybe Dominic told them.' She spoke quickly and irritably, as though she'd had too much to drink. Most likely she hadn't slept. *Wired* was the word that came to Stephen. She might have snorted something, except he knew her better.

'I thought you said you were staying in Gulu,' Tessa continued. 'Why have you come back here?'

'Because the connection at the hotel is crap and I need to use the computer again.'

The door opened and Dominic entered carrying a large stack of papers. He looked surprised, as though he had expected to see Tessa, but not Stephen. He greeted them coolly, nodding his head in Tessa's direction. 'Are you all right?'

Tessa hesitated. 'I'm okay. And you?' she asked, indicating the Elastoplast bandage on his head.

'I am good,' Dominic replied, but his tone was neutral.

'What about the others?' Tessa asked anxiously. 'Have you heard any more?'

'The others—yes, I have heard that John Alphington has gone back to the US. He sent you an email?'

Tessa nodded.

'Perhaps that is for the best; he will get better medical treatment there. He can finish his report.'

'Have you heard about his ankle?'

'They are going to reset it. And Gideon will have his sutures out in a few days.'

The debt Tessa felt mounted. Shame, too. Alphington and Gideon had both been injured trying to protect her. She thought of Gideon, with his hatred of foraging baboons and his throwaway line, '*Wi-lobo*—that is the way of the world.'

'I have spoken with an official from the Ugandan army,' Dominic went on. 'There will be a preliminary hearing: questions for you to answer about the brigadier—the priest, Obed Lokodo. There are reports to say he is dead, and now there are fears that there might be reprisals by the rebels, possibly further attacks in the Congo. But I think that is just talk. They are held in check at the moment; they know it will only make the situation worse. For you, later, a formal inquiry is meant to take place, although by the look of it,' he said, indicating the folder of documents, 'no one expects anything to happen anytime soon.'

The generator thumped. Stephen lifted his sunglasses and ran his hand through his hair as if pushing a thought away.

Dominic's face clouded. 'I've found out what I can about Francis. His parents were farmers. Cattle and cassava. His father also made pots, but their village was one of the worst affected. The rebels slaughtered everyone; reports say they hacked them to pieces then burnt the place to the ground.'

Tessa's stomach churned. 'So there are no survivors?'

'None. The village doesn't exist anymore. I have been searching for other relatives, but I can find no one. Francis has asked what happened to his family and now I must respect his need for honesty. I will speak with him shortly.'

'I was hoping Francis was mistaken, that there'd still be someone here for him,' Tessa ventured.

'Perhaps we will find somebody who knew him,' Dominic replied. 'Then, with luck, he will have a new place in the community. We must try to rebuild his life.'

Tessa thought of Oraako and saw the deft strike of the panga through the hen's sternum, its blood seeping into the earth. 'But what if that doesn't happen?'

'It is the only way—with cleansing, with *mato oput*, there can be acceptance, sometimes even forgiveness, and he will be taken back. We will try to help him rehabilitate.'

Dominic had said things like this before, although Tessa had not understood his hopefulness until now. That despite everything, including the failed peace talks and his own devastation at the result, optimism was still his default position. He had often spoken of *kanyo*, or coping, and of gritting one's teeth—rather like her father, who would say that unless you were able to solve something outright then you were probably better off to just accept it and get on with life. Face up to things.

'And what if Francis has other ideas?' It was Stephen who spoke. He was leaning against the metal filing cabinet, his arms crossed. Above him was the whiteboard with the list of returnees' names on it.

Dominic tossed the file onto his desk with a thud. 'Forgiveness and acceptance are the only ways to get rid of the violence. Francis was a young boy when he was abducted; under normal circumstances he would not do what he has done.'

'Francis is not a boy now,' Stephen replied. 'He knows too much. He knows what you have to do to survive.'

Dominic looked at Stephen and straightened his shoulders as if throwing some unseen weight from his back. Tessa watched his face; he was making a point now and it cost him: 'People can be talked into doing terrible things,' he said. 'Then, later, as we say here, *the brain eats itself*. Unless the boy asks for forgiveness, the wrong he feels will remain. It will stay and feed on itself, gnawing away at his soul until one day he is no longer able to free himself from the bitterness. He must make peace with himself and then he can make peace with God. What he did was against life, against himself.'

Dominic looked out the window and Tessa followed his gaze. She could see Francis approaching. He walked with his head down, his hands dangling at his sides.

'He has done bad things,' Dominic said. 'Some would say evil things.' He lightly touched the crucifix he wore around his neck. 'I know this, I have travelled his path. We who have killed—' he glanced at Stephen then back at her '—must learn that reconciliation is the only way.'

He went to meet Francis. Together they walked across to the

bench seat and sat down beneath the compound's shady kigelia tree. Tessa could see them through the window. Dominic angling himself to face Francis, while Francis shrugged or moved restlessly, as if checking to see who was behind him.

Someone—Beatrice, perhaps—had given Francis one of the standard-issue Bibles they usually kept in the classrooms. At one stage Francis lifted it up and pointed to it, but when Dominic shook his head, Francis pitched it across the grass as though it had caught fire, then stuck out his chin, a gesture that seemed hostile, almost threatening. Then, just as quickly, he turned away again and, dropping to the ground, he crouched with his face buried in his hands, the curve of his back convulsing.

Tessa would have gone to him but Stephen stepped forward and held her by the upper arm. She could feel his fingers dig into her flesh. She struggled against him, but he held her fast.

'Leave him,' he said, and in that moment Francis got to his feet and ran off, his legs scissoring with long powerful strides.

Tessa pulled herself free from Stephen's grip and stepped away.

'There are boys like him all over this country,' Stephen said.

'Oh, right,' Tessa said and shot him a furious look, but Stephen held her gaze as if issuing some kind of challenge.

'Yeah right, so do you really think you can change things?'

Her stomach clenched, she wanted to strike him, just as she might have done when they were kids. 'What are you saying?' she asked in a low whisper. It was the certainty in his voice that sickened her.

'Look, Tess, I'm sorry if life doesn't meet your expectations—maybe you think your idea of "humanity" can work, but let's face it: you're wrong. People who want to change the world burn out from disappointment. Humanity is nothing more than a biological label for the animal species we belong to.'

'Oh, fuck your self-serving philosophy, Stephen! Cherie was right, you're a complete arsehole. You know, not everyone's an opportunist like you. You think your theories justify your behaviour? They don't. You make them fit to suit yourself. You go into business, Reba's Firearms. What's that, anyway? You provide people with guns.' She glared at him, but his face remained impassive. 'That's what you do, don't you? You provide people with a means of killing each other and then you go off and swill expensive wine. You . . .' But her voice faltered.

Stephen's jaw tightened. 'I run a legitimate business,' he said in a reasonable tone. Then he smiled and gave a dismissive shrug. 'Besides, everyone who comes here, whether it's the celebrity do-gooders who organise anti-poverty campaigns or the geologists or the aid agencies, they're all the same. NGOs replace missionaries. They all stake their claim. How am I any different?'

Tessa threw her hands in the air. 'Because what you do—oh my God—because what you do has different consequences.'

Stephen laughed. 'Does it? And why should that worry you?'

'Because you're my brother!'

'Right. But there's something you never seem to get, even after everything that's just happened to you, and it's this: I'm no different from anyone else. We're all here to make a buck, including you.'

'That's not true.'

'Really? You say you're here to do some good, but just like everyone else you've got something to gain. Or have you forgotten you're advancing your career, Dr Lowell?'

He had circled her, worn her argument into the ground. His ability to turn the blame from himself and call her bluff gutted her. He had risked his life to rescue her—what right did she have to call him out when she had followed her own impulses, put others in danger? But worse, and she knew it, was that she had come all this way only for Stephen to show her what she most feared about herself, and there was a flicker in his eye that told her he understood: *You're the problem; you should think more about yourself before judging me.*

30

After landing on Gulu's bumpy tarmac the plane came to a standstill. In the window seat, Neil waited for the engine to shut down. The sun was just beginning to rise, and in the early-morning light he could make out the thick tufts of grass that grew between the cracks in the asphalt.

An infant in front of him was crying—desperate gulping sobs, its fuzzy head just above the headrest. Its mother, whose bangled arm jingled as she cupped its small plump shoulders, cooed, until finally it stopped and, laying its head against her neck, smiled back at him.

Neil glanced across at Leigh. She appeared older than she had before they left—drawn and tired, her eyes puffy and her skin had a pale greyish tinge. It had been a long journey, with numerous delays and too many stopovers. Since their argument in the hospital he had been trying to reconcile the tension between them, but the gap was wide and he felt it extending both back to old grievances and beyond them, into the future. They had said things to each other that could not be unsaid and had spoken little throughout the journey, both understanding that if they did it would only make things worse. He knew that Leigh was trying to work out what she could on her own. It was what made her a good doctor, perfect in an emergency, although she could close off. Still, he could hardly criticise her for that; he too took charge and had the same tendency to shut people out. It was why they were here, wasn't it? Neither of them could leave things to others.

He reached for her hand and squeezed it gently. On her lap lay a map that included Murchison Falls. At any other time, they might have been setting off on an adventure instead of coming to this troubled place to try to help their daughter. The details were still unclear. Tessa was back at the centre, although there were concerns. 'She is not doing so well,' Dominic Oculi had said, his voice becoming reserved and formal when he told them that she had been to the medical clinic and had admitted to shooting one of the rebels. 'According to the reports, the man died.' He wouldn't say any more. All he told them was that he didn't have enough information himself. The image of Tessa being assaulted and shooting the man left Neil with a rising sense of panic, his thoughts scrambled as if he'd taken a dangerous drug. What good was his knowledge of coelacanths and earthquakes or geological timelines, all those obscure facts that had consumed him—that octopuses have three hearts, that sharks close their inner eyelids for self-protection—what did any of that matter, the endless hours he poured into understanding the world, when he could not keep his own family safe?

As the other passengers gathered their belongings and waited to disembark, he pulled out his phone and switched it on. Gulu airfield was little more than a large paddock with a small makeshift terminal at one end and a dozen or so junked planes—UN mostly. On the other side of the runway he saw a spray of headlights where a business jet and a couple of four-wheel drives were parked. The figures standing there were too small for him to make out the details: a group, probably all men, two of them white, clustered together. As far as he could tell, some kind of uneasy meeting was taking place. He tapped the camera icon on his phone and, holding it to the window, snapped a series of shots in rapid succession. He might have taken more, but Leigh was already standing. 'Come on, let's get going.'

As they descended the stairs they were met with a warm breeze. Neil tried to stifle his apprehension by taking in their surroundings. The sun had lifted above the horizon to reveal the landscape just beyond the tarmac. It was intensely green with waist-high grass and shea trees in clumps, their crowns branching against a brooding sky. On either side of the runway, dirt roads cut away, exposing the russet-coloured soil. A crowned crane lifted from the grass; he heard its hooting call and watched until it disappeared from sight. He'd produced half-a-dozen documentaries in Africa, although he'd never had the opportunity to come to Uganda, this wet fertile country of thunderstorms and purple skies. As they walked towards the terminal the smell of the earth rose; it filled his nostrils and he absorbed it—a sickly-sweet scent, the kind he associated with other warm places where people with few means lived close to the ground and in tight proximity. Cow manure, sewage, burning rubbish. In the snow, you could bury those kinds of smells, but not here where everything flourished in the fetid air and seeped into every pore.

When he looked again at where he had seen the men on the tarmac, no one was there. The four-wheel drives had gone and the business jet stood motionless, like a giant insect drying its wings in the morning sun.

He left his phone in his pocket—the battery had run flat over the course of the long journey—and followed Leigh, who was moving through the crowd of people towards the battered carousel. They collected their luggage then located the driver they'd arranged to pick them up. A thin man with a gold-capped tooth, he stood with their names written on a torn piece of cardboard and a welcoming smile at the novelty, or perhaps predictability, of their white faces.

'Hello, sir, madam. How are you?'

'Fine, thank you,' Leigh replied. One side of the man's face drooped and she found herself trying to identify the cause—the possible result of a mild stroke, or Bell's palsy, maybe. 'How are you?' she asked as he wiped saliva from his chin.

'I am blessed,' the man said without irony. 'I am blessed. Are you UN? What NGO?'

'Neither,' Leigh said. 'We have come to see our daughter.' She told him they wanted to go to the rehabilitation centre. 'Afterwards we will go to the hotel. Will you wait?'

'Yes,' he said, 'I will wait.'

He drove badly, pointing out certain landmarks that apparently held interest for him: a new road that the Chinese were building, an authorised car dealer, a motley herd of longhorn cattle. At one point, they passed a cluster of shops where coffins were stacked against a breezeblock wall. An old man in a red T-shirt was working on one, cutting a window into the lid as if to offer the living a view of the dead, or perhaps the dead a view of the outside world.

On the Skype call Tessa had sounded detached, at times almost incoherent. 'I don't know what I mean,' she had said, and Leigh fretted that if Tessa didn't sleep, she might become even worse. What was going through her mind now? What state had she been in when Stephen found her? His brief text message had given nothing away; Stephen would avoid scrutiny at all costs. She reached for Neil's hand, and although he took it in his, he did not look at her.

When they reached the rehabilitation centre, a group of teenagers was playing a game, kicking a handcrafted football and shouting loudly to one another. Leigh asked them where Dominic Oculi was, and one of the girls pointed to a low run of concrete buildings along which Leigh recognised the cheerful mural of laughing, blue-armed children from a photograph Tessa had sent.

As they approached the building Tessa appeared, opening a door and stepping outside, almost as if she had stepped out of the painting itself. She was thin and gaunt and there were dark circles around her eyes and purple bruising along her jaw. She smiled and hugged them tenderly, then quickly withdrew.

'It's okay,' she said, as if echoing the parental voice they might use with her.

Leigh smiled anxiously. It was all she could do to stop herself from touching her daughter again—the lobe of her ear, the bruise along her jaw; she wanted to feel her forehead, check if she had a fever.

'How are you?' she asked.

'I'm okay, really.'

'You don't look it,' Leigh replied. Even as she spoke she noticed Tessa's broken fingernails and, standing so close to her, could smell her ketotic breath. Had she eaten anything? She wore no make-up and had gathered her hair into an untidy ponytail. Her face was drawn, no longer young-looking. You could not re-create that youthful look—the *before* look, Leigh thought; once it was lost, it was gone for good. She shook her head. 'Sweetheart, this is not entirely your fault, you couldn't see how it would play out.'

'Mum, please don't.'

'What?'

'I'm sorry. It's just—please don't look at me like that.'

'What do you mean? How am I looking at you?' Leigh took a breath and Tessa's eyes darted to where some of the returnees were watching them curiously.

'Perhaps we can get something to drink,' Leigh said. 'A glass of water?'

They went to the canteen and sat at a table where there was a stack of tin cups and a jug of water. Leigh rested her elbows on the sticky plastic cloth and felt the jetlag take hold. A wave of inertia spread over her; the heat was thick, and it was an effort to inhale the air. In the water jug, insect larvae squirmed—juvenile mosquitoes, or wrigglers, as she used to call them when she was young: vectors, disease carriers, as she knew them to be now. She studied Tessa's complexion and thought it yellow;

her eyes were dull, she looked as if she might have a vitamin deficiency—vitamin A, or perhaps malaria. But there were deeper concerns—the fact Leigh could barely admit to herself: her daughter had been to the centre's clinic, Dominic had told them, the word 'rape' said once. It lodged in her brain. She tried to out-think it and found herself worrying about pregnancy, STDs, HIV, the list went on. There would be at least a twelve-week wait before any seroconversion results. Leigh began to diagnose; she wanted a fixable problem for which, even here, among the limited medical supplies, she might find the right medication. Something achievable. She studied the dark bruises around Tessa's throat and another, she saw now, like a thumbprint in that soft place just behind her ear. Her eyes kept returning to them.

Neil began to fidget. 'We need to get you home,' he said in a voice that did not even sound like him. 'But first, why don't you come back to the hotel with us? It would be more comfortable there.'

Tessa looked at her father with his hooded eyes and three-day growth; her mother too, wearing a silk scarf that she had knotted around her neck. They were like two people in a boat at sea, and she suddenly felt a new burden that extended to her parents—of how what happened to her could not be contained behind the facade she was working so hard to maintain. She knew she couldn't tell them not to worry. Her father crossed his arms and it seemed like an awkward gesture.

'Dad, thanks. But for now, I think I should stay here.'

'Come on, Tess, you're in bad shape. Come to the hotel, then come home.'

'I can't,' Tessa said. 'I need to stay, at least until the inquiry.'

'Why? Even if an inquiry goes ahead, it's unlikely you'll be required to remain in Uganda. We can argue that it's not safe for you. You can return to Australia.'

Tessa shook her head then said, 'Maybe if I show you around you'll understand.' She stood.

They went across to the school and the small room that, at her suggestion, had become a library. When Tessa spoke, she seemed herself again. In many ways, her parents' arrival had made her stronger. They were a reminder of restraint, and she needed that now; if she was to stay in one piece she needed to have self-control. She noticed the way her father avoided speaking about his health and saw the tension in her mother's face—but somehow it helped.

Like Francis had said when they had waited for the rain to ease: you must forget what had happened. Forget what had been done. Be strong. The question was whether or not that was possible.

When they reached her room, Tessa pushed the colourful curtain divider aside and ushered them in. Leigh recognised the clothes that were crumpled on the floor and the camera she'd wrapped as a Christmas present only four months earlier. Such things gave her a sense of comfort, although the bottle of local gin and the tablets in a foil pack alarmed her. Was this how Tessa was coping? Xanax, Temazepam. That she had not even attempted to hide them concerned Leigh even more. She sat on the bed, making room for Tessa to sit beside her. It was a single bed with a mosquito net above it and a slumped mattress that sagged with their weight. There were two pillows.

One was without a covering, yellowed and lumpy, the other encased in a pillowslip with a faded Disney print. An ironic Western legacy that Tessa might have dryly commented on at any other time.

Leigh touched her daughter's arm and felt Tessa flinch. An awkward silence followed and the shell of brightness Tessa presented threatened to crack. There was a strange hesitation in her manner that suggested there was something else she wanted to tell them.

Reaching down, she scratched the scabby insect bite on her ankle.

'You shouldn't do that,' Leigh said in her doctor's voice. 'It'll get infected.'

Tessa brought her hand back to her lap. She didn't say it was the hand that had held the gun or that it still burnt. She didn't say what had happened exactly or that Francis was right when he said, *You find a place to leave—you go out of your body. Your brain opens a door and you go through it*. In this way, you learn how to kill.

She tried for normality. 'You've come all this way,' she said. 'And now you see how badly I've fucked up.' She took in a breath and shook her head at her own statement—it was bizarre that, after everything, she was still seeking her parents' approval. She still wanted that. Wanted them. Wanted to confess.

'Tess,' Neil said, 'you were trying to do something that matters.'

'No, Dad. I've done nothing anyone can be proud of.' And suddenly there was a need to correct them. She was accountable. She had failed them, failed herself.

'I want to know what you think is worse,' she said.

Leigh looked at her. 'What do you mean?'

'I mean as a crime against another person . . .' Tessa reached back and gathered her ponytail, then brought it over her shoulder and ran her hand down it with a taut wringing action. 'Do you think it's worse to rape or to murder?' she asked.

Neil started to speak, but Leigh raised her hand, feeling some of her old frustration at Tessa's tunnel vision. 'Tess, darling, you were defending yourself.'

'Was I?' Tessa replied. She plucked at the fabric of her trousers. 'I murdered someone.'

'You killed someone in self-defence—that isn't murder,' Neil countered. 'A murder is deliberate, it requires premeditation.'

Tessa shook her head.

Neil looked astonished. 'Tess, he deserved it.'

'Did he?'

Her parents were staring at her now, clearly confused. She could sense their alarm, but it only added to her shame. She looked back at them, although she wished she could turn away.

'Don't do this to yourself,' her father said. He laid his hand on her shoulder and for a moment a rush of gratitude filled her; here was the reassurance she needed. But in the next instant the weight of his hand seemed unbearable.

Tessa dug her fingernails into her palms. 'Murder is not the same as other crimes,' she said. 'If you steal you can give it back. If you're raped . . .' She hesitated. 'If you're raped, the rapist can ask for forgiveness. Neither is possible with murder.'

Neil shook his head. 'Come on, Tess. This doesn't help.'

Tessa looked at him. His grey eyes held her. 'You're right,' she replied. 'This doesn't help. I'm sorry, and this is not a family celebration. Neither of your children—' She stopped there.

'What?' Neil asked. 'What were you going to say?' He saw the way Tessa had begun to rub the knuckles on her right hand, repeatedly pressing her thumb over them until they blanched a whitish blue. 'You and Stephen have gone through a great deal—'

'Stephen—' Tessa interrupted, then stopped again.

'What?' Neil demanded. 'What about Stephen?' He was alert now, as if a warning bell had sounded. He could see how Tessa shifted uneasily, and there was something else, a flicker in her eyes that suggested there was a loose thread at the edge of her, a thread which, if pulled, might unravel her completely. She began to scratch the bites on her neck and arms. Some started to bleed again.

'Tess?' Leigh whispered. 'If there's something else we should know, then maybe you should tell us.'

Outside the generator cut out and Leigh could hear a group of students chanting the times tables. She caught the rhythm of their voices—the singsong mathematical pattern that reminded her of nuns and blackboard rulers a lifetime ago.

She watched Tessa nod her head as if to make some private pact with herself. Tessa's lips were bloodless and when she spoke her voice sounded hollow. 'Stephen's staying in Gulu,' Tessa said. 'You need to speak to him before he leaves.'

'What about?' Neil asked.

Leigh took Tessa's hand, and Tessa squeezed it in response, then softened her grip before saying, 'You need to ask him.'

31

The Acholi Inn had high ceilings and cool corridors. It had been built by the British as a luxury guesthouse in the 1930s and was the only three-storeyed building in the area. Usually frequented by government officials and NGO workers because of its well-stocked bar and spacious dining room, it required armed security guards and a manned gatehouse. An established garden surrounded the pool. Otherwise the rooms were small and run-down.

At the reception desk, Neil signed his name and handed over their passports together with his credit card. The receptionist, an impassive man with a resigned manner, gave him the room keys and pointed them in the direction they should go.

As they were gathering their luggage in the lobby they saw Matt Reba, who appeared to be waiting for them. Blond-haired, thick-necked and robust, Reba greeted them awkwardly then drove his hands into his pockets and lifted his chin in the direction of the open door. 'Stephen's out there by the pool,' he said.

Neil nodded. The light through the doorway was soft, almost lime-coloured. He looked back at Matt Reba.

'You've seen Tessa?' Reba asked.

'Yes. She told us you came with Stephen to find her.' Neil hesitated. 'How long are you staying in Gulu for?'

'We fly out in the morning,' Reba replied. 'Or as soon as we get clearance.'

'Matt,' Leigh said, stepping forward and unwinding her scarf. Her face felt hot, her smile brittle. She could still picture the bruises on Tessa's neck and the way she had twisted her hair, wringing it in her hands as she brought it over her shoulder. That worried her; it was such a small detail, but it worried her—added to the worry. Tessa's experience ran through her and now it was as though her own nerve endings were exposed. 'You helped Steve to get her out, right? We want to thank you—it must've been a pretty awful ordeal.'

Reba rocked from foot to foot. 'Yeah, well, Stephen's a hard man to say no to. I drove, that's all.' He laughed uneasily, and Leigh felt that he was on the verge of saying something more, but had checked himself. She studied him dubiously as he stood there in his safari-style shirt and hiking boots, privy to so much they didn't know about either of their children. He'd grown up to look a lot like his father, she thought, recalling Derek Reba, who'd travelled to Melbourne from Cape Town for the school valedictory. Loud and opinionated. The only surprise was that he could be funny—until, too drunk, he wasn't. A month later, he died from a brain haemorrhage, leaving his entire business to eighteen-year-old Matt. His obituary, she remembered, read like a lie.

'Can I talk with you?' Reba asked. He was looking at Neil now, not her.

'What about?' Neil asked, and straightened.

But Reba's phone began to ring and, distracted, he took it out of his pocket and said over the ringtone, 'I'll catch you before I go. But for now, you'll have to excuse me—I need to answer this.'

In their room, Neil put their bags on the battered Queen Anne bed and plugged his phone into the charger. He felt it vibrate and saw the battery icon come to life again as he placed it on the bedside table. He turned and opened the curtains to look out at the pool.

'Is that Stephen down there?' Leigh asked, walking across the room to stand beside him.

Neil nodded and pointed to a lounge chair by the pool, and for a long moment they observed their son from their unseen vantage point.

'We should go down and speak to him,' Leigh said.

'You go,' Neil said, rubbing his hand across his chin. 'I need to check something first.'

Leigh hesitated. She was about to object, to say that they should go together—present a united front—but she decided not to press the issue. She wanted to talk to Stephen by herself, anyway.

Outside the heat was muggy. Stephen sat by the pool with a half-empty glass in his hand. His eyes were closed. His hair was wet and his tanned body glistened after swimming. Leigh was struck by how fit he looked. He was more toned now than he had been in Melbourne. Stronger. Leaner. He wore a pair of blue board shorts, and when he opened his eyes and smiled Leigh saw that his teeth were very white—so white that his sclera looked cloudy. He lifted his glass as if to salute her. 'Do you want one?' he asked. 'The mojitos here aren't bad.' Leigh shook her head. Around his wrist he wore a plaited leather cuff along with an expensive-looking watch. There were a few nasty scratches on his arms and insect bites that were slightly infected, although somehow they made him appear more adventurous than injured. He was good-looking and he knew it, Leigh thought, knew how to cultivate it in an easy-going roughish way. He sat forward and smiled at her. He didn't get up. No hug, although an intense energy radiated from him.

Leigh sat on the chair beside him and when the drinks waiter came up to them she waved her hand in a gesture of refusal. Stephen lifted his forefinger. 'The same again,' he said, and nodded at his glass.

'We've been to see Tessa at the centre,' Leigh began. 'She seems . . .' But she couldn't find the words. 'I don't know; she's in shock. After all that's happened, God, who wouldn't be? Although I can't help thinking there's something else. She's ashamed, she judges herself for what happened, and—I don't know, maybe there's something she can't tell us.'

In addition to the security guards, there were a couple of dogs—mangy tan-coloured mongrels with heavy collars that trotted around the boundary with a proprietary air. Stephen watched one of them stop and sniff at something in the flower-bed then said, 'I reckon you should leave her be.'

Leigh gave him a searching look. 'What do you mean?' she asked.

'Let it rest, Mum.'

'No, Steve, this isn't something I can just stop worrying about. I have to know what happened. I'm her mother. How else can I help her if she won't tell me herself?'

Stephen drained his glass then set it on the table beside him. Slowly he flexed his neck from one side to the other then made a face that suggested he didn't know what she was talking about—but there was, Leigh knew, something more, some price. Despite the humid air, she felt a cold chill run through her. 'I need to know what you know,' she said. Her voice was insistent, almost accusatory, and she saw a flicker of irritation cross Stephen's face.

'Why?' he asked. 'What good do you think it will do?'

He watched the dog begin to dig in the flowerbed and felt his mother's eyes on him. Yes, she would want to know. She would ask questions. She was good at that. He looked at her, then glanced down at her feet. She was wearing a pair of sandals and her toenails were painted red. He saw that her second toe was slightly longer than her big toe. No surprise that his feet were shaped like hers—the same DNA; there was no getting away from biology, even if he wished to. Nor could he escape their history; they were like the opposing sides who could be counted on to make each other feel like shit.

He lifted his empty glass and, pushing the mint aside with the straw, stirred the ice. 'All right. So, you heard she was raped?'

'Yes,' Leigh replied.

'One of their so-called leaders. Some kind of priest.'

Leigh nodded.

'And you know Tessa shot him?'

'Yes.'

'So that's it, she pulled the trigger—not just once, but until there were no bullets left. Even after she splattered his brains across the floor she kept shooting. I had to pull her away so we could get the fuck out of there. And you know what? It was easy for her, second nature, that's why she's acting so weird.'

There was a self-assured look on Stephen's face. Leigh felt hot. She lifted the shirt she wore away from her throat. 'No. You're wrong. That's not how she is.'

'Of course, you would say that. Because that's how *I* am, right?'

'Jesus, Stephen! What is it with you?'

'What is it with me? Do you think Tessa is incapable of doing anything wrong? That she is incapable of violence?'

Leigh eyed him with disdain.

'What?' he said in a mocking voice. 'You asked me to go after her, you said you would accept the consequences. And I went—not just because of Tessa. I went because of you. I risked all kinds of shit, because you asked me to.'

The waiter returned with Stephen's follow-on drink and a bowl of something fried. After he left, Stephen popped one of the delicacies into his mouth, chewed, swallowed and then wiped his lips with the back of his hand.

'Grasshoppers,' he explained. 'I've seen the guards catch them at night. They use a trap made from a piece of yellow plastic and bait it with molasses. It's supposed to attract them.' He wiped his mouth. 'Although people around here think that the grasshoppers get lured into the trap because of the smell of their dead relatives—an instinct that's not limited to insects, wouldn't you say?'

Furious, Leigh was about to respond, but before she could Stephen got up and dived into the pool. One moment he was there, the next he was gone, leaving hardly a ripple behind him.

Back in their room Neil sat on the end of the bed. Hunched forward, he was tapping his mouth with his fist. In the other hand, he held his phone.

'Why didn't you come down and speak to Stephen?' Leigh asked, closing the door behind her. 'I waited for you, but . . .' She didn't finish. She came and sat on the bed beside him. 'What's wrong?' she asked cautiously. 'Neil? What have you been doing up here?'

Neil passed her his phone. 'It's him, isn't it?' he said.

Taking the phone, Leigh began to scroll through the photographs. They had been taken from the window of the plane when they landed that morning. She didn't know what he was talking about, but when she used the touchscreen to enlarge one of the images it was as if she'd received an electric shock. She lifted her finger away then allowed herself to take in the details. The pale pink shirt was the same as the one on the back of Stephen's chair by the pool, and the leather cuff and watch were recognisable on his tanned wrist, but it was the distinctive way he stood with his shoulders squared that told her it was him—the stance from goals kicked or arguments won, a confidence that clearly identified him.

She glanced back at Neil and saw the lines on his forehead deepen. His eyes burnt cold.

'Why would he do something like this?' she said.

Neil stood up. 'For fuck's sake, who knows why?' he exploded. 'The money, to get Tessa out—because he could, because he likes to live on the edge. Or maybe it's because he thinks he get can away with it. Any number of explanations.'

Leigh closed her eyes. The image on Neil's phone detonated in her head—Stephen presiding over a cache of semi-automatic rifles—and the unwanted, awful epiphany came to her that this was their son. He could do this.

'So, he's made some kind of a deal?' she said.

'It's more than that,' Neil replied. 'I've just spoken to Matt.' Neil glared at the phone that Leigh still held in her hand. 'Stephen's a middleman, an arms dealer. This is not a one-off, it's the kind of thing he does. It's who he is.'

Now he understood what Thompson had been hinting at when he said Stephen had been trading outside of the business and was in over his head—it made sense, didn't it? They sold guns for sport; what was to stop them from moving to contraband? The policing was lax, the money astonishing. Neil's heart thumped. Jesus, it was like watching his son drive drunk and get away with it.

'No,' Leigh whispered to Neil, and looking past him, she thought she saw something move—a shadow, a nightmare image, as the carefree sound of people splashing in the pool outside filtered into their hotel room. Laughter across water and the tinny sound of pop music contrasting with the terror inside her head.

32

Stephen lay on the hard mattress and looked at the ceiling fan. His skin still felt cool and had a comforting chlorine smell after swimming. He had dressed again—except for his socks and boots, which lay on the jute rug beside the bed—and now he let his head sink into the pillow.

In the rebel camp, he'd felt the adrenaline kick in at being able to convince the thuggish, if clownishly dressed, colonel of what he could offer. 'Ah, yes . . .' Kolo had said once he understood what Stephen meant. He made a shooting gesture with his hand. 'What have you got?'

'AK-47s, Ares, grenades, good stock.'

'And how can I trust you to deliver them?'

It was pretty clear, though, that Kolo had already taken the bait. The deal was arranged within a few minutes, collection to be organised with sympathisers across the border. Good as done, except that Stephen heard Tessa's scream and broke away to find her. And now, because the priest was dead, they had demanded that he pay out more.

Earlier that morning he and Reba had driven to Gulu airport, where Stephen handed his passport to a security guard, a thin man with hollow cheeks who opened it to see a wad of shillings slipped between the cover and the flyleaf. Without comment the guard took the money and let them pass through the gate. Reba parked the hotel courtesy jeep next to the Gulfstream and turned off the headlights. It was still dark. Stars studded the sky, yet along the horizon the first light cast a luminous glow and a pink line steadily appeared along the black surface of the land as though it was neon-lit. There were groundsmen about and, above the engine noises, Stephen could hear their voices. On the runway, a small domestic carrier had just landed; he smelt jet-fuel fumes on the updraft. He would have preferred to meet when there was no one else about, but on second thoughts it was probably good to have a few other people around—no isolated clearing here. Somehow it balanced out the risks; if they were out in the open an ambush was less likely.

He unlocked the Gulfstream's hold and began to make a quick inventory of the cargo. It was all there, loaded and secured, just as he'd arranged it before leaving Cape Town. He counted the wooden crates, then randomly opened two or three of the lids to reassure himself. Good—perfect, in fact—packed in like oily sardines, gleaming and brand new from leaky stockpiles, the tail end of a complex supply trail that by now would be virtually impossible to trace.

A covered jeep drove up and stopped beside them. The driver cut the engine and, leaving the headlights on full beam, got out.

In the glare it was hard to tell how many other men were in

the jeep; four, possibly five. The driver, who introduced himself as Kolo's brother, was a large thick-lipped man in army trousers and a sleeveless jacket. In one hand, he carried a satellite phone. 'You've got the consignment you promised?' he asked.

Stephen gave a curt nod.

The man waved in the direction of another open crate, the lid of which had just been jimmied off by Matt. 'What good are these?' he demanded when he saw the AK-47s. 'This is the crap you offer? This is old shit.'

'Old, maybe,' Stephen replied. 'But unused. You ought to be pleased—it's war surplus, stock left over from Bosnia and Afghanistan. Good quality. Everyone knows the Russians build them to last.'

'You have American?'

'Yes, I have American. Ares if you want, but they'll cost more.'

'I do not need to pay more; I have instructions,' he replied, and lifted the hand in which he held the satellite phone. 'It seems you have violated the agreement.'

'There was no violation.'

'My brother said no killing.'

'No killing, that's a good joke—it's your lot who do the killing.' Stephen smiled and Kolo's brother laughed, then stopped abruptly and clenched his jaw so that the muscles in his face worked as he ground his teeth. 'I would be careful if I were you. Right now you are not in a position to make such remarks.'

Another truck pulled up and half-a-dozen men got out, forming a semicircle around them. *Mapogos*, Stephen thought. Rogue lions.

'Okay, so now you show me the Ares.'

Stephen looked at Reba, who shifted uneasily then pulled out another crate, and together they dragged the case forward and opened the latches.

'You will like these,' Stephen said. 'The serial numbers have been ground off.'

'I do not care about serial numbers,' Kolo's brother replied. 'Real soldiers do not think of such things. Tell me, how many do you have?'

'Twenty, with ammunition. But there are Uzis too, take your pick.'

'I will take what we agreed upon, plus the Ares.' Picking up the slick Ares Shrike, he ran his fingertips along the hand-guard. 'Ah yes.' He grinned. 'In the golden West, you have machine guns named after war gods and birds of prey. You have everything. You are excessive. Excessive with your habits, so you are excessive with your guns. But you understand that these are not enough. You owe us more.'

'You'll get it,' Stephen had said brusquely. 'Tell your brother he will get what he wants.'

Kolo's brother smiled. 'What I will tell him is that you can definitely improve your odds.'

In minutes they'd unloaded the cargo, leaving the hold like a shucked oyster. Stephen watched their battered four-wheel drives leave. By then, the sun had already crept above the tree line, and across the tarmac passengers were disembarking from the domestic carrier in a haphazard line.

He glanced at them. It felt like a game, standing next to the sleek Gulfstream jet in the early morning, having just traded more than he bargained for; a game of chance, except the stakes were real.

'You're familiar with the markets?' Frost had asked him in the bar that night in Cape Town.

'You mean your distribution channels?'

Frost nodded. 'Spot the right deal and you might get yourself a promotion. Maybe a chance to cut out some of the other middlemen.' He smiled. 'Let's see how you go.'

Now, following this morning's handover on the tarmac, it was clear he would need to up the supply to meet the rebels' new demands, meaning he'd have to cut a better deal with Frost's suppliers too, and that would cost him big time.

Stephen wondered where Reba was; they would need to clear out of here. Back at the hotel where they'd had breakfast in the dining room, he listened to Reba complaining over a second or third cup of the awful brewed coffee. 'What do you mean, "Money's money?" Shit, Steve, this isn't the first time you've got us out of our depth.'

'Yeah, right—poor you.'

'You saw that village, the stinking carcass in the campfire; what makes you think you'll be treated any differently?'

'We got out. Now you know why—it costs.'

'Great, well maybe you can pick up the tab for me.'

Stephen was surprised; he hadn't expected Reba to brood.

'Jesus,' Reba continued. 'I can't believe we're doing business with these people.'

'Why?' Stephen asked. 'Who did you think we were doing business with? The Tooth Fairy?'

Reba's face clouded. 'I tell you, Steve, what you do is like thumping your opponent behind the play—you might think you're going to get away with it, but in the end, you'll always find there's someone on the sidelines who's watching you.'

Stephen wanted to laugh or make some quip, but none came to him. Normally he was able to second-guess how people were going to react, but every now and then someone would surprise him and pull some unexpected shit, like Reba becoming philosophical or Tess blowing the preacher's brains out. Six rounds straight into his face.

What he had to do now was think first, then act. He would have to contact his bank in Cape Town and move some money to make up the shortfall. Reba's payment could wait. Cherie's too. Despite her protests and threats of lawyers—whom he would need to stymie—she would have to wait the longest.

He could do with a backup plan though. He sat up and poured himself a shot from the bottle of Scotch on the bedside table. It slid down the back of his throat and, as he put his glass down, his phone buzzed with a text message from his father. Jesus, what now?

33

Neil waited at a small table on the second-floor balcony. The sky was milky and streaked with purple clouds; it would be dark soon, although the heat had not yet gone from the day. Sweat dampened his collar, and it seemed the fruit hanging from the trees in the garden continued to ripen in the quickening dusk. Insects hovered in the warm air while overhead he heard bats wheep.

When Stephen approached he was still putting together what information he had—wondering how much of it was true, how much was pure speculation—and thinking about what he needed to do . . . what he should have done a long time ago, in fact. Neil watched the confident way his son moved, the definite footfall as his heavy hiking boots struck the tiled floor, and he noticed the way the muscles in Stephen's arms flexed as he placed a bottle of Scotch and two whisky glasses on the table in front of them.

'Want one?' Stephen said, and before Neil could answer, he poured a glass for himself and another for his father then handed it to him. 'So, you wanted to talk?'

'Yes,' Neil declared firmly, placing the glass to one side. 'There are a lot of things I want to talk to you about. Things I should have spoken to you about months ago when I planned to visit you in Cape Town.'

'But you didn't.'

'No. I didn't.'

Stephen rolled his shoulders then sat down. He looked striking. His sandy hair was well cut, and he wore an expensive chambray shirt with the sleeves rolled up. His watch, a heavy Rolex, had two or three smaller dials on the face.

Neil pressed his lips together. 'Anyway, I'm here now. Look, Steve, you found Tess and got her out of there, although she's . . .' He hesitated, then said, 'I just wish I'd got here sooner.'

'Why?' Stephen replied. 'Tessa's safe now, so there's no need for you to be a hero. Besides, Dad, you weren't up to it, remember?' He smiled, then leant across the table and patted Neil on the shoulder.

Neil flinched as Stephen gave him a small, patronising squeeze. Shrugging off his son's hand, he said, 'Stephen, listen to me, I want to get something straight: you helped Tessa escape and I'm grateful for that—'

'But?' Stephen interrupted.

'But now I want some honest answers.' He heard the hostile tone in his voice and tried to tamp it down. It sounded like such an insistent, old-fashioned thing to demand, and for a second, he saw his own father bang his fist on the dinner table. The inevitable violence of his upbringing. Tempers unchecked. Heavy Irish drinkers.

'I know what it is you do,' Neil said, still trying to control himself. 'I know what your business is here.'

'Yeah?' Stephen replied with dry sarcasm. 'And what's that?'

Reedy music came from somewhere and, above it, a faint call to prayer. So many fucking religions, Stephen thought. Someone was shouting in the street. *Boda-bodas* tooted. Stephen heard his father, but he was still thinking about Kolo's so-called brother. He would have to watch his back and, at the same time, sweeten the deal. No surprise that, given he hadn't delivered what they'd demanded, there might be trouble. Here, where reprisals were the norm, it was like a Molotov cocktail: the slightest spark and everything could burst into flames. He didn't have time to talk to his father. He needed to leave, and then, after he got back to Cape Town, he'd need to lay low for a while, maybe even spend a few weeks in the US or, better still, go to Asia, and work from there.

'Did you hear me?' Neil said. 'I saw you at the airport.'

For a brief moment, Stephen felt a flicker of alarm. 'So what?' he said. 'You see me at the airport with a couple of thugs and you think you've got a whole story figured out?'

Neil moved his glass further aside. 'Well, tell me how it is then. Fill me in. What have I missed?'

'You want answers?'

'I want the truth!' And Neil's fist did strike the table, causing it to shake.

Stephen sat back and folded his arms. 'Really?' He smiled. '*You* want the truth? I don't think that's ever been what you wanted. You're a filmmaker, remember. No such thing as the truth.'

Neil's heart pounded. He had met with Matt Reba in the downstairs bar. The South African's boyish face had been flushed and his accent heavy as he said, 'I'm telling you, man, Steve thinks he can do anything. He doesn't care what the rules are. When you're with him, he says what you want to hear. The moment you leave the room, he's someone else.' And all at once it fell into place with startling clarity. Who would stop Stephen? Who would tell his son 'no'? The violent tingling that began in Neil's heart and in his head ran down his spine. What, in fact, could he make his son do? No matter what course of action he took, he might not be able to turn things around or stop Stephen from doing whatever he wanted. Yet he had to. He must. If there had been one guiding principle in the way he parented, it was that he would not father as he had been fathered. But all he could think of now was how to cut Stephen down—expose him, then shame him into a confession. He wanted an admission from him. Justice after that—and, yes, punishment.

Stephen sculled his drink.

'Answer me,' Neil repeated. 'What is it you do? I want to hear you say it, these deals you make—for fuck's sake, you have the freedom to choose, and you choose to be a criminal. You destroy people's lives. You exploit them for your own gain.'

Stephen refilled his glass. 'It's free enterprise,' he said dismissively. 'Besides, if not for what I do, Tessa would still be in that shithole.'

'For Christ's sake, Stephen, what the hell's wrong with you?'

'Nothing's wrong with me. I'm a problem solver. I'm from the West, remember—here to help.'

'Haven't you had enough to drink?'

'Ah, so that's the issue now.'

'Listen, Steve, don't imagine you can make light of this. What you're caught up in isn't on the periphery of some distasteful little business, it's the dirt trade of the world. What the hell makes you think it's okay, or that you're in any way justified?'

Stephen raised his eyebrows. 'Who's talking about whether it's justified? I offer a means of protection. Haven't you noticed? In the markets around here they sell guns and knives alongside children's toys and Omo washing powder.'

'You're exaggerating.'

'Am I?' Stephen turned his glass in a circle in front of him, then lifted it up and took another swig. The hair on his arm was sun-bleached but Neil focused on his hands, the shapely knuckles, the square nails. A smart kid, a greedy man.

The air smelt rank. Slightly rotting flowers lay on the grass. A groundsman was raking them in the near-dark while elsewhere the hotel staff went about their evening routines. Women walked past with folded towels balanced on their heads while, by the pool, glasses clinked and people dived into the blue-lit water.

'When wolves are successful,' Neil said, his voice becoming thick with anger, 'they do not eat in moderation. They are extreme, often devouring more than they need; a single animal can consume up to a fifth of its own body weight in one go. It's instinct—to balance out the lean times when their resources are scarce, but *you*, your greed—'

'My greed,' Stephen scoffed then sat back. 'It's not *my* greed. It's just the way the world works.' He waved his hand in the air carelessly, then sat forward again. 'But you know what? As fucked and unfair as that might be, the truth is it's consistently fucked and unfair.'

'Wait a minute, Steve . . .'

'No, you wait. Do you really think there'll ever be peace on Earth? Look at the history books, read the news. This isn't one of your documentaries, some easy-viewing TV show with voice-overs and tribal music that can be confined to a forty-five-minute time slot. Shit, Dad, what do you think goes on?'

Neil tried to cut in again, but Stephen held up his hand. 'Let's start with this place, the Acholi Inn. It's owned by a top Ugandan general who fills his rooms with some of the worst of the rebels who have defected. At an exorbitant rate, he promises them, and us, a security his military can't promise the Ugandans—those people, may I remind you, who are actually screwed over by this conflict. So don't sit there and think your choices are all that innocent. What I see is what most people see, but they don't admit it because it's easier not to give a shit. Besides what I do would continue to be done whether I was here or not. Maybe you think you know what's going on, but let me tell you, the reality is worse every time.'

Neil raised his hands and let them fall heavily into his lap. 'Jesus, Stephen, listen to yourself! What about the consequences of what you do? I'm telling you, you have to stop. *Now*. Do you hear me?'

Stephen jiggled his knee and looked away as if the conversation bored him.

'Christ Almighty!' Neil shouted. 'You think you're so smart, and yet what have you done with your life? Is this what you make of the opportunities you've been given? You come here, to this amazing place, and all you do is destroy what you find.'

Stephen turned back to face him, his expression almost smug. 'Why don't you save your platitudes for someone else?' he said, then pouting in mock sympathy, he added, 'Save them for Tessa, who's always wanting to do the right thing by you, and is now a complete mess.'

What Neil felt then went to another level, beyond fury, beyond reason, as if something had unleashed itself in him. He leapt to his feet—knocking the table over—drew back his fist and punched Stephen in the face. It hit with the entire force of his rage and, in that instant, it was as if all his disappointment and frustration had found a single outlet. His whole body radiated violence which, once released, continued to strike with a savagery he could not contain. He heard the cartilage in Stephen's nose smash—felt it give way as if it were plasticine, then drew back and once again aimed for Stephen's upper jaw, knowing in that instant the violence of what he might do was real. As Stephen's head jolted backwards he understood that he could break his son's neck.

'Neil!'

Leigh's voice was loud and insistent, and when he heard it again, he wanted to ignore it, and yet part of him was grateful to her for saving him from himself. He felt her hand grip his arm.

'Neil! *Stop!*'

He sat down and brought his bloodied fist close to his chest. For a moment the pain beneath his ribcage threatened to overtake him. His heart contracted, and he feared he might black out again. He leant back and let his head rest against the wall.

Stephen was still staggering from the blow, his face bloodied.

'Jeez,' he snorted. 'Who do you think you are? A cop?'

Leigh moved towards him, but Stephen held up his hands to prevent her from coming any closer. He looked disoriented, and shocked, as if he could hardly believe what had happened. He wiped the blood from his nose with the hem of his shirt and swayed for a moment. Then he steadied himself and, picking up his tumbler of whisky, raised it to his parents. 'If you had a choice between leaving Tessa for dead or doing what I did, what would you do?' he asked flatly. 'What would either of you do?' He looked from one parent to the other. 'Well, what?'

Neil's face was red. 'Not what you have done,' he said.

Stephen shook his head. 'How do you know that? Huh? The truth is neither of you know, and you never will, because I saved you the trouble.'

Neil looked at his son's bleeding mouth. His fist smarted. If he was to make any difference at all, then he needed to act now. 'You're wrong,' he said in a low voice. 'And don't think for a minute I won't stop you. This isn't something you did for your sister. Your sordid deals: the contraband you're trafficking. There are photographs—'

'Photographs,' Stephen repeated dismissively.

'Yes, photographs, taken at Gulu airport. Photographs which I can use to incriminate you.'

'Fine, but what do you think will happen to Tessa if I'm implicated? Do you think she's immune? Do you think they won't come looking for her if what I have promised them fails to materialise?'

'You're bluffing.'

'I don't think so.' And picking up the bottle of Scotch, he walked away.

Neil turned to Leigh, who was still looking towards the faint light on the stairs where Stephen had gone. Finally, she faced him, her expression incredulous, as if he were someone she had never met before.

He shook his head. 'I'm sorry,' he said. And then, after a time, 'If you hadn't stopped me, I would've killed him. I wanted to.'

34

The next morning they sat at a breakfast table in the shaded courtyard, drinking orange juice and eating scrambled eggs. They might have been in a cafe in Melbourne if not for the dread they both felt. The waitress wore a magenta hairpiece that looked like a streak of fluorescent paint in her crinkly black hair. She served them extra toast, and when she left their table Leigh leant forward and put her hand on Neil's arm. 'What are we going to do?' she repeated. Her eyelids felt gritty, her mouth pinched. She had been awake since 3 am going over the violence of the night before, her anxiety escalating. She pictured Stephen by the pool—the silver droplets of water on his tanned skin and his half-smirk, later bloodied by Neil's fist. She believed the discovery of Stephen's dealings had been the tipping point for Neil, defaulting him back to his own dubious upbringing—and shockingly, it now seemed to her, a loss of control in order to gain control. And there was Tessa too, troubled and agitated, her sleep-deprived eyes strangely lit and flicking away as she tried to avoid the scrutiny she and

Neil had put her under; her stiff shoulders and the purple bruising on her neck where a dark undertone of blood had pooled beneath her skin. The whole family mess, where no one could pretend that violence was something they would not participate in. How could they right what was wrong? How could they restrain Stephen, or persuade Tessa to return home?

Neil stared at the garden. 'Tessa will stay on—you know that, don't you? At least for the time being.' Then, as if he was working up to what he really wanted to say, he glanced at Leigh and added, 'The inquest into the shooting will fold, but Tessa will stay here. She will feel she cannot leave until she is ready. Until the boy, Francis, is settled. It is who she is. The best thing we can do is support her.'

At first, he had refused to let Leigh bandage his hand. He had done it himself and made a bad job of it, rejecting the idea of an icepack and only giving in when Leigh said she was almost certain he had broken his middle finger; then, reluctantly, he let her strap it for him. He struggled to cut his toast now, then gave up and lifted the whole piece to his mouth, but before he could take a bite he put it down again.

'But Stephen . . .' he said in a low furious voice.

'What about Stephen?' Leigh replied. A knot tightened in the base of her stomach, and as she spoke a shot of bile rose in her throat. Shame and protectiveness, and again the recollection of Neil's rage erupting into physical violence. Fear too, that his fury was not yet spent. 'Be careful,' she said softly. Warned.

When the girl came back, Leigh watched her pour coffee into two large ceramic mugs. Milky and lukewarm, it smelt like nutmeg, and when she took a mouthful she thought it tasted like a child's drink, something to induce sleep rather than wakefulness. Leigh set her mug down on the side plate with a clatter. There were remembered conversations, arguments, omissions—even when Stephen was at school there were problems. He was forever getting into trouble, but somehow he always managed to get out of it. Usually someone else, whether from goodwill or through Stephen's coercion, helped him out; *they* helped him out—she and Neil made excuses, paid fines, looked for solutions. But this was not some high school prank gone wrong—it was a nightmare from which they could not wake.

Leigh put her knife and fork together and pushed aside her uneaten breakfast. 'All right,' she said. 'We give Tessa our full support. We respect her wishes and allow her to work things out for herself. I can do that. Even if we go back to Melbourne, I can offer her that from a distance, and perhaps you're right, with time she'll be okay. But Stephen? Neil, what are you thinking? How the hell do we stop him from being a part of this appalling business if he refuses to give it up?'

She watched Neil tap his coffee mug and waited for him to speak again.

Finally, he looked up, but he didn't say anything.

She continued, 'When I checked at reception half an hour ago, they told me Stephen and Matt had already left. They've gone.'

'I know!' Neil replied with renewed frustration, thumping his bandaged fist on the table as though he had forgotten his injured hand. The force rattled the plates and they both watched as blood slowly began to ooze through the dressing.

Leigh inhaled then reached across and gently put her hand on his arm. 'Don't,' she said, and tears filled her eyes. 'Look, I know you want to try to repair this. I do too.' And she gave him an awful smile that suggested they were both complicit. 'We make a pact as parents to be responsible and then we see the accommodations people like us make, the thousands of tiny adjustments where we give in or simply give up, and suddenly we realise our children have gone too far.'

'And now?' Neil asked.

'Now, we must face something that feels beyond us.'

Neil held his smarting hand. In a way, he was glad of the pain; it kept him alert and he needed to be awake now. If this were a moral tale he would dive into the depths of the ocean or descend into the crater of an active volcano to save his son, but it was not a moral tale—his son was not moral. And he himself, as Stephen reminded him, was no hero. No Hercules subduing the three-headed Cerberus.

It shamed him now to recall a memory of Stephen at about twelve years old, stealing money from his desk. He'd seen him open the drawer; seen not just his stealth but a look of—what? Intoxication? Pleasure in the forbidden act? Later, Stephen didn't even seem to care that he had been caught. Rather, he lied and continued to lie in the face of any accusation. Would it have made any difference if they had done things differently? If they'd punished Stephen more severely, held him accountable, rather than opting for lenience—the liberal tolerance that he believed was a better, more modern parenting style than he had known when he was growing up? Perhaps it would have; perhaps everything comes down to one indulgence too many. His heart pounded in his ears, guilt merged with terror, for there had been other times too, when he knew what Stephen was capable of: the incident with his Gerber Gator fishing knife, and other allegations dropped for lack of evidence, a gambling debt he'd covered for him, or the time he had known him to walk away from a parked car he'd sideswiped—all small enough acts and, at the time, Neil had thought them pretty harmless. But he'd had the opportunity then, hadn't he? It had been like looking into a crystal ball—a match struck in a darkened room where he'd been given a glimpse into what the future might hold, each incident a foreshadowing which he might have chosen to address, and yet what had he done but allow Stephen free rein? By omission he had become the absentee father who relied on school fees to cover ethics and on team sports to instil fairness.

Leigh touched the bandage on his hand. The bleeding appeared to have stopped, although she told him she wanted to get some more antiseptic and change the dressing. 'But first,' she said, 'we have to agree about Stephen. What's the best thing to do? Do we get him put on an international watch list? Should we report him to the police, the army?'

The girl with the magenta hairpiece came back and took their plates away. When she had gone, Leigh's voice was ragged. 'God, darling, you look awful, are you okay? Have you had more chest pain?' She shot him a look he didn't quite catch.

'I'm okay,' he replied. 'My heart's fine.'

'Then what is it? Are you holding something back?'

What could he say? That he didn't regret hitting Stephen, that there had been currency in it—Stephen's surprise, even if it was short-lived.

Leigh rested her elbows on the table and put her head in her hands. There was grey hair under the blonde. He remembered when it had been thick and long, and she used to dry it in the sun. He wanted to touch her and say that they would get through this, but he kept quiet. It was not that she would not understand; what worried him was that she did. She knew him in a way that surprised him, knew him at times better than he knew himself.

She lifted her head and fixed her gaze on him. Feeling her suspicion, he sat back and folded his arms. Her eyes were very blue.

'All right then,' she said, 'if you don't want to talk, I'm going back to the room. I need to speak to Tess anyway.'

She got up from the table and walked back across the courtyard. He watched her leave, and when she had gone he followed the weaverbirds as they ducked and dived—tiny arrows that shot in and out of the acacia tree, tending their small basket-like nests, those intricate circular works that took days to weave with their delicate beaks and feet yet which, despite their efforts, might fail to become a home, might fail to have a purpose.

Last night, when he couldn't sleep, he'd gone down to the hotel lobby where there was better internet reception. By then there was hardly anyone left, only the nightwatchman who sat dozing at the main entrance with an AK-47 across his lap. At the computer, Neil's hand had throbbed. He was clumsy, and the connection was still slow, but he managed. Using his phone he called Thompson, who told him that some of the bigger operators were ex-military; a bloke in Cape Town called Frost and another supplier known as Alex Vadim, who was probably part of a larger syndicate. Multi-tentacled, hydra-headed was how Neil was beginning to understand it, and right then the knowledge fired something in him. He spent the rest of the night furiously digging for facts and came up with more incriminating details than he could stomach—other suppliers, distribution channels, not so difficult to uncover now that he had ceased to defend his son. He felt sick. Once you begin to see someone in a different light, it's impossible to go back to what they were before. It was like opening a door on another world and not being able to close it again.

An email from Thompson confirmed that the plane in the photograph Neil sent him had been leased by Stephen from Frost. 'One of our Spider Men, I now see,' Thompson added, referring to their collaborative research—since it was with Thompson's backing that Neil began his documentary series in the nineties: deforestation as a result of drug crops, a scam that extended to the transporters, the so-called 'Spider Men' with their connections into illegal markets, money laundering, trafficking—anything from exotic animals to weapons for dirty wars. Organisations that ran front companies, shipping grain and machinery.

'Stephen must have taken it to heart,' Thompson said dryly, 'because we're not just talking about flowers or frozen chickens, it's what else they carry: the kind of stock even Reba's Firearms might have trouble clearing. Some of it—especially the light weaponry, which isn't that light, since it's just a term for what's portable—gets approved by governments, some doesn't.'

'Could it be a mistake?'

Holy shit, he had thought, let me find a way out of this.

'The first time it might be a mistake,' Thompson replied flatly. 'After that it's more like a pattern.'

Back in their room, the bedside lamp was lit, and a soft orange glow filtered through the gauzy mosquito net. Leigh had been awake too, notebook and pen still on the coverlet. Neil thought he would tell her what he had in mind, but in the next second he decided not to. No, she would want to protect Stephen. It was her instinct, a mother's love, no matter what. She was like that. Fierce. Defensive. If he said anything, she might try to block him in some way. He couldn't tell her. Not yet. He would let her know in the morning, or later that afternoon when he got word back, when he knew more. But at that hour he just wanted to lie with her until morning came and try to put everything out of his mind—to sleep. But mostly he wanted to hold her and hope she might hold him in return.

In the acacia tree, the weaverbirds, like small, yellow-lit flames, continued to dart as if in a frenzy, and although their workings appeared random, he saw they were actually meticulous. He would need to be like that: careful and meticulous. He would need to wait.

35

Entebbe

Stephen tapped his phone. 'Now they're telling me the guns are shit,' he said. 'Kolo's brother wants another consignment.'

His left eye had swollen, and his top tooth was missing. Where his once-perfect smile had been, there was now a gap. The night before his tooth had gone black and that morning it had come out in a gob of bloody saliva. He'd tried to push it back into the socket, but it came out again, so he rinsed it, wrapped it in a piece of plastic then put it in his shirt pocket, although he suspected he would have to throw it away. By the time he got back to a decent dentist in Cape Town, too much time would have passed for it to be worth keeping. He pushed his tongue into the tender, vacant space, unable to feel the violence of his father's fist now, only the pissed-off feeling that he'd been beaten.

It had been a shock to see such rage in his father, like a wounded animal turning to attack. Well, let him have his moment. Let him make his point.

'Did you hear me?' he said to Reba.

They'd flown from Gulu to Entebbe that morning, but

engine trouble meant they had to wait until the plane was cleared before flying on—a blockage in the fuel line or a cylinder problem, no one seemed to have any idea.

Now grounded, Stephen checked his bank account. He had trouble with his password at first. And then the zeroes were not there. He shifted between accounts, double-checked and checked again, but as he scrolled through, he realised he was looking at a debit rather than a credit.

'Fuck,' he said. 'What the hell?'

Reba, who had been staring intently at something on his phone, finally glanced at him.

'Someone's hacked my bank account,' Stephen said.

But Reba only waved his hand as if what he said meant nothing. 'It's probably a mistake. Nothing you can do from here, so you may as well shelve it for now.'

'What are you talking about? I'm not about to shelve anything. There's no money in my account. Either there's been a stuff-up, or I've been shafted.'

Reba looked towards the busy departure area, where someone was shouting.

'Didn't you hear me?' Stephen demanded. 'Someone's put the word out that we're selling crap.' He raised his phone. 'They want new terms, more stock, but Frost won't release it unless I pay upfront. And we've got no money.'

'Listen, Steve—' Reba began.

But before he could finish, Stephen got to his feet. 'Come on, what is it? There's a shit storm brewing here, and we can't afford to hang around. I need to get back and speak to these people in person.'

Airport announcements stuttered, and rattled passengers moved out of the way as Stephen hurried out of the terminal onto the tarmac. When he reached the Gulfstream, he clambered into the cockpit. The mechanic told him that although the engine trouble had been fixed, he still wanted to go over a few things. Stephen waved him away and began flicking the control switches, then he started up the first engine. A groundsman shouted and flapped his arms in the air, but Stephen ignored him too.

The cabin door swung open, and Matt climbed into the co-pilot's seat next to him. 'All right then, let's go.'

Stephen started the second engine, then rammed the throttles to full and released the brake. He told air-traffic control there was a medical emergency and the plane was needed back in Cape Town for a patient transport.

The air-traffic controller cleared them to go ahead and Stephen taxied onto the runway, jumping the queue in front of a domestic carrier.

As they lifted, the landing gear drew up into the body of the plane and they went into a steep climb. The runway receded beneath them, and they arced away south across a murky Lake Victoria, the engine humming, instrument panels reading as they should.

Beside him, Matt began rummaging in his backpack. He took out his phone and passport, then began reshuffling the cards in his wallet and checking them repeatedly as if he was doing a stocktake. A tsetse fly that must've got into the cabin when they were grounded landed on his neck. He swatted at it and missed.

Stephen gave him a sidelong look. They hadn't spoken since take-off.

'Listen,' he said. 'If you know something I don't, then this would probably be the right time to fess up.'

Reba didn't respond; only a slight stiffening of his jaw suggested he had heard.

They were above the clouds now and the sky was clear and very blue. Stephen stared ahead. 'What's going on?' he asked.

'What do you mean?' Reba mumbled. He had gone back to scrounging in his backpack.

'Well, something's weird,' Stephen said, and when Reba didn't look up he continued, 'All right, should I tell you what I think?'

'If you want,' Reba replied, making it sound as if he had zero interest.

'Okay, the way I see it, it's simple: we provide arms to everyone—government forces, villagers and rebels alike. We don't do the killing. They do that. Half the time they don't even need guns to do it. Machetes, hoes, it's all the same. What we do is business—*your* business, Matt, fifty-one per cent, which you stand to lose if you're not on board. You can't have it both ways. Get it? If I'm shafted, so are you.'

Matt succeeded in jamming the tsetse fly into the window seal with the corner of his passport. There was a tiny bloody crunch against the glass. 'Fucking thing got me.'

He spat on his fingers and wiped saliva onto the bite on his neck, then began fidgeting with his headset.

'Did you hear what I said?' Stephen asked.

'I heard. Except maybe you've got the wrong information.'

'Really? Then enlighten me.'

They flew south-west. Below them the clouds were beginning to turn crimson as the sun set. Matt adjusted his sunglasses and Stephen thought he might be mistaken; maybe Reba was still just a big-boned jock without imagination, the same sixteen-year-old yearning for home. 'So, let's get this straight,' he said. 'Are you trying to tell me that you want go back to your uncle's farm in Bloemfontein where everything's safe? That you want to go and live like a *japie*, hey? Like a Boer?'

Reba shook his head. 'Tessa was right—you don't know shit.'

'And she does?' Stephen cast him a triumphant look, but then suddenly something of the last couple of days began to fall into place. The times at the Acholi Inn when Reba went off—looking, he said, for some space—and his all-out panic when he bolted back to the four-wheel drive in a bid to get out of Garamba. 'You knew about this, didn't you? You're in on it.'

'Hey, man, I was the one who tried to warn you.'

'Is that right?'

There was a long pause before Matt replied, 'Come on, don't pull that shit on me. None of this is my problem.'

'Oh yeah, and why's that?'

'Because I'm getting out, man.'

'What do you mean, you're getting out? You say that as if you've already got something sorted. Did you cut a deal with someone? With Kolo's brother, maybe?'

'Why would I do that? I told you, Steve, I don't want to do that kind of business.'

Stephen scoffed. 'Come on, you can't quit so easily. Besides, your fingerprints are already all over *that kind of business*.'

A long silence followed, and when Stephen spoke again it was slowly and confidently, as if he was already claiming victory. 'Bring me down, Matt, and you bring yourself down.'

He checked the fuel calculation and increased their airspeed, then lifted his tongue to the vacant spot where his tooth should be.

There was a chill in his brain. What he wouldn't do now for a drink.

36

Gulu

Earlier that morning Tessa had washed her hair and now, in the cabin of the jeep, she breathed in deeply in order to smell the soaps and creams she had used. Camomile, sage leaf, lemon balm: travel-sized bottles that were among the small gifts her mother had insisted on giving her. She'd had dinner with her parents at the hotel the last few nights and now she was picking them up to take them to Gulu airport. Her head throbbed. The past four days had been a constant round of negotiations, the conversations skirting around the same two topics: Stephen, and when she would be coming home.

Every time her father spoke of Stephen it looked as though there was a sour taste in his mouth. Her mother would glance at him with an uneasy look. Her face was lined, and there were things she said then: 'I don't see how anyone can get out of this unscathed . . .' But last night her parents had argued in a way Tessa had never heard before.

Her father had protested, 'Your fantasy, Leigh, is you think he'll change. But he won't. Trust me, some people do, most don't.'

'I can't believe that,' her mother had replied, pushing her plate aside and wiping her mouth with the green table napkin.

'Dad,' Tessa had intervened, 'if you've already called Steve out on what he's doing, then maybe Mum's right, and that might bring him round. He might have second thoughts.' She was not about to say she had her own doubts—her parents were struggling now, and struggling so spectacularly when, to her, they had always seemed so capable.

If her father noticed her uncertainty, he didn't say. He was still intent on arguing his point. 'And do what?' he demanded. 'Stop? Say sorry? When have you ever heard Stephen apologise? No, he's not sorry, and he's not about to stop his role in this business. In the meantime, what do we do? Do we stand by and let this happen? Do we give in to him?' It was clear that he wanted their support. In his voice there was a pleading tone, fraught and uncharacteristic. 'We have to do this. We need to put him through the courts. We have to tell him: *The game's up*.'

Tessa's mother frowned and shook her head.

'Come on, hear me out!' he insisted. 'There are things we can do: Stephen can be reported to Interpol or the UN. None of the local authorities are equipped to handle it, this is a global problem. If he won't stop of his own accord, then our only option is to force him.'

'But that could put him in harm's way,' her mother objected.

'Think what he's doing, Leigh! Who *he's* putting in harm's way.' Her father inhaled sharply as if he wanted to say something more, but instead he kept quiet. It was there though: *This is not what I want, it is what I must do.*

Tessa drove the jeep that Dominic said she could use. It was still covered in mud. The front windscreen had smeared arcs where the wipers had ineffectively swiped the glass. When Tessa had asked to borrow the jeep to visit her parents, Dominic had said dryly, 'At least your brother has left us a full tank of fuel.' She wondered what Dominic would do if he knew the truth about Stephen. Would he contact the national police, the army, the government? Dominic, with his sense of justice and broken desire for peace. But her father was right: this was not up to Dominic, it was their responsibility.

As it turned out, her own suspicions about Stephen were only the start. He was an arms dealer, yet more involved than she had first thought—a middleman, hand-picked for and by those higher up the chain. Someone called Frost, although that was probably not his real name, and others; the main operator, rumoured to have mansions in Belgium and South Africa, as well as a gated estate in Riyadh. 'Someone profiting from all sides, a friend to rebels and governments alike,' her father had said. But if it was shocking, then it was not altogether surprising, and it certainly wasn't so difficult to imagine Stephen being drawn to such a world. He had always been attracted to what lay beyond reach, had always been the one to climb the highest mountain or run the fastest race. He got pleasure from being illicit and admired those who beat the system. *The game's up*, her father wanted to tell him, but Stephen loved the game, even more than he prized the results.

Tessa listened to her parents, although she had her own version of Stephen. As a child she had idolised him but later as a teenager she had resented him, and that meant she was always watching him—she knew how competitive he could be, how unbending and, now, how their relationship would be this intensified thing, more wide awake and vigilant. He would know she had alerted her parents to him. It didn't matter that her father had dug up information on those he was in contact with, or taken photos that might incriminate him; at some point Stephen would work out her part in calling him into question and he would pay her out for it, of that she was certain. And just like when they were kids and she had chased after him, she knew she wouldn't keep up, not least because there were no clear rules that he played by.

She braked to allow a pickup truck with twenty or more people sitting precariously in the back to veer in front of her. Men, women, children. She didn't know what would happen now, if her parents would agree or which course they would take. But even though she suspected Stephen of being ruthless, she still wondered whether it would make a difference to him if he was disowned by his family. She hadn't spoken to him since they'd argued, and she was unlikely to hear from him any time soon. Apparently he had left Uganda, yet he had risked his life to come after her. Why? *Because someone had to*, he said. Was he being funny? Ironic? She couldn't tell.

Her parents were waiting for her when she arrived, standing in front of the hotel, their tension obvious in the way they carried themselves. Her father straight-backed, his hand bandaged and his grey head tilted to the side, her mother's mouth drawn downwards. They put their luggage in the back of the jeep and then her mother turned to her with an anxious expression on her face. 'Oh, Tess,' she said softly.

Tessa tugged at her shirt, but still her mother reached out and touched her where the bruise on her throat was beginning to fade. It was a natural thing for her to do and Tessa tried to smile. She had seen the bruising herself in the mirror that morning, the ugly way it looked on her neck with the edges already dappled yellow. Her mother nodded then gently put her arms about her, and in her embrace, Tessa was her child again. It was a brief moment which Tessa broke, taking a small step back. 'Come on, Mum,' she said, moving towards the car. 'We have to go if you're to make your flight.'

It was a short distance to the airport, but slow going through the town, where dozens of people sauntered along the road on their way to the big market and cyclists wove through the traffic with branches of green plantains roped to their bikes. Horns tooted. Tessa passed a thin man with an unwieldy bedframe tied to the back of his *boda-boda* and tried to make conversation with her parents about anything other than what was on her mind.

Her mother shifted uncomfortably in the passenger seat beside her then asked, for what seemed like the hundredth time, 'So, Tess, have you decided how much longer you plan on staying?' Tessa heard the strain in her voice, although she could tell that her mother now seemed resigned to the fact that she wouldn't be returning home with them.

'I'm still not sure how long,' she replied cautiously. 'Maybe another month. After that I don't know; I might come home for a while and then come back here. If they'll have me.'

'Oh, Tess, I thought you wanted to leave this place,' her mother said.

'This place,' Tessa repeated. 'No, Mum, I love this place. That's what I've been trying to tell you.'

Leigh nodded, her gaze directed towards the children on the street. One leaning against a doorway chewing sugarcane, others chasing chickens and flapping their arms.

'This place,' Tessa said again. 'But especially the people here, they're amazing. Even after everything they've been through, there are those who can still forgive so much. It's like Beatrice says: they bring relief to their tragedy. I see it sometimes in the way they talk about things other than the war. How they get on with life; their laugher, their jokes—about their shoes, or lack of them.' She gave a wry smile, then lifted her shoulders and let them fall. 'It's what drew me here in the beginning—how people cope in the aftermath of civil war. How they cope at all. And . . .' She faltered.

'And you'd like to see Francis resettled,' her father said from his position in the back of the jeep.

Tessa nodded. 'Dominic calls it deradicalised, although Beatrice says that's just a word, it will take the rest of his life. But yes, I want to see how he gets on. I said I would help him learn how to use a computer.'

'And you? How will you get on?' asked her mother.

Tessa hesitated, then replied, 'I'm not sure, although there's something I want to do.'

'And what's that?' her mother asked warily.

'I want to make peace with the preacher's family—through a *mato oput* ceremony.'

'Oh, come on, Tess,' her father said.

In the rear-view mirror his face had gone slack and jowly.

'*Oh, come on*, what, Dad?'

'You don't really want to do that, do you?'

Tessa glanced again at her father. 'I do, if his family does. I've heard that his mother and sister live here in Gulu.'

'But the man—'

'I know,' Tessa said. 'And he probably did worse to others.'

She turned on to the airport road and picked up speed. There had been times when she could feel the weight of Obed's body—it made her skin crawl, although now there was also something pitiful about the sound he had made. She heard it sometimes when everything else was quiet: the small wanting noise in the back of his throat that spoke to her not of anger or even violence anymore, only of pain.

She waited for her parents to say something else, but they were quiet. A young boy with one leg hopped along the side of the road. It made her think of Oraako with his infected foot. 'When a life is taken here,' she said, 'many people believe that unless there is *mato oput* there will be no peace. They say the dead are not dead, that they will continue to come back and cause atrocities to their own family as well as the family of the offender.'

'And what about you? Do you believe that?'

'Yes, I do. I believe that now.'

She imagined the ceremony. The reddish roots of the *oput* tree like bleeding hands. It was what had been intended for the boy, Oraako. That after his cleansing ceremony, reconciliation would follow, except his uncle had refused to accept him back.

Civil war in his country, civil war in his family.

And in her family? The awfulness of it settled over her like a miasma. For the truth was her actions had set off a chain of events that had caused them to fracture along fault lines she hadn't known ran so deep.

'I'm sorry,' she said, stumbling over the words, inadequate to convey what she wanted to express. 'For what I've brought you into, and what I've put you through.'

Together her parents made small objections, but there was hurt there too, and irritation. Over the last few days they had been building towards this, towards some kind of reckoning. Tessa was aware of her parents' support and grateful for it, but she craved consolation not just for herself but for them. To find some kind of resolution. 'What about Stephen?' she ventured.

Her mother pushed the hair from her face and took an inward breath, but before she could answer her father replied: 'What Stephen does is beside the point. The point is that he should be stopped from doing any more damage.'

Tessa heard the resolve and then the agitation in her father's voice as he caught her mother's expression in the side mirror. 'Lu, don't look at me like that,' he said. 'Don't shake your head as if you don't believe me. I *will* stop him.'

Her mother made an odd sound, challenging, almost disbelieving.

But her father continued: 'We have to act,' and after what felt like a very long time he added, 'If we can't change him, then we have to change his circumstances.'

'You sound as if you've already sentenced him,' her mother said sharply.

'Actually, it's the other way around: *he's* sentenced us—Stephen is corrupt,' her father stated, and it sounded as if the word had stuck to his tongue. 'He makes us all complicit.

'And Cherie isn't as dumb as he thinks; there's evidence of payments in the form of electronic receipts, banking details. Even a halfway competent lawyer could punch holes in Stephen's story.'

'My God,' her mother exclaimed. 'When did you speak to Cherie?'

A few nights ago Tessa recalled her father asking for Cherie's phone number and, assuming he wanted another way to contact Stephen, had given it to him.

'When?' her mother repeated. 'When did you speak with Cherie?'

Her father cleared his throat. 'Two or three days ago,' he said. 'I don't remember exactly. She was happy enough to help. She knew how to get into Stephen's house in Cape Town.'

'What for?' her mother asked. She turned around in her seat to face him.

'To access his computer for one.'

'Oh my God, Neil, what have you done?'

Her father took a breath in through his nose. 'Leigh, listen: we can't let Stephen get away with what he's doing. Besides, he's not a major player in this—not yet, anyway. With the right information, he could lead the authorities to bigger fish. What I've done is put pressure on him, enough for him to implicate himself and those he's doing business with.'

'What?' her mother said. 'I don't believe you're telling me this. You want to bypass the legal options you've been insisting on and go rogue yourself? Have you thought about where this could end up? And what do you mean exactly? What pressure have you put on him?'

'I made a decision,' her father said, and Tessa could hear the resolve in his voice. 'Matt told me he was skint and that their partnership was a verbal agreement. I guess I figured it wasn't possible to have that information and not do anything about it. I offered to buy out Matt's share of Reba's Firearms. Good thing we can afford it.'

'You bought Matt out—and what else?' she heard her mother say, her question already a kind of foreknowledge.

'Steve's bankrupt. I got access to his account with Cherie's help.'

'Christ,' her mother whispered. 'You went ahead and did this without my knowing?'

'You would have stopped me, Leigh.'

'You don't know that,' her mother said, but it sounded as if her reply was built on quicksand.

They entered the small dusty terminal, which faced the runway. In the distance, there was a squat air-traffic control tower on a crisscross frame. Painted in red and white stripes, it looked like a giant jack-in-the-box. Two light planes were parked on the tarmac, but nothing to alert Neil this time. A few passengers disembarked by the rear stairs of the smaller aircraft and made their way to the departure gate. On a freestanding flagpole a Ugandan flag fluttered in the breeze. Neil checked their tickets and passports. He wondered if he would hear whether Stephen was back in Cape Town and if he would stay there. The transactions he had put into place, moving money from various accounts, contacting Thompson in Joburg and, through him, those who might be able to destabilise a trade path, had been its own complex maze. At first, he thought he would not be able to bring it off and then he'd been surprised that shifting Stephen's money had gone through with little more than a keychain sequence of numbers and passwords. Cherie had said, 'Nail him,' and the fury of first discovering what his son was involved in, a fury he had unleashed on the hotel balcony, cooled to something more purposeful.

He had searched Stephen's computer via his file-hosting service. Cherie was accurate with those passwords too, and he found the metadata he was looking for. It was not as sophisticated as he might have imagined, but it was still satisfying to discover it was there and that he was able to isolate it. The legitimate option was to pass it on to the UN office for disarmament, but the urgency to implicate his son and those he was collaborating with had set off a twanging discord in his brain, and if he regretted withholding what he had done from Leigh and Tessa, and felt their censure now, he didn't regret acting on the impulse. In fact, it was a relief of sorts; he reasoned that the UN Security Council was still waiting for the Arms Trade Treaty to be ratified before they could act, and that could be years away, while he needed to do something now, before Stephen did more harm. His jaw tightened. He thought of Tessa's case for *mato oput*, but how could he and Stephen bury the hatchet? Any thought of reconciliation was inconceivable unless Stephen ceased what he was doing, and even then he doubted it was possible. He loved his son in a furious, fractured way, but he was not going to wake up each day feeling despair that Stephen was beyond redemption or that everything had gone to shit. What he needed to do was to rediscover a world that was just. What terrified him was that such a world might not exist.

He sat on the tandem plastic seats, with Tessa on one side and Leigh on the other, and waited to board the flight. There was a whiff of rain in the air. Nimbus clouds rolled in from the west, causing the greenness around them to intensify. It was a contrast to the glass hub they would pass through in Dubai and, another thirteen or fourteen hours after that, the ordered streets of Melbourne. Neil watched the other passengers with their lives packed into cardboard boxes and rolling suitcases. He could forget people lived elsewhere and had lives so different from his own, but airports were threshold places. You could walk out of one world and into another, as if stepping through a magic wardrobe into snow.

He ached to put his arm around Leigh and have her rest her head against him, but he felt the chasm between them now. Standing in the hotel lobby when they were waiting to check out, Leigh had said they needed to stop blaming each other and work together. She was right, of course, but how would they begin now, with this new knowledge that he had deliberately chosen to place their son in danger—the child they had first dreamt of together, the child they had once marvelled over. He used to believe that he could keep the things he cared about safe. But it took more than strength or desire; it took stubbornness and blind hope too, in the face of all that could go wrong.

The boarding call was announced, and they walked to the gate. Nearby a young family was rearranging their luggage. The mother, a slender woman with auburn hair, was trying to appease a small child. They looked like foreign aid workers; the man had a Médecins Sans Frontières logo on his bag and spoke rapidly in French. Neil was aware of Leigh watching them. Mother, father, son, daughter—the ideal of a united family. He saw the distress in Leigh's face as a mix of recognition and loss, and, as if by way of a pledge to his own family—or, more urgently now, to ease the furious beating of his heart—he put his hand flat against his sternum and closed his eyes. When he opened them again, Tessa was looking at him. She leant forward and gently kissed him on the cheek, and when she stepped back he could see himself reflected—two small silhouettes blurring as tears brimmed in her eyes.

He wanted to speak, to utter words of explanation, but she shook her head. She hugged him then, and at the same time she reached out and put her arm around Leigh, knotting them briefly in the intense kind of connection people achieve best on departures.

37

Cape Town

For a moment, Stephen pictured the clearing where the speckled jackal had slunk in close then trotted across to the charred body in the campfire. He had not wanted to think about what he had seen at the time, had simply shut it out, although the image came to him now, unbidden and with startling clarity. He pictured the man's body in the smouldering coals, and for a fraction of a second it became vivid and real to him. Again, he saw the gabardine trousers where they had melted into the burnt skin and recalled the crooked position of the limbs. There was the stench of scorched hair; it filled his nostrils and he tried not to gag while the dentist held the temporary crown in place and pressed down as the glue set.

There would need to be at least two more visits before the permanent crown was fixed to the implant. The dentist's hands were as large as a boxer's and the dry latex glove pushed against his upper lip with a force that spiralled through the implant into the bone. His nose was tender and still slightly swollen, but at least the break was straight and would heal that way.

Just before they had touched down in Cape Town, Reba had made a sound as if he was clearing his throat. 'Your father,' he said with a slight catch in his voice.

'What about him?' Stephen had shouted over the engine noise.

'He's the one who put out word that you're selling crap.'

Stephen felt his face tighten. 'And what? You're going to tell me that it was my father who emptied my bank account?'

'Would you rather I lie to you?'

'I think that's just what you do.'

The runway came into view. Parallel lines of steady white edge lights, telescoping to yellow then to red.

'He wants to liquidate the business.'

'He can't.'

'Can't he? It's not like we made a solid partnership agreement. No lawyers, remember.'

Which meant what? That his father now owned Matt's controlling share of Reba's Firearms. Should they rename it Lowell & Son? If it wasn't so messed up, it might make him laugh.

There had been a warning of sorts; a cryptic text message from his father—*This can stop here if you want*—but he'd deleted it. He didn't want to bargain. Maybe he should have handled that better. Jesus, he thought, his father might just see this through. He tried to remember their conversation on the balcony at the Acholi Inn, the whole drama of paternal authority. Okay then, bring it on, if that's what you want—the Gulfstream making a thud as the tyres hit the tarmac—and suddenly it occurred to him that he might have missed something. Something vital.

His father had his buddies from his documentary film-making days, and there was Matt trying to save his own skin, but he would've needed more help than that.

It took Stephen until he got back to his house in Camps Bay to figure it out—someone had accessed his computer—and now he clenched his fist. His father might have outplayed him, but what mattered was getting ahead again. No more surprises. One fact he felt certain of was that his father had no real idea of the extent of the network he was dealing with. He was smart, but he didn't see the whole picture. That was the trouble with intelligent people: they often focused on what they were good at and were blind to the rest.

'All done,' the dentist said, and the nurse took the protective glasses off Stephen's face. He blinked, his eyes adjusting to the bright fluorescent lights, and sat forward to rinse his mouth. Then he looked at himself in the hand mirror. It was a pleasing result, and not even the final one. He ran his hand through his hair and handed the mirror back to the nurse.

His phone buzzed in his pocket then pinged with a text message alert when he didn't answer. On the street, he shielded the screen from the sun. It was from Frost, asking if they could meet in half an hour at a harbourfront restaurant.

When Stephen arrived, Frost was already there with an open bottle of tempranillo, an award-winning Stellenbosch.

'Here, sit. Have a drink,' Frost said expansively. There was music playing in the background, some cheesy song from the eighties. They sat outside under a white umbrella and looked across the Victoria & Alfred Waterfront to Table Mountain. Luxury yachts were moored in the marina under a blue sky.

The waitress filled Stephen's glass, and took the menus away when Stephen said he wasn't eating. Frost ordered a wagyu burger.

'If you want to get out of this, you go in deeper,' Frost said. 'Your partner, what's-his-name, Reba, was always going to be dispensable. I'm telling you, you're better off without him.'

Stephen ran his tongue across his new tooth. The dentist had offered to set a diamond in the permanent crown. The idea appealed to him, although it made him think of money—or rather his lack of it—and, now, how much he owed. On returning to Cape Town he'd thought his best bet was to clear out and go to LA or maybe Shanghai—he had contacts in both places—but now he was having second thoughts.

'What are you looking confused about?' Frost said, topping up his wine. The expression on Frost's face might have appeared hostile to anyone observing him from the next table, but then he broke into a smile. 'You stick to the policy, okay? Only rarely turn down an offer and never take sides. Everyone, whether mercenary, militant, rebel or an ordinary gun-happy civilian, is a prospective customer, and if necessary, we arm both sides in the same conflict. It's all about foresight,' he said. 'And,' he added, 'neutrality.'

The drumbeat in Stephen's head picked up—an adrenaline rush that made it seem anything was possible. He felt like he'd lost a stack of chips on the roulette table only to win them back again.

The waitress returned with Frost's burger, chips spilling off the side of the plate. 'You learn to make friends with everyone,' Frost went on, picking up a chip and biting into it. 'And everyone tolerates that because they have no alternative. They want what you deliver. You're the postman, right? And they don't want to shoot the postman.'

Stephen wiped his hand across the back of his neck. In the rebel camp, they would have shot and killed him. He remembered the swiftness with which they'd ambushed him and pinned him to the ground, the muzzle of the gun driven into the side of his head by the boy who'd leapt on his back. He now knew the boy as Francis Amayo, and the one who had been leading the small patrol party that had probably seen him long before they jumped him. But as he scrambled to his feet, Francis murmured in his ear: 'If you help me, I can help you too. I will help you get away.'

It went quickly after that. He was brought to a campfire where Kolo, dressed garishly in a full military uniform, sat drinking from a gourd. 'What is it you want?' Kolo demanded, although his smug look suggested that he already knew, and watching him, Stephen found himself strangely pleased. 'I've come for the *muzungu*.'

In the firelight, the rain on the plastic chairs glistened. '*You* are a *muzungu*,' Kolo said, laughing. 'Ah, but yes, I see, you want the woman. And what is she to you, this woman? Is she your wife? Your girlfriend?'

'I don't know anything about her,' Stephen lied. 'I'm just doing someone a favour. But I can assure you that it would be worth your while to hand her over.'

'Is that so?'

Kolo drank from the gourd, then wiped his mouth with the back of his hand before adding, 'Because money, even the folded kind, is no good to us here.'

'I'm not talking about money,' Stephen replied, and Kolo's eyes lit up with interest. A quick deal. They even shook hands, although what Stephen had not anticipated were the complications that followed: the cry he recognised as if from some distant childhood game, and his own immediate response as he ran towards it, his chest burning, to find Tessa struggling on the dirt floor, and rising within him the flood of rage. He was too late. And then something primal, the instinct to protect his sister and forget himself—a better part of his nature, as he grabbed the priest, took a punch in the gut, and fell, to hear the first gunshot blast and then the frenzied look on Tessa's face. A force that burnt white-hot as she fired in rapid succession until the gun was empty.

'Move! Get out!' he shouted, and they fled, his ears ringing with the sound of gunfire. And the miracle was they got away, Francis leading them through the bush like a fish moving through water. A smart kid. Smart and quick. Quick enough to confuse the rebels who came after them.

Frost finished his burger, washing down the last mouthful with more wine before wiping his mouth with the linen table napkin. 'Have you got anyone else who might cause problems—a girlfriend, perhaps?'

'No,' Stephen replied. The wine he'd drunk on an empty stomach and the quick shot or two he'd knocked back before going to the dentist had worked. A mood of bravado had set in.

'Better still.' Frost raised his eyebrows. 'No complications.'

'None.' Stephen smiled. Though not complications exactly, there were loose ends. He had watched Cherie on some back-dated CCTV footage from outside his house. Light on her feet, she moved like a long-legged bird. He missed that, missed her sassiness.

Maybe he would have to sell the place to pay off the mortgage, but for now he probably needed a guard dog. Even if Cherie had already left South Africa and Reba had disappeared, security helped, everyone knew that. He hadn't been able to contact Reba since returning to Cape Town, although he'd spoken to Cherie on Skype. She made no bones about it; said his parents—his father in particular—had asked her to help him, her pixelated face indignant. *What?*, he thought when she widened her eyes. *Had she started to play the part of the unfairly put upon innocent?* She made out that what she had done was in his best interests. 'You can turn your life around, you know.' An ex-girlfriend acting like a psychologist; who needed that? Tessa was enough, along with his mother, who had tried to contact him. What did they want him to say? That he had changed his ways? Cherie had finished up by telling him she was getting married in three days. 'Good luck with that,' he said, and after a pause, 'You'll be hearing from me—a few outstanding bills.'

'I won't be hearing from you,' she replied, and after the call, she blocked him as a contact.

He realised he was hungry and looked at Frost's empty plate. The dentist said he could eat in an hour, soft food.

'This Colonel Kolo, or his brother, or whoever you made a deal with,' Frost said, 'tell them we can make up the shortfall. That should hold off any reprisals. In fact, we can probably secure a further distribution. There are rumours that the US are planning to support an offensive. Operation Lightning Thunder or some such bullshit—ha! If they want to stop the LRA or catch Kony, I can't think of a dumber thing to do. Still, they'll try, and what everyone will need then is more guns and more ammunition.'

Stephen looked past Frost to Table Mountain, which loomed in the distance. He'd climbed that mountain numerous times, scaling the escarpment where the rock disappeared into the side of the ridge. On the more difficult routes he'd had to scramble for natural handholds and grip with the tips of his fingers. Looking down, he might've been flying, the same thrill of rising high above everything. *Why leave this place?,* he thought. He had made it his own and, like the *Mapogos*, he would stay.

He glanced at the table next to them, where an attractive woman and three men sat drinking champagne. The maître d' went from one to the other offering coffee and dessert. Stephen lifted his glass and drank the last of his wine. He was at home here, and besides, he had protection. Frost had contacts, some ex-military, others bigger players—people like Alex Vadim, business moguls, even politicians.

'My suggestion is you never forget who is connected to whom,' Frost said as though he was already one step ahead. Then he leant back and clasped his hands behind his head. 'Watch your back, Stevo, and I'll tide you over for now. You're a good pilot. Risk and safety. A survivor, huh?'

38

Gulu

Tessa entered the dormitory, where a bed had been provided for Francis, although he preferred to lie on the floor. 'I do not sleep on this,' he said, nodding in the direction of the cast-iron bunk. 'It is not for a soldier.'

His bed was the last in a row of twelve. As she came towards him, he sat up and wrapped his hands around his legs. She nodded and smiled, but he looked at her impassively. He had refused to go to the woodworking class with the other boys and was the only one here in the middle of the day. The dormitory was cool compared to the heat outside, and it was dark except for a long oblong strip of sunlight that came in through the open door.

Since arriving a week ago, Francis had been treated for scabies, his head shaved to rid him of lice and the wound on his face cleaned. He'd been reluctant to talk, and initially the other boys at the centre were wary of him, although Dominic said it would not stay that way.

'There is a pattern we see when they come back, an initial

period of silence, but then most begin to speak. Some are given pencils and paper—you have seen their drawings?'

'Yes,' Tessa said, she had seen their drawings, but she didn't share Dominic's faith.

'Hope is our guide,' Dominic insisted. 'Like others, he will remember first, and then he will forget. It is the only way to forgive, to heal.'

Beatrice agreed. She had spent hours with Francis, speaking to him in Acholi and then in English while Francis hung his head or picked at the callused skin on his hands.

Time, she told Tessa. He needs time.

Francis shifted his weight forward. The welt on his face had almost completely scabbed over except for a small point of yellow pus that still festered near his ear. Within a few months it would become just another scar. He squared his shoulders. He wore clean clothes now, issued from the various boxes supplied by charities and stored in the main administration building: Nike runners, jeans, a tight T-shirt with a picture of a seal on it. The T-shirt was a souvenir from SeaWorld, and the seal was pup-like, with innocent eyes and long wiry whiskers. Francis would never have seen the ocean, much less an actual seal, and he probably wouldn't know what SeaWorld was. What, Tessa had found herself wondering, was the attraction of this item out of the mountain of charity clothes?

Francis looked at her. 'And you? How do you sleep?' he asked in a sullen voice. 'You do not, hey? Because you killed the preacher and so now you are afraid.'

It was as if he knew what was troubling her, as if he'd been watching her all along. It was the type of intelligence he had:

shrewd, observant, with a keen sixth sense. He rattled her.

She had come looking for him because Beatrice suggested she might be able to encourage him to join the other boys. It seemed reasonable, since it was felt they had made a connection because of her experience with him in the bush, and because she'd been present during the counselling sessions held by Beatrice, but now Tessa was not so sure. This was the first time they'd been alone since the rebel camp and what he said so suddenly had startled her. She ran her hand through her hair. There was a constant tautness in the back of her head that gathered behind her left temple and reached in as though a bird had gripped her eye with its claw. Images of the major's blood on her hands and of repeatedly shooting the preacher in the face persisted, memories that kept turning in on themselves to become increasingly distorted and surreal.

'Why should I be afraid?' she asked him softly.

'Because you must watch for *cen*,' Francis replied. 'You must catch them and cork them in a jar or they will come for you in the middle of the night.'

It made bizarre sense—*cen*, spirits, recurring dreams. It went back to her research, which centred on the idea that for many people the memory of trauma lay just beneath the surface and could be triggered or even heightened under certain conditions. More importantly, if the memory of something terrible worked as a survival tool, if it reminded you how not to let that happen again, it had a purpose—but, and that had been her preoccupation—how was it possible to stop it from going into overdrive and becoming its own force of destruction? To ultimately learn to have some control over it? Was forgetting the way, as Francis said, or was reconciliation necessary, as Dominic proposed?

Without a family, children on their own did not cope so well, she had concluded in her early thesis. Now it seemed as if she had been writing with her eyes closed. No one coped so well on their own.

Stuck to the wall behind Francis was a small devotional card depicting a merciful Christ. Tessa glanced at it and then back at Francis, but it was as if a dull detachment had fallen over him. 'If you think too deeply, you become sick,' he said in a muted voice. 'Every night I wake up, thinking and thinking, and I cannot get back to sleep.' He kicked the floor. '*Nen!* Look! There are worms in the ground. Spirits come up.' His mood shifted, and now there was an urgency in his tone. He stopped kicking and looked at her. 'What will you do? Where will you go?' he asked.

I don't know, Tessa wanted to say. *I have no idea what's in store for me now*. But before she could answer, he added, 'And where have your family gone?'

She hesitated. 'They have gone home,' she replied. She remembered their troubled faces—her father with his bandaged hand and need for retribution, her mother's desire for resolution. 'We will work this out.' The three of them standing in a knot at the airport.

When her parents had voiced their concerns, she had told them not to worry. She insisted she would be all right, even as she felt a part of her wasn't. It wasn't that she couldn't believe what had happened, only that she kept trying to fix it. There had been a small ceremony arranged by Dominic, a version of *mato oput*—with Obed's cousin as it turned out—but it had been less than Tessa imagined, hollow somehow and dislocated, and the thing that became clear to her was that although she might have crossed into this world, she could not be truly part of it.

In the past few days she'd had moments of fanciful thinking when she imagined she might understand or wipe away everything that had happened and start again, only to realise with a complicated sense of guilt that she couldn't, that everything had changed.

Francis was watching her.

'My parents wanted me to come home,' she said, 'but I told them I can't leave here yet, that they should go without me.'

'And your brother?'

'I don't know where he is,' she said, shame pulsing through her when she thought of Stephen, and confusion too. After all, he was the reason why she and Francis were both here.

Francis gave her a calculating look 'Because he is flying away, but he does not take you with him?'

'No, he does not take me with him. For now, I will stay. Dominic says there's going to be an inquiry, the army will go over what happened.'

'And then you will leave?'

'I'm not sure. Yes, probably.'

'You should go back to your own country.'

He pressed his lips together and his eyes widened with a look that could have meant anything, yet seemed to say, *You don't belong here,* just as easily as it begged her to stay.

Tessa sat down on the bunk bed opposite him. 'But what about you, Francis? How are you?'

He lifted his chin and when he spoke he was guarded. 'My home is gone, my family . . .' Lowering his head, he began to rock back and forth. He made a small choking sound.

She wanted desperately to comfort him. She tried to think of the right thing to say—*this is so hard for you*—but he quickly wiped the tears away, and straightened. 'It is too late for me to go back to school,' he said.

Tessa studied him, wondering how she could help. Perhaps she could appeal to the sense of pride she had witnessed in him in the bush? 'I remember you telling me how you liked school, that you were the best student,' she reminded him.

But Francis shook his head as if she was making it up and made a strange noise which she realised was a muffled kind of laugh. 'That is what no one understands,' he said. 'School will not help me.'

Before she could respond, he got up and went to the door, where he stood with his hands dangling at his sides. Other youths ran past, shouting to each other. Beyond them a small boy spun from a rope that hung from a tree. Twirling, he called to the others to join him, their laughter pealing as it might in a playground anywhere.

Francis pressed his lips together. In ten years' time, Tessa thought, he could be a teacher standing in front of a classroom, or a pot-maker like his father, or . . . Or perhaps not; perhaps he was right and those options were closed to him now.

'I do not want to go to school,' he repeated. His voice was angry, almost violent. 'I do not want to read stories meant for babies or look after skinny cattle. Here, they teach you only so much—they keep you from learning.' His mouth twitched.

'School is stupid. It is *kijinga*—fucked.' He gave a small smile.

He was still focused on the children playing outside. 'This is wrong,' he said. 'I am in the wrong place here. I do not remember it.'

Tessa felt her breath catch. Did he really believe what he said?

His eyes glazed over as if he were in a trance. 'I never had a family here,' he continued. 'I never had a brother.'

It was a declaration that made her heart ache. *He will remember first, and then he will forget. It is the only way to forgive, to heal*—Dominic believed that, just as other experts in her field did. They concluded that those who could forget became less angry, felt less hurt, were more optimistic. Counsellors said they were also more compassionate and self-confident. But at what cost? To forget who you were, who your family was? In the end to forget what you had done? And then forget that you had forgotten? It was a type of amnesia which required if not amputation, then a kind of oblivion. No, there had to be other ways of moving forward. *Post-traumatic growth* was the phrase Tessa had once lifted from some paper or other. Look for happiness in the corner, Beatrice would say. Tessa clung to that now. Reconciliation, acceptance.

'Francis,' she began tentatively, 'there are people here at the centre who can help you—Beatrice, Dominic. . . .'

But when he turned to face her, his mouth had hardened. 'What can they do?' he asked. 'What can anyone do?'

'They—' Tessa began.

'Ha! You are green,' he said. 'Like a green soldier.' Then he faced the wall and began to kick it, slowly, repeatedly. 'What do you know? You hardly know anything.' And looking over his shoulder, he asked the question that lay between them: 'How can I have a better life here when everywhere it is the same?'

Tessa searched for the right thing to say. 'Francis, you are so clever. You can learn. I have seen you. You learn by watching.'

He frowned. 'Yes, I can learn. I can learn how to use a computer and become like you—or like your brother. I can fly a plane. Is that what you mean?' He sniffed, a mucus-filled breath, and wiped his nose.

There was a time when she used to think that if she studied enough and passed the right exams, she would carry that knowledge with her—jump through certain hoops and she would discover the answers. But the truth was she would never know enough, and that every day she would need to start all over again.

She watched Francis roll his shoulders. A cold remoteness had returned to him, and now it was as if the loss of control he'd shown earlier had humiliated him, and he would not allow that to happen again.

'I am going now,' he said, and abruptly turned and walked out through the open door into the sunlight.

39

'In Acholi we have a saying: *Pii pe mol dok tere cen.* River water does not flow back to the source. You know this? Some things cannot be reversed.'

Dominic rested his spoon on the side of his plate. He spoke once more of acceptance, of moving forward—at all costs you must keep going; some things you must leave behind—although for the past month it had seemed to Tessa as if she were holding her breath under water. Even if what he said was true, she doubted it was possible. Moving forward involved taking the past with her. It was not just a matter of living in the present, as Beatrice said, but of being present. Forget, and she believed there was a dangerous sense of dislocation that threatened to unmoor her completely.

Cicadas started up and she took another mouthful of soup, cabbage and onion with too much pepper.

'He will need continual guidance,' Dominic added and looked across to where Francis sat at a long table with several other youths. 'And yet that may not be enough.'

Tessa followed Dominic's gaze. It had only taken a couple of weeks for Francis to establish himself as a popular leader among this group, a group that included the strongest personalities at the centre. Oraako, who now walked with a distinctive limp and who, as yet, had not returned to his village or been offered a place to live with another family, was sitting next to Francis with his arm draped affectionately around Francis's neck. When not attending classes or counselling sessions, they sat around talking. Most of the time a current of unease ran through them, especially at night, when they were given more free time. It was then that Tessa heard them become increasingly vocal and she watched from a distance as Francis became more confident.

The SeaWorld T-shirt he had worn when he first arrived had been replaced by a khaki shirt not unlike the one he wore in the rebel camp. He'd adjusted it by rolling the sleeves up to display his muscular shoulders. His hair had begun to grow, and he'd put on weight. He looked fit and strong and had acquired some long cargo pants with multiple pockets down the sides as well as a new pair of black army boots which, like the previous pair, he polished obsessively. More recently, she noticed, he had repaired the preacher's devotional scapular, re-covering it in clear plastic so that the image of the young Kony with his cornrows and mesmeric eyes seemed to lie behind a gauzy veil. It surprised her that he'd been allowed to keep this, that it had not been confiscated in the way his rifle had, but Dominic and Beatrice had a range of priorities—a gentle easing back, they called it. 'You cannot rob him of his entire identity.'

*

Entering Dominic's office later that day, Tessa found Francis in front of the computer. The light from the screen highlighted his face and she could see that the scar on his cheek had erupted again. It was inflamed, and along the ropy red line there was a new thread of pus.

'You might need more medicine for your face,' she said.

He wore headphones and leant forward on the spindly legs of the plastic chair. Right from the beginning he had been keen for a Facebook account and had learnt how to navigate the web browser with surprising speed. He was reading something now as his mouth followed the words, but by the way he tilted his head Tessa was certain that he was also listening to her.

Eventually he looked up. 'My face will heal,' he said. 'I am protected. I do not want the medicine they give me here. It makes me sick.'

He nodded at the screen then clicked on another tab to bring up the Google image page. Before him was a tiled wall of guns. He flicked through the images, lingering on some for much longer than others. The pictures he favoured were of the more elaborate weapons, those that were automatic, belt-fed, or the sleek sniper rifles that had a longer range.

'Francis learns quickly. Look how well he is coming along, how his English continues to improve,' Dominic had said. 'We must find him a purpose that will allow him to come back into the community. He knows the bush well; maybe he could eventually work as a park ranger.'

Dominic's face had lit up, as though the thought alone might make this happen, and there was such faith in his voice that Tessa found herself sharing his enthusiasm. She had taken on the role of showing Francis how to use the computer, and although she knew her time here was coming to an end, she felt not only indebted but also that she had a responsibility to do more. Should she adopt Francis, like some well-meaning aunt? Take on his welfare, educate him, even try to take him back to Australia, where he might learn a trade or a speciality and then return to Uganda as an IT technician or a doctor?

A more honest feeling warned her against such impulses, and Beatrice, who saw more clearly what was achievable, held her hand and squeezed it as though they were school friends. 'When you go, we will miss you, but not for too long.' She laughed. 'Maybe for three days!'

Tessa felt a mix of anxiety and accountability. 'Francis is eager,' she told Dominic, although seeing the arsenal on the screen now, she was afraid she had made a mistake in encouraging him to spend so much time surfing the Net.

'Why do you want to look at these?' she asked cautiously.

Francis didn't take his eyes from the screen.

'Francis?' she repeated.

He shrugged his shoulders. 'Because I am still a soldier,' he replied. 'And because I will always be a soldier.'

He scrolled down the screen—American, Russian, Chinese guns. Gleaming, precision-built. They might have been beautiful if not for what they were used for.

'There are so many,' she said, remembering how she had pulled the trigger, which had not, *had not* been an involuntary act. For her, then, the Seventh Circle in Dante's world; a place for murderers.

Francis clicked on an image of a lightweight automatic rifle and enlarged it. It looked like a weapon from a science fiction movie.

'I would rather die a soldier,' he said, hunching forward.

His words filled her with dread. 'So that is why you want to join the Ugandan army?'

He looked at her.

'I have heard some reports,' she said by way of explanation. 'Dominic told me you wanted to do more training.'

He shrugged. 'No, it is not to join the Ugandan army,' he replied. 'If you say that then you are wrong.'

'What then?' she asked softly.

He did not answer, and it was only in that moment that she understood. 'You mean you want to go back to the bush? To Kony?'

'Yes.'

'But Francis, you told Beatrice you wanted to get away and begin again, you wanted to learn new things.'

'And I have learnt new things. I am more now than just Francis Amayo. I am Francis Amayo, the LRA rebel—and I will always be a rebel. But because I come back, this doesn't change anything. I can't stay here; I am not wanted.'

Tessa frowned and shook her head.

'Yes,' he said. 'They think I am evil, they want me on the *wii oduu*—you know this, the garbage heap?'

'Who wants this?'

'The community,' he insisted, nodding his head in the direction beyond the gates of the centre.

'No, Francis, you are an Acholi. You belong here, this is where you can be safe. Even help your people.'

He turned and looked at her. 'Can't you see that is what I am already doing? I *am* helping them.'

'How?' Tessa ventured, although her voice wavered. 'By going back to what you did before? Aren't you afraid? They might punish you for being a traitor.'

Francis took the headphones off. His eyes were steady and when he spoke his voice sounded shrewd. 'Here they want *mato oput*. You want *mato oput*, but I do not want that.' He sat up straighter. 'Dominic says, *There is reconciliation, we go on*. You say, *Go to school, go to school*,' and he nodded towards the books on the desk. 'Everyone thinks that will stop the killing, and people will no longer be unhappy, no longer poor, but I do not want to go to school when what they tell me there is wrong. Here, they want me to tell them about the rebels. They say I can be charged with *trea-son*,' he said, drawing out the word. 'What do they know about treason? Only Kony knows the way forward. He is a freedom fighter. Look,' he added, gesturing to the computer screen. 'He will not sign. He is smarter than all of them.'

Tessa glanced at the newsfeed on the screen. The picture of Kony was old, although the item Francis had indicated had been posted only an hour before. The headline read: REBEL LEADER AGAIN FAILS TO SIGN PEACE AGREEMENT.

Francis sat back. 'They will want me to return.'

'Francis, listen to me, you can have a life here. A better life.'

'No,' Francis said and stood up. His eyes shone, and, as he stepped forward, he pushed the pile of books off the desk so that they hit the floor with a loud thwack.

He raised his hands above his head, then stopped, as if struggling for control.

Finally, he sneered, 'Look at this place. The Ugandan government doesn't know how to look after its people. They don't know God. If I stay here I am dead. But Kony will not die. Even if they shoot him he will not die. He can never be killed. That is why I will return. The rebels are the only ones who know how to win, they are the only ones who can give me a future.'

'No, wait,' Tessa said, then she sat down at the computer as if to outdo him at his own game. 'Look at this,' she added, her fingers rapidly tapping the keyboard.

There had to be another ending, she thought, where even if Francis returned to the bush, even if his faith and loyalty took him there, he would not be able to accept all that he was asked to do. She'd seen that kind of intelligence in him before, the spark that allowed him to question. Everything hinged on it now.

She would find some article or piece of information that would build her case. She would do as her mother might, and search for a way to make things better, a solution in the face of the odds, or she would apply her father's stubbornness; she was good at that. A strategy, but as she clicked on the screen, Francis's Facebook page came up, and there in the corner was a message from Stephen. *I can help you. What do you need? Name it. I can supply whatever you want.*

Tessa opened her mouth, but before she could say anything Francis put his finger to her lips. Shhh. It was an unbearably intimate thing for him to do.

Her heart pounded in her ears. She sat back. He was telling her to keep quiet. He was asking her to watch his back. Had she been kidding herself? They're way ahead of me, she thought. Both Francis and Stephen were survivors; they knew how to utilise what was available to them—a skill. For one born of necessity, for the other because he could, and together they were stronger. They had learnt that too.

Her father may have hoped to break the circuit, and she may have told herself she understood that, but deeper knowledge can come in an instant and illuminate everything.

Francis logged off. He sat breathing hard and watched as the computer shut down.

No, Tessa thought, looking at the blank screen. No, she was not done yet.

Acknowledgements

Special thanks to Melanie Ostell, whose honest eye and inspiring support has been instrumental. To Jane Palfreyman, for opening the door. To Rebecca Starford, Ali Lavau and the team at Allen & Unwin for their insight and editorial care.

To Andrea Goldsmith, for her enduring mentorship, and Doreen Baingana, who brought Uganda into focus for me.

Deepest gratitude also to my early readers, those colleagues and friends who gave this story reason to grow.

And as ever, most of all, to Paul and our children, you have been with me the entire way.

The following books were particularly helpful in the writing and imagining of this one: *The Lord's Resistance Army: Myth and reality* (Zed Books, London, New York, 2010) by Tim Allen and Koen Vlassenroot (editors); *Drink the Bitter Root: A search for justice and healing in Africa* (Douglas & McIntyre, Berkeley, CA, 2011) by Gary Geddes; *The Shadow World: Inside the global arms trade* (Hamish Hamilton, London, 2011) by

Andrew Feinstein; *Living with Bad Surroundings: War, history, and everyday moments in Northern Uganda* (Duke University Press, Durham and London, 2008) by Sverker Finnström; *Virtual War and Magical Death: Technologies and imaginaries for terror and killing* (Duke University Press, Durham and London, 2013) by Neil L. Whitehead and Sverker Finnström (editors).